SPACE ACADEMY

Space Academy

Published by The Conrad Press in the United Kingdom 2020

Tel: +44(0)1227 472 874
www.theconradpress.com
info@theconradpress.com

ISBN 978-1-911546-94-8

Typesetting and Cover Design by: Charlotte Mouncey, www.bookstyle.co.uk

The Conrad Press logo was designed by Maria Priestley.

Printed and bound in Great Britain by Clays Ltd, Elcograf S.p.A.

SPACE ACADEMY

HANNAH HOPKINS

For Samuel and Anthony

1.

THE JOURNEY BEGINS

She was running through the night, clutching the small, precious bundle under her cloak tightly to her chest.

It was deathly quiet, the only audible sound coming from the flickering streetlamps as they hummed and struggled into life.

Her breath caught in her throat, a ball of burning exhaustion rising in her chest. She had been running for what felt like hours, but there was no time to stop and rest.

As she sprinted down the street, she caught glimpses of the houses left desolate and empty, abandoned by their owners in fits of panic and hysteria. Cars were parked diagonally across driveways, their doors flung open, awaiting owners that would never return.

Dustbins had been overturned and rubbish littered the street as far as the eye could see. Front doors had been left ajar, revealing eerily lit hallways. She wondered how much longer it would be until the power went out altogether, plunging Earth into a permanent darkness.

She turned the corner and continued to flee down another deserted road, the smell of the salt and seawater filling her nostrils and telling her that she was getting closer. She reached a metal sign cemented into the ground, twisted and warped from the heat of a passing solar flare. The top had come askew, but she could still make out the white lettering against the faded green background informing her that Pentewan train station was half a mile to the left.

Before she moved off, she peered into her cloak to check that her journey so far had not disturbed her cargo.

Satisfied that all was well, she began to walk, continuing down another derelict street, the flickering lights taunting her as she went. She closed her eyes to block out her surroundings.

For just one moment, she imagined that she was walking down the street on a perfectly ordinary evening, perhaps going to meet friends or returning home after a hard day's work. She felt the echo of excitement rise inside of her as the sound of faint laughter filled her head, conjured somewhere from the depths of her memories from a time when normality still existed.

The Wars on Earth, as they were collectively referred to, had broken out when she was barely a teenager and she struggled to remember a time when conflict and strife hadn't dominated the day-to-day life of every citizen on Earth. The poverty and lack of resources that had ensued after the numerous wars had resulted in the rise of gangs and looters, causing the fight for survival to move from the battlefield and onto the streets. Once the peace of a mundane life had gone, nothing had ever been the same again.

Her thoughts had clouded her vision, but her legs had taken her to the right location. She arrived at the decrepit train station, flinching slightly at its ghostly appearance in the dark.

She pulled a battered pocket watch from her cloak, a prized relic from the old days that she had found on her travels, and clicked it open to read the time, her cold breath illuminated in the clock's glowing face.

It was 11:40 p.m., which meant her train was due any second. Terrified she might have missed it, she began scanning the inky black tracks desperately, relief spreading through her body as two headlights pinpricked the horizon.

The silver metallic train pulled up and halted to a silent stop. Two of its doors opened smoothly, splitting in the middle and coming away so that they blended with the side of the carriage. Without hesitating, she stepped aboard, moving quietly through the dimly lit compartments. She didn't need a ticket. There was no driver, no conductors and no ticket inspectors. They had all gone. The magnetic system that ran the trains had been left on, with nobody bothering to switch them off. The trains continued to run, picking up no one and taking them to nowhere. Occasionally, though, they had come in useful, allowing her to move about the country undetected as she had made her vital journey.

The seats were laid back in their reclining position, ready to take tired commuters into the night. A single coffee cup sat upright on one of the cold, white tables that connected one pair of seats to the other. She wondered how long it had been sat there for and under what circumstances it had been abandoned.

The faint smell of sweat lingered in the air, almost completely masked by the steely odour of metal that emanated from the train's walls. At the head of the carriage was an interactive screen, blinking slightly from years of damage and neglect. She walked over to it and activated it with a touch of her finger and was greeted by a clinical female voice as the screen sprung to life.

'Welcome to the I-Train,' the voice said. 'The pioneering way to travel brought to you exclusively by The

Interactive-Tech Company.'

She selected the main menu, bringing up a display that featured information on the journey. A small icon of a train moved along a virtual winding road, heading towards Charlestown, Cornwall which was marked by a large, red circle. Elsie pressed on the screen and the estimated time of arrival appeared before her, letting her know that she had only fifteen minutes before she would reach her destination.

She swallowed, the fear of failure creeping into her mind like an unwanted pest. She was yet to come up with a proper plan of action to take when she arrived at her journey's end, and she had so little time to prepare. She was about to sit down and begin detailing a plot with all the information she had gathered so far, when a noise from the next carriage along startled her, causing her to stagger backwards.

She paused for a moment, unsure whether she should run and hide, but instinct told her not to be afraid. Boldly, she pressed her hand to the small sensor by the side of the door that divided the compartments, causing it to slide open.

As she stepped across the carriage's threshold, she was greeted by a blonde-haired woman, sitting on a rear-facing seat, a tartan push-trolley sat between her legs. She was leaning forward on its handle, smiling coyly up at her new visitor. A middle-aged man sat hunched on the floor opposite her, his legs drawn up to his chest and his arms wrapped protectively around his body. He was so thin that he was almost skeletal. His sunken eyes stared fixated on the floor and his mouth hung open, forming whispered words that only he could understand.

'Hello, love,' the woman said cheerfully. 'Come and take a seat.'

Elsie hesitated, glancing over at the man with alarm. The woman followed her gaze.

'Oh, don't worry about him, he's harmless,' she smiled.

Warily, Elsie moved through the carriage and sat on one of the forward-facing seats, swinging her body around carefully so that she could see the other woman.

'The name's Grace,' the woman grinned toothlessly. She didn't look particularly old, but her face was haggard, prematurely aged by hardship and sorrow.

'Elsie,' she replied. She wasn't sure why, but she trusted Grace. It was clear she had suffered great stress and loss and that somehow gave them a common ground to stand upon.

'I didn't expect to see anyone on these trains,' Grace said after a moment. Her accent was hard and callous. Wherever she had grown up had left a lasting impression on her inflexion.

'Neither did I,' Elsie replied.

'We're going to see them off, Bernard and me,' Grace continued, gesturing to the man. He did not seem to recognise the sound of his own name and continued gawking, wide-eyed at the floor.

'Them?' Elsie asked.

'You know who I'm talking about,' Grace hissed. 'Those who are dearly departing on *The Mayflower*. I reckon we ought to give them a great send off. Let them know how sorely they'll be missed. Bunch of fools!'

She spat on the floor and wiped her mouth with the back of her hand. There was a fury resonating from her eyes that Elsie had never seen in another human being.

'They think they've got it all planned out,' Grace ranted. 'Leaving us less important people behind to rot like pieces of rubbish while they fly off to start their new world. Well, they're on a fool's mission anyway. Mark my words they are. There is more to this than any of those stuck-up fools can begin to get their tiny minds around.'

Her eyes flashed with a passion that Elsie could only interpret as excitement.

'Are you talking about the conspiracy theories?' Elsie asked, beginning to feel she was trapped on the train with a madwoman.

'You've heard them too?' Grace said, her voice ragged with enthusiasm.

'Yes, I have,' Elsie replied flatly, her heart twinging with pain as she recalled the fate of the last person she had known to believe in the theories.

The bundle beneath Elsie's cloak began to wriggle, causing the fabric to rearrange itself suspiciously.

'What have you got there?' Grace asked, her beady eyes detecting the movement.

'It's nothing,' Elsie said quickly, stealing a glance through the cloak's neck hole.

'Are you sure about that?' Grace pressed her, as a soft cooing noise emitted from beneath the swathes of cloth.

Elsie said nothing, she knew her secret was out but had no desire to discuss the matter. The true magnitude of what she would lose if she failed to make it aboard *The Mayflower* was too terrible for her to acknowledge out loud. Grace seemed to understand this, continuing to speak without receiving a response.

'My husband left me, you know,' she informed Elsie. 'We were married fifteen years. He had another son by his first wife.

It caused a lot of problems between us. I can't have children, you see, and I resented the boy for existing.'

Elsie nodded, unsure how best to respond to such a personal revelation.

'Anyway, his boy's mum died. She was killed by looters in one of the cities. Everything changed after that. My husband and I had both agreed we would stay on Earth come the day of the Split, whatever that meant. He believed in the theories too, you see. Had real evidence for them as well. But when he took his boy in, he changed his mind. Suddenly he was applying for *The Mayflower*, saying he had to give his son a chance of living. I told him I wasn't going, no matter what, but he left anyway. Have you any idea how bad that feels? Being left to suffer and die by the one person who's supposed to love and protect you?' she asked. The question was rhetorical, but it brought a fresh wave of pain to the surface of Elsie's mind.

'I do actually,' she said. Grace regarded her shrewdly, a moment of silent understanding passing between them.

'Well then,' she nodded. 'You know why I have to go and see them leave for myself. It's not just humans on that ship, you know. I've heard whispers.'

Elsie nodded but said no more on the subject. She was well aware of the conspiracy theory Grace was referring to and didn't think it wise to voice her harsh opinions on the matter. The only thing which surprised her was how widespread the theory seemed to have become. Stupidly, she had assumed she was among the only few people to have heard it.

'What happened to him?' Elsie changed the subject, regarding Bernard with concern.

'Him? His family abandoned him. His parents have been

dead a long while, mind, as most of ours have. He had a sister, though, but she married some rich bloke, got her and her kids a place on board and left him here to rot. Apparently, there was 'no room' for him. Truth is I think she was ashamed. He doesn't have any skills, you see, or money so he's of 'no use' to *The Mayflower* or the continuation of our species,' Grace explained with disgust.

'That's terrible…' Elsie said after a moment. Grace nodded curtly. Whatever pity she had had for Bernard seemed to have been doused by the overpowering anger she felt towards all those leaving after the Split.

'What about you then?' Grace asked brazenly. 'You got any nearest and dearest? Other than the obvious,' she nodded at Elsie's cloak.

The question hit Elsie like a knife to the throat. She felt her chest closing in on itself in a futile attempt to cushion the pain to her heart that the words had caused her. She closed her eyes and bore the agony, letting it peak to an unbearable torment before it subsided, allowing her to breathe once again.

'All dead,' she said thickly, hoping that would be enough to deter Grace from pressing her any further.

'They been gone a long time?'

'Years,' Elsie lied.

Her parents were long dead it was true, but it wasn't the discussion of their absence that was causing her to silently crumble into dust. She could not even think of her more recent loss, for fear the pain would rip through her body and destroy her completely.

Grace seemed to accept this response and the conversation drifted into a comfortable silence. Elsie allowed herself to be

14

lulled into pleasant numbness, concentrating on the whirring sound of the train's mechanism as it pulled them forward into the night. Every so often, she stole a fleeting glance at Bernard, who hadn't moved or changed his posture the entire time she had been in the carriage. She wondered what would happen to him and Grace after the Split, fighting the panicked thought that she might still be on Earth to find out.

The time fell away like raindrops sliding off soft skin and soon enough the robotic, female voice was announcing that they had almost reached Charlestown. Grace rose to her feet immediately, heaving a dazed Bernard into a slumped standing position beside her.

'Well, 'she said, regarding Elsie with a look of comradery. 'Good luck to you, love. We're heading up the hills to get a good view of them leaving. If you need to, you can find us up there.'

Elsie attempted a smile, causing Grace's previously hardened expression to be abducted by unconcealed pity. She raised two fingers to her head in a strange sort of salute and then turned to face the steel doors of the train, which was now slowing to a standstill. With one final lurch, they became stationary, the doors sliding open in one swift movement.

Without looking back, Grace disembarked with surprising elegance, dragging Bernard limply behind her. They disappeared into the night. Suddenly, everything was quiet.

Mustering all the courage she could find, Elsie stepped onto the platform. Immediately, she was hit by two powerful sensations. The first was the sharp, crisp air that engulfed her body the moment the train doors shut behind her. It was a deeper degree of cold than she had felt earlier in the evening, and she clutched her arms around her travelling cloak protectively, drawing in as much heat as she could from her body. The second was the bittersweet sting of nostalgia as she took in the familiar appearance of Charlestown, the place that had made her heart leap with joy as a child.

She could still picture it now. Her mother curled up on the corner armchair in their holiday cottage, engrossed in a novel on her I-Reader, her father popping in and out from cooking in the kitchen to sing silly songs and take requests. Elsie would be sat on the window ledge, her bare feet swinging freely as she relished the relief of the cool evening air after a startlingly hot summer's day. Her parents would put the 3D television on for her to keep her entertained while they went about their various tasks, but she sat with her back to it, ignoring its persistent noise as she stared out across the moon-bathed hills, that rose and fell all the way to the silent black sea beyond.

Shaking these thoughts from her mind, she made her way to the green, perforated steps that would lead her out of the train station and ascended, quickly reaching the street above. The shops and houses that flanked the road had once been bustling with tourists and cheerful residents, but were now haunted by echoes of voices and laughter.

She walked past the Tall Ships sat bobbing gently in the bay, their decaying masts rising gloomily out of the mist, and rounded the final corner, leading her to the beach. She stopped still, her feet finding balance on the pebbled shore. She had arrived.

THE MAYFLOWER

Elsie had heard many stories about *The Mayflower*, but nothing could have prepared her for seeing it in the flesh. The spacecraft was gargantuan, its metal frame stretching higher than the eye could see. It rested delicately upon the water, the sheer mass of it covering the entirety of the ocean. Its dark titanium sides ran down the coastline, attached to the shore by open walkways that were manned by intimidating guards. People were still queuing across the beach, waiting anxiously to board in the remaining minutes before take-off.

Elsie gulped and began to move towards the spacecraft with leaden legs. Somehow, she had to get past the guards and onto *The Mayflower* without being exposed. She had never received formal permission from the government to board.

All of *The Mayflower's* passengers were required to either have a special skill that could be used to rebuild civilisation or be rich enough to be allowed to board from status, although the latter was kept secret from the general public. The applications had been rigorous and had taken up to six months to be processed. It had been an agonising wait and she had waited every day with bated breath, wondering if she would be delivered a message of safety, or one of doom.

Despite all her hard work studying at college, her request to board the ship had been denied with no explanation. All she had to cling onto now was hope. She had found the location of *The Mayflower* by following whispers on the streets and the tales of fellow travellers, but there was no way to guarantee that she would successfully make it aboard.

She reached the cobbled beach and made her way towards the nearest queue, which had dwindled into a number of thirty people or so. She slipped inconspicuously to the back of the line behind a middle-aged married couple, who were chattering among themselves about what lay beyond the giant metal doors in front of them.

'I heard *The Mayflower* has its own water park and multiplex cinema,' the man told his wife. 'Apparently, all the luxury apartments have their own coffee machines too!'

'Honestly, Jared you shouldn't listen to ridiculous gossip. How on Earth would they be able to make coffee in space?' she replied with a roll of her eyes.

'It's true, I'm telling you!' the man named Jared insisted. 'Colin from next door said his brother is part of the team who make all the food and drink on board. They use some sort of cloning procedure to replicate organic food. All they need is one coffee bean from Earth and they can use it to make thousands of pots of coffee.'

'Well, I certainly hope you're right. I'm not sure I could handle many early mornings with you without a cup of coffee,' his wife scathed. Elsie knew immediately that they must be from one of the wealthier communities which had guards protecting them and the best pick of resources delivered to their door for an exceptionally high fee. To be worrying about something as insignificant as coffee after all the devastation that had ravaged Earth for the past decade was unthinkable to Elsie.

The line moved forward, and the woman in front drew her damask cloak around herself. She inched ahead with her husband, the moonlight illuminating the taught tweed patches on his overcoat. Elsie followed them closely, trying to stay silent so as not to draw any attention to herself. The woman began looking around wistfully, her arms folded against the wind. She had pulled her scarf over her mouth to keep out the cold, distorting her voice so that her husband could no longer hear her.

'All the coffee in the world won't make it Earth,' she muttered, glancing at *The Mayflower* with disdain.

Elsie stood on her tiptoes, vying to get a glimpse past the gruff guards who were blocking the entrance to *The Mayflower*. She counted ten of them, each one checking the prospective passengers thoroughly before they were allowed to enter. Soon, it would be her turn.

A wave of nausea swept through Elsie's body. She was certain that her legs would disappear at any moment, sending her crumpled to the floor.

She tried to distract herself, looking up towards the beautiful velvet sky, with hundreds of stars visible across its dark canopy. They twinkled majestically, their shiny light winking at her from across the galaxy. This would be the last time she ever saw the Earth's sky, regardless of whether she was successful in her mission or not. No matter her own fate, she was determined that she would save her son, whatever it took.

He had been sound asleep for the entire journey, the motion of her movement lulling him further into the sweet ignorance of his dreams. She peered down to look at his peaceful face.

He was only a few months old and had no idea of the suffering and torment that had passed in his short life. It was her dream that he would never know the pain she had felt. Even if she was not allowed on board, she would plead with the guards to take her innocent son. There was no way she was going to let him die on the disease-ridden Earth.

She closed her eyes and thought of Austin. If she was going to die tonight, that meant she would see him soon. She imagined him greeting her and the two of them sharing a joke. She terribly missed the way he used to laugh, his head tipped back, his eyes closed in hysteria as a loud and infectious noise burst from within him.

Elsie was pleased by her ability to accurately conjure Austin in her mind, even after spending months trying to erase him from her brain. Despite his final act of betrayal, she found that thinking of him still brought her great comfort, particularly in what she was beginning to feel certain would be the final moments of her life.

Reluctantly, she opened her eyes to re-join reality and found that the woman in front had been staring at her most curiously. She gave her best apologetic smile, hoping that she wouldn't fear her insane and alert the guards. She was just about to turn to her husband and say something, when a stern voice from ahead distracted her.

'Next!' it called. They were at the front of the line. As soon as one of the guards finished with their passengers, Elsie would be next. She desperately scoured the reaches of her mind for something clever to say when questioned, but found she could think of nothing. All too soon, she was called ahead.

'Ma'am,' a guard to her left called, motioning her forward.

She reached *The Mayflower's* entrance and stood perfectly still, awaiting his next instruction with a sense of dread.

'Present your fingers please, Ma'am,' he told her, holding up a DNA scanner. Elsie sized him up. He was tall and stocky. The lines around his eyes and mouth placed him in his mid-forties. He had scars on the back of his hands and across his face from years spent in service. One of his eyes was discoloured from a blunt trauma, the other dark and beady. His body language was indifferent, his gaze unseeing. He was a man who was simply doing his job. There was no point trying to plead with him.

'Your fingers please, Ma'am,' he prompted her. Unsure what to do, she pulled her arms out of her cloak, careful not to disturb her son. She delicately placed her hands on the screen of his scanner. A whirring noise and a blue light indicated that the reading of her fingerprints was taking place. After a few seconds, the screen flashed red with a large thick 'X' in the centre.

'Access denied,' a woman's voice informed them. Elsie tried to keep her expression neutral, fearing that any show of emotion would give her away.

'Ma'am, can you confirm that you have received permission to board this spacecraft from the government of the United Kingdom?' he demanded.

'Er... I... yes,' Elsie stammered, not knowing what else to say. The guard's eyes narrowed suspiciously and then began roaming over her, looking for a clue or a sign of danger. He faltered upon the bundle beneath her cloak and froze, his whole stance changing from nonchalant to alert in a matter of seconds. He reached into his back pocket and pulled out his weapon, pointing it directly at her.

'Put your hands in the air,' he said, his voice shaking.

'No! It's not what you think! Look!' she motioned to undo her cloak and reveal the sleeping baby underneath, but this only riled him more.

'Do not put your hands under the cloak!' he yelled. 'Keep your hands where I can see them.'

Several of the other guards turned to see what was going on, running over and abandoning their posts as they rushed to join the confrontation. The last handful of passengers waiting to board on the beach gasped and screamed in horror.

'It's not a weapon!' Elsie pleaded, but it was no use. None of the guards could hear her over their frenzied shouting. The man who had first discovered her was talking into his personal device, strapped tightly around his wrist.

'Do I have permission to shoot, sir?' she heard him say.

She tried to scream, but the sound caught in her throat before it could escape. Her vision began to blur, the world around her whirling faster and faster. It was happening. The guard was going to shoot her dead.

She took a deep breath to steady herself, wondering with desperation if there was any way to protect her son from the bullets that would surely hit her at any moment.

'Hold on,' a voice said from the other end of the personal device. The voice sounded eerily familiar, but Elsie couldn't place it over all the commotion.

'Stand down, stand down,' the guard informed the others. They stopped yelling and lowered their weapons.

Elsie remained frozen, petrified that even a slight movement would give them the incentive to shoot. A black silhouette appeared in the long corridor that led inside *The Mayflower*.

The guards stood statue still, their backs to the approaching figure and their faces fixed in a new expression of calm.

Suddenly, a man stepped out of the doorway. Elsie blinked. There was a moment of confusion followed by a crippling sense of relief. She knew this man. She knew him very well.

'Alfie,' she whispered, her voice hoarse. Alfie smiled, his unmistakeable features coming into focus.

'It's 'Captain Alfred Sommers' now,' he grinned.

She took in his uniform; the white high-neck jumper made from a smooth airy material, the sleek black trousers that seemed to fit perfectly, the golden badge depicting two planets with a dotted line between them. Her mouth hung open. Alfie noticed her expression and began to laugh. She flinched, momentarily transported back in time by the musical sound.

'Come inside, Elsie. We can talk,' he said. His voice enveloped her in a warm blanket of comfort and, without having to think for a second, she stepped over the threshold of *The Mayflower*, watching as he motioned for the guards to return to their posts and continue their duties, the entire event forgotten.

'Just wait there a second,' Alfie smiled. Elsie standing still in *The Mayflower's* entrance, watching as he conversed with the guard who had discovered her.

'If they show up, don't let them board, their apartment is no longer vacant,' she heard him say. There was some murmuring before the guard nodded and saluted, rotating back to face out into the night.

Alfie returned to her side and indicated for her to begin walking down the long passage. She did so, looking around with hesitation. High walls of sheeted metal rose up around her, spanning over her head to form a strange titanium archway.

Yellow lamps had been fixed into the wall at periodic intervals, their dim artificial light leading the way to another door a few yards ahead of them.

'I can't believe you're a captain now,' she said to Alfie as they walked. He looked at her with confusion, perhaps wondering how she could make light conversation after having been seconds from death.

'Yes, I applied for my captaincy after we left college,' he explained.

'Well, congratulations,' she praised him.

'Thank you,' he replied, his face suddenly twisting into an awkward expression of discomfort. 'Sorry I didn't keep in touch, Elsie. I meant to, I really did, but I was so preoccupied with all of this...' he gestured to *The Mayflower*. 'Time got away from me.'

'We were all busy,' Elsie smiled. As she spoke, her baby grizzled from beneath her cloak and began to stir.

'What was that?' Alfie asked.

Elsie pulled the cloak over her head and revealed the sleeping baby underneath, his little head resting daintily on her chest. Alfie craned his neck so that he could look into his face.

'It seems you've earnt a 'congratulations,' too,' he beamed. 'He looks just like you. What's his name?'

'William,' Elsie replied.

'After your father,' Alfie nodded.

'Yes, I thought the world could do with another William James. Although,' she paused, her voice faltering with confusion. 'I'm not sure if I can even say that anymore- 'the world'. There is no world anymore, is there?'

Alfie grinned.

'There will be,' he assured her.

'I assume Austin is the baby's father,' he said after a few moments, his tone matter of fact.

'Yes,' Elsie answered.

'Where is he?' he asked as casually as he could, keeping his eyes fixed on the door ahead of them.

'He's dead,' she said wearily, the extreme emotions she had experienced that day beginning to take their toll. Alfie standing still, immobilised by the news.

'He's dead?' he repeated in shock. Elsie nodded. He began shaking his head back and forth, his eyes darting from side to side as if he were trying to solve an equation that had no answer.

'How did it happen?' he asked, deep confusion spreading across the recesses of his usually composed face.

Elsie gave him a meaningful look and he nodded, piecing the clues together in his mind as he began to understand.

'He didn't let it go, did he? His belief in the 'great conspiracy'.'

'No, he didn't,' Elsie replied.

There was a brief moment of silence, during which Alfie cleared his throat several times, stalling as he determined how best to phrase his next question.

'Do you ever think about…them?' he asked, his tone suddenly fearful. Elsie sucked her breath inwards.

'No,' she told him. 'I don't. If I did, I'd end up driving myself mad like Austin. Besides, there are bigger things to think about now.'

Alfie nodded, folding his arms behind his back and straightening his posture as they came to the end of the passage. A sensor on the left-hand side of the door flashed impatiently, demanding a fingerprint to scan.

'Well, Elsie, are you ready?' Alfie asked her. Elsie smiled at him weakly. She lacked the energy to indulge his schoolboy excitement as he prepared to show her his shiny new toy. She longed to find the oblivion of sleep and lose herself in it, exhausted by the emotional toll of her long journey. She was certain that nothing could impress her enough to keep out the sadness that was slowly creeping into her mind, pouring through the floodgates that had been opened by her painful thoughts of Austin.

The door opened with a touch of Alfie's finger and the pair of them stepped into the heart of *The Mayflower*.

They found themselves in a gigantic lobby, the size of at least two football pitches. The floor was made from smooth white marble that gleamed and glistened from the reflections of the numerous lights that were fixed overhead. Large oval-shaped elevators made of glass were transporting people from the ground to the floors above, moving smoothly at first before suddenly jolting in all directions.

The lobby itself was circular, and transparent walkways ran around its outer edge on every floor. Elsie could see passengers hurrying along them, some carrying bags and suitcases, others strolling with their families, pointing with enthusiasm whenever they saw something new.

The ground floor was filled with venues designed for the passenger's entertainment, with coffee shops, clothing boutiques and toy stores making up just some of the available outlets.

Elsie's eye was drawn immediately to the familiar 'I-Tech' logo hanging above one of the shop windows, every gadget and device imaginable laid out on display. A gigantic wafer-thin screen hung from wires in the centre of the floor, presently displaying the fifteen-minute countdown to the Split.

'It's… so big,' Elsie mused, her bleary eyes struggling to comprehend the wealth of new sights in front of her.

'Come this way,' Alfie urged, leading her towards the nearest lift. The lights seemed to become a hue brighter as she stepped somewhat dubiously into the oval pod.

Alfie tapped on the glass and an interactive screen appeared, his fingers moving across it at such a speed that she could not discern what he was typing.

'I'm taking you to your apartment now,' he informed her.

'I have an apartment?' she replied with confusion.

'Yes, you'll be on the top floor with me,' he confirmed, pressing a final button that caused the lift to begin vibrating wildly.

In a flash, they were flying up towards the ceiling, with Elsie certain she had left her stomach behind on the ground floor. Their speed increased as they shot past the different levels of living accommodation, the blue carpeted corridors blurring into one gigantic sea of cotton.

Elsie closed her eyes and turned away, the sight beginning to make her dizzy. By the time they had reached the top floor, they were travelling at such a speed that she was convinced they would break through the ceiling, launching into space independently from *The Mayflower*.

Mercifully, the lift slowed to a smooth stop, and they disembarked into a small but extravagant atrium. A large chandelier hung from the ceiling, casting dancing shadows across the floor, which was paved with marble in hues of swirling gold and bronze. Five sets of wide double doors stood at precise intervals around the walls, each marked with a number. The doorknobs were made of crystal, and silver-plated archways twisted around the doorframes. Alfie led Elsie to number 'three', delicately taking her hand and touching her finger to the sensor pad beside it.

'You'll be able to gain entry yourself now,' he explained. She nodded, her head swimming as she attempted to take it all in. Alfie's mahogany eyes and dark eyebrows blurred into his brown hair when she tried to focus on his face, leaving her to wonder how much longer she could stay awake without collapsing.

She followed him into her apartment, a vast space that was as lavishly decorated as the atrium would suggest. Plush rugs spilled across the laminate flooring, so soft she could almost feel their tenderness through her worn and beaten boots. Large mounted paintings of vivid landscapes from Earth hung across the room, providing a comforting reminder of home. A shiny electric fireplace was attached to the wall at the end of an elongated black glass table, complete with matching chairs. A series of white sofas and chaises were arranged in the living room around a quartz coffee table, a variety of brand-new tablets laid out on its surface, never having yet been touched.

'This is it,' Alfie announced. 'There are also three bedrooms, two bathrooms and a kitchen.'

'Oh...' Elsie replied. 'That's good.'

'I expect you'll be wanting to get some rest now,' he noted, and she nodded readily, allowing him to lead her semi-conscious body into the master bedroom.

Once inside, Alfie strode over to the large wardrobe and produced a pair of red, silk pyjamas from its depths. He laid them on the bed and then turned his back to her, tapping on a small rectangular screen that was fixed into the wall. Elsie undid her travelling cloak and removed it, along with her boots. She carefully detached William from her body and placed him gently on the bed, his sling falling to the floor with a delicate thud.

Hastily, she pulled off her mud-covered trousers and fraying jumper and put the fresh pyjamas on in their place. Her whole body sighed with relief as she found herself physically comfortable for the first time since she could remember. She sat down on the bed, ready to fall asleep at any moment.

From across the room, there came a whirring noise. Alfie's head snapped to the direction of a hatch carved into the furthest wall. It was protected by a curved, metal door which opened upon Alfie's touch, revealing the contents within. Elsie gasped with surprise. Sitting inside was a beautiful cream cot, complete with a holographic mobile depicting whirling planets and zooming spaceships.

In one swift motion, Alfie heaved the cot into position next to Elsie's bed.

'You can order anything you want from there,' he said, pointing to the rectangular screen. 'The people downstairs will send it up.'

Elsie wasn't sure what any of this meant. She watched somewhat distantly as Alfie picked William up and placed him into the cot, pulling a soft, blue blanket up to his shoulders and tucking him in.

'Thank you,' Elsie murmured, falling backwards and allowing a feathery pillow to catch her head. 'For everything.'

'You don't have to thank me,' Alfie replied, putting the warm duvet over her aching body. 'So long as you're aboard my ship you'll never have to worry about a thing. You're safe now.'

There was a moment's pause as he stared into the distance.

'You should remember I said that,' he advised her mysteriously, turning on his heel and walking from the room, his arms folded behind his back.

Elsie lay in the dark for a moment, letting the silence swallow her up. She looked over at William's peaceful face, his mouth hanging open as he slept deeply. She had done it. She had saved him. She was victorious in her quest, yet the strangest feeling of emptiness engulfed her as *The Mayflower's* engines burst into life, shaking the room from floor to ceiling.

Unable to cling on any longer, she succumbed to the lull of sleep, knowing that by the time she awoke, they would be deep in space. Life on Earth was over.

THIRTEEN YEARS LATER

Will opened his eyes, blinking as they adjusted to the light in his bedroom. Reluctantly, he kicked off his duvet and sat up, swinging himself out of bed. Feeling groggy, he walked across the room to his wardrobe, his bare feet padding across the dark blue carpet.

He opened the doors and picked out a maroon jumper and pair of sleek black trousers to wear. Even though he was thirteen years old, his mother still chose his clothes for him. She had them specially made by an upmarket designer who lived alongside them on Floor One.

He shrugged out of his pyjamas, the light grey material crumpling into a pile at his feet. Once he was dressed, he folded his nightclothes carefully and put them in pride of place in his top drawer. They were adorned with images of his favourite rocket racer, Pablo Pianthus and his famous Solo Rocket XR2. Last year, he had broken the record for the fastest ever journey undertaken in a one-man rocket.

When Will grew up, he wanted to be just like Pablo, though he hadn't told anyone about this particular dream. He was certain that his friends would make fun of him and that his mother would panic at the thought of him catapulting through space at top speed in a small metal rocket. She wasn't the biggest fan of flying, mostly due to Will's father dying in a mysterious spacecraft explosion before he was born. Will had never been told the full story, but he knew enough to be sure that his mother wouldn't be cheering him on should he choose racing as his career.

After he had finished getting ready, Will headed over to the computer screen fitted securely into the wall above his desk. He sat down and turned on the display, which told him the date – 1st of September 2113. A large dialogue box popped up, flashing to announce a message of some sort.

'Good morning, Will. This is a reminder to inform you that you will be departing for the Space Academy today at 11.11 A.M',' the robotic voice notified him.

Will swiped the notice off the screen. As if he could have forgotten! He suspected that Marie, his private tutor, had logged the event into his computer's diary.

He brought up another screen and checked his inbox. A small speech bubble icon informed him that he had one new message from Spencer Hullington, his friend who lived across the hall. He opened the message and began to read:

'Hi Will,

Just letting you know that my father has pulled some strings and managed to arrange for our rooms to be on the same floor at the Academy, just like here! He designed a lot of the school's architecture and they owe him a few favours. Anyway, I'll see you later on the shuttle. It leaves at 11.11 exactly so don't be late! I'll try to save you a seat.

From Spencer.

P.S Have you packed yet? I think I'm going to ask Anita, our maid, to do mine. She's so much better at folding than I am!'

Will frowned as he finished reading. He supposed he should be excited that he and Spencer would be living near each other at the Space Academy, but instead he felt a thud of disappointment. He had looked forward to making a fresh start and experiencing something different, finally free from the confines of his life on Floor One.

Spencer's message had reminded him about packing. He had promised his mother that he would finish it before he went to bed the night before, and yet he hadn't managed to pack a single thing. He had spent the evening playing his favourite virtual reality game 'Earth Wars' instead and had been so absorbed in it that he had completely lost track of time.

He had been in the middle of killing the last evil general, jumping about his room with his virtual sword and fighting the holograms that were spawning around him, when he had suddenly noticed the time and realised it was far too late for him to be awake. He had shut the game down with haste and scrambled into bed, shutting his eyes and willing himself to fall asleep before he was caught still awake in the small hours of the morning.

Rummaging under his bed, he found the brand-new suitcase his mum had got him from the lobby the week before and pulled it out, yanking his clothes from their hangers and throwing them inside in a haphazard manner. He wasn't sure how many outfits he would need, and so decided to pack his entire collection. He left his Pablo Pianthus pyjamas in their drawer, selecting a few pairs of plainer nightwear that were less likely to embarrass him.

He scanned his room carefully for anything else he would need. His personal device that would allow him to send and receive messages was already attached to his wrist after he had fallen asleep wearing it. Other than that, he didn't have many possessions that he treasured, save for a photograph of himself and his mother that had been taken when he was a baby.

He walked over to the picture, smiling at the image of himself sat on his mother's lap, wearing a pair of green dungarees over a stripy T-shirt, beaming at the camera with very little teeth. Carefully, he picked up the frame, wrapping it in his dressing gown and placing it in his suitcase with the rest of his things.

When he had finished packing, he pulled the zip on the case to ensure it was secure and positioned it in the middle of his room, making sure it would be immediately noticeable should his mum come in to check on him.

He stepped out of his bedroom, the doors sliding apart automatically, and walked down the hallway into the dining area. His mother, Elsie, was sitting at the long glass table, drinking a cup of hot coffee while reading her day's schedule from the tablet in her hand. When Will entered the room, she looked up and smiled.

'Good morning, darling,' she said, motioning to the chair beside her. 'Come and sit down'.

Will went and sat where she had gestured and began delving into the breakfast spread that the family's assistant, Derek, had laid out for them. Derek insisted on being referred to as an 'assistant' and not a 'maid', 'butler' or 'cleaner', or else he refused to do any work. Will could hear him in the background as he ate, cleaning the bathroom and muttering curses under his breath. He heard something heavy drop and smash, causing a string of obscenities to pour from Derek's mouth. Will took a long swig of his orange juice, concealing the laughter that he knew would earn him a scolding.

'Well, today's the day,' Elsie said, leaning on her hand and looking at him wistfully. She was smiling, but her voice was choked with emotion. In all his life, Will had never seen his mother cry. However, he had learnt to look for the sadness in her eyes, which often gave her away.

'I know,' Will answered, suddenly becoming fascinated with his breakfast muffin.

'How do you feel?' she asked, folding her arms and leaning back, as though he were one of her clients.

'I don't really know,' Will answered with a shrug, devouring the rest of his breakfast.

'School was very different back on Earth, you know,' Elsie began. Will tried to fix his face into an expression of interest as he prepared himself for another 'Earth' story.

'We didn't learn nearly as many interesting things as they teach at the Space Academy,' she continued. 'Only college was really exciting, and people were lucky to be able to get a place there. That's where I met the Captain, you know.'

'And Dad,' Will said casually. As soon the words had escaped his mouth, he regretted them. He scrunched up his face and cringed at his unfortunate mistake. Elsie swallowed and looked away. Composing herself, she turned back and continued chattering brightly.

'I've cleared all of my appointments this morning so I can take you to the shuttle,' she informed him. 'We haven't got long until we have to get going.'

'Already?' Will asked incredulously. He felt as though he had only just got up.

He glanced out of the large windows that hung along the

right-hand wall, but it was impossible to tell the time of day by looking through them. Special UV lights had been installed on Floor One to give the impression of sunlight flooding through from outside. However, the illusion could easily be broken by sitting in the same room for a long period of time. The lights were set to a timer, coming on with a sudden burst at eight in the morning and disappearing again abruptly at eight p.m. From what he had been told by old Earth dwellers, this had nothing on the real beauty of the rising and falling of the sun.

'Get your coat on,' Elsie's voice interrupted his reverie. 'We'll be meeting Alfie and Lois soon. Have you packed?'

'Of course I have Mum, what do you take me for?' he replied. His mum narrowed her eyes but said nothing. She called for Derek and asked him to fetch Will's suitcase from his room. He nodded and repeated the word 'certainly' several times before balling up his fists and storming pointedly into Will's bedroom.

A moment later, Derek returned with the black suitcase, wheeling it to the front doors before stepping away and heading off to continue with the day's chores.

There was a loud knock on the door and Will jumped up, racing across the room to answer it. He pressed his finger to the sensor pad beside the door, which opened to reveal Alfie and his daughter, Lois, standing in the atrium.

Alfie was standing behind Lois, his large hands fixed on her shoulders as he grinned in a bemused sort of way. Lois stood stony-faced, not seeming to have inherited her father's cheerful nature.

Her long, blonde hair was scraped back into a high ponytail, fastened with an over-sized black hair band. She wore a green tartan dress with a black shawl, bright white tights and a pair of brown, clunky shoes. Will thought she looked like one of the frightening china dolls available to purchase in the toy store. She was clasping a large, pink travelling bag between her hands and had three more suitcases on a golden luggage rack behind them, currently being manned by one of their many staff.

'Hello, Elsie. Hello, Will,' Alfie greeted them each with a nod of his head. 'Are you ready to go?'

Lois frowned deeply and rolled her eyes, the difficult task of standing still in the doorway apparently causing her some great inconvenience.

'Yes, we're all ready here,' Elsie beamed.

'Great!' Alfie grinned. 'Lois is really excited, aren't you, Lois?'

Lois could not have looked less excited if she was being chased by a ten-legged alien. She continued to scowl furiously into the distance, refusing to look any of them in the eye. An involuntary laugh burst out of Will before he could stop it, causing Elsie, Alfie and Lois to glower at him with confusion.

'Sorry. I just... remembered something funny,' he stammered feebly.

With Will's suitcase added to the luggage rack, the group set off through the atrium, their footsteps echoing across the walls as they walked.

They reached the lift and stepped inside, Elsie tapping the screen on the glass to select their destination. There was a sudden lurch to the left, causing them all to lose their balance as they began whizzing away from Floor One.

They whooshed up and down and side to side, hurtling in all different directions until finally the lift slowed and turned a corner, its mechanisms clicking as it shuddered to a halt.

Will stepped out, blinking as his eyes adjusted to the sudden stillness of their surroundings. The section of *The Mayflower* they had arrived in was unrecognisable to Will. The carpet was a worn beige, and the walls were painted in a dull shade of grey. There were several heavy-looking brown doors running down the hallway, which appeared to open manually with a handle instead of by the touch of a sensor pad. A small sign stuck to the wall informed them that 'Loading Deck E' was to the left, a helpful arrow pointing them in the right direction.

Alfie took the lead, guiding them to a set of thick steel doors. He turned around to face the rest of the group.

'Well, this is it,' he announced. 'Are you two ready?'

Will and Lois exchanged a nervous glance, the first time they had interacted on their journey thus far.

Will nodded, a sudden surge of nerves passing through him as Alfie opened the doors.

The group stepped forward, and found themselves on the largest loading platform Will had ever seen. The vast space, usually used for the purpose of transporting goods from *The Mayflower*, was bustling with hundreds of people.

Mothers and fathers were saying goodbye to their children, brothers and sisters were chattering with excitement and friends, separated by the long school holiday, were gleefully calling out and waving to each other. An exceptionally large transporter ship was sitting stationary on tracks that ran across the shiny white floor, unmoved by the gathering hordes of Space Academy students and their families.

There were five doors along its side, which, as Will watched, opened to reveal comfortable blue leather seating inside the ship's belly. Crowds of students began moving towards the doors, hugging their families goodbye before hustling forward.

Will and Lois looked at Alfie and Elsie for guidance, but all they could find was their own dumbfounded expressions reflected on the adult's faces. Their uncertainty was addressed a few minutes later, when the sound of a strong, female voice carried across the platform.

'All new students this way!' the voice called.

The four of them followed in the direction of the voice, bustling through the crowd with Alfie's butler close behind them, the wheels of his luggage rack squeaking as they dragged across the cold, hard floor.

They edged their way past a family of mousy-brown haired children. The mother had her hands on the youngest boy's face and was talking to him in a soft voice, her eyes full of tears. An older boy and girl were standing to the side, their arms folded around their chests as they rolled their eyes and huffed in the direction of their mother.

There was a younger girl too, clutching her mother's hand. She looked around apprehensively, craning her neck to see into the faces of everyone who was passing by. When Will's group drew level with the family, the girl's eyes widened and she let out a gasp, tugging on her mother's coat and pointing at them with her mouth open.

'Mummy, mummy it's the Captain! Look! It's the Captain!' she shouted. Her mother turned and stared at Alfie, as did the rest of the family.

They all stood perfectly still, gawking as though they had never seen another human being before. As they stood in their strange, fascinated unison, Will couldn't help but notice the tatty and worn state of their clothing.

The mother's canary yellow coat was fraying at the edges

and the younger boy, who looked to be about the same age as Will, was wearing trousers that were slightly too big for him, their hem trailing on the floor. The older girl and boy's clothes had been hand stitched together by someone who wasn't very skilled, and the youngest girl's flowery dress and navy coat were obvious hand-me-downs, their once richer colours faded with time and use.

Will knew these sorts of clothes were not produced by the designers on Floor One and he had never seen a family dressed in such a dishevelled manner before. He pulled at his own jumper, suddenly conscious of the rich quality of its material.

'They must be from a very low floor.' Lois whispered to no one in particular.

The family stood out vividly against the sea of smooth fabrics and dark colours that swarmed the platform, making it hard not to notice them. Alfie smiled diplomatically in their direction and then continued to steer Lois through the crowd.

It soon became evident that the little girl's shouts had attracted more attention than she had intended. A ripple had started to spread across the platform, and a tide of faces turned to watch as the Captain passed.

Lois' cheeks flushed a dark shade of magenta as she tried desperately not to meet the eyes of their onlookers. Will saw her face visibly flood with relief as they caught sight of their old tutor group from Floor One. She moved with haste, settling herself in the midst of the other girls, while Will went to stand quietly between Spencer and their friend Alasdair.

The tutor group was standing among a crowd of about ninety other students their age, every single pair of eyes fixed on a young woman who was standing at the head of the gathering.

The woman's arms were folded behind her back as she waited with impatience, scanning the crowd for anyone new approaching the group. Her dyed-blonde hair was scraped back tightly against her head, and her lips were fixed in a permanent pursed position. Will turned to follow her gaze, which was currently patrolling over the perimeter of the platform, and wondered how much longer it would take for everyone else to arrive.

While looking for other students, he was pleased to see his mother and Alfie standing close behind them in a small congregation of parents. He felt a rush of relief as he realised he hadn't missed his chance to say goodbye.

After a few more minutes, the severe woman began to count heads, whispering to herself as she did so. Once finished, she clapped her hands, immediately commanding the attention of everyone around her.

'Hello,' she boomed. It was more of an announcement than a greeting. After flashing a brilliant white smile in the direction of the parents, she began to speak, directing her words over the student's heads.

'My name is Miss Fortem, and I am a teacher at the Space Academy. It is part of my job to look after the first-years and make sure that their transition into life at the Academy is a smooth one,' she explained with a carefully inflected tone of voice.

'As you can see, we are standing next to a large transporter ship, which will be taking us to the Academy shortly. For many of you, this will more than likely be your first ever journey through outer space and you may be feeling quite anxious about the experience. Rest assured that the shuttle has been tested by both the Academy and officials aboard *The Mayflower* and is one of the most safely built spacecrafts we have.

'Despite knowing this, the first time flying can still be a nerve-wracking experience. I urge any of you who are feeling scared on board to approach me, and I will do all I can to ensure the rest of your journey is more comfortable.'

She smiled her dazzling smile, her eyes still fixed on the parents as she stressed her point. Will started to wonder if Miss Fortem was always on the platform to give such an encouraging welcome, or whether the school had simply got wind that the Captain's daughter would be starting that year.

'Right then,' Miss Fortem clapped her hands together again, causing several members of the crowd to jump. 'Without further ado, I must ask you to board the shuttle,' she gestured to the giant spacecraft next to her.

'We will be leaving at 11.11 am precisely! First-years must board through the first door on the left. I ask parents and those helping to take any luggage to the stewards, who you will find at the back compartment of the shuttle.'

At these words, the parents poured upon their children and began their emotional goodbyes, as butlers and staff began to hurry away with the suitcases.

Will found Elsie, who was standing in a clearing of people and smiling proudly at him from a distance. He walked over and she crouched down to his level, readjusting his coat and smoothing out his hair, which he immediately ruffled again. Elsie smiled and cupped her hands around his face.

'Well,' she said. 'I suppose this is goodbye.'

'Don't worry, Mum, it's not that long until the school holidays.' Will smiled.

'I'm sure you will have a fantastic time,' Elsie said, her voice strained, 'but I will miss you.'

'I'll miss you too, Mum,' he replied. 'At least you'll have Derek to keep you company.'

Elsie laughed. It was a lovely sound, and Will wished he had heard it more often in his childhood. The two of them embraced briefly, then pulled apart, Elsie struggling to blink back tears as she released him.

'Make sure you call!' she ordered him, though her voice was light and weary.

'Of course I will! You can't get rid of me that easily,' Will grinned.

He would miss home, it was true, but the excitement of starting a new adventure at the Space Academy was luring him. He could be anyone he wanted to be there. He no longer had to be 'Will from Floor One'. He had always felt a powerful conviction that there was much more to life than he had come to know, and he was filled with a burning curiosity for all the things he was yet to discover and for the people he was yet to meet.

He took a deep breath and closed his eyes, forcing his feet forward and onto the shuttle.

The voices of the other first-years filled his ears and the smell of new fabric shrouded his nostrils as he entered the large transporter ship. He allowed himself a moment's pause before he opened his eyes again and began the next chapter of his life. His entire transition from a boy into a man would occur at the Academy and he struggled to comprehend the significance of the moment.

'Erm, excuse me?'

A voice snapped him out of his reverie, forcing his eyes open as he whipped his head around to see a tall, lanky boy with dark hair standing behind him, clutching a rucksack with a bemused look on his face.

'Did you know you were just standing there with your eyes shut?' he smirked. 'You're holding up the whole queue!'

Will tried with all his might to stop the inevitable flush of red that was making its way up through his neck and to his cheeks. He looked over the boy's shoulder to see a line of students peering around one another, struggling to see what was holding up the line.

'What were you doing?' the boy pressed him. 'Were you having a seizure or something? Should I go and get a medic?'

A few of the boys behind him began to snicker. They were all staring at him, trying to work out if something was genuinely wrong, or if he was just incredibly strange.

Will's mouth moved soundlessly as he tried to think of something to say that would save him from eternal social damnation. Those who were already seated around him had stopped their conversations to see what was going on.

Whatever he said next would determine their first impressions of him, and yet he could not come up with a single reasonable explanation as to why he had been standing completely still in the middle of the shuttle with his eyes closed.

'Leave him alone Rudy, he's probably just nervous,' said a girl's voice from within the queue. Will was both simultaneously grateful for her intervention and morbidly embarrassed that he had to be rescued by a stranger.

He turned and began making his way towards the rows of seats decorated with navy blue upholstery that filled the first compartment, wishing that the metal bottom of the shuttle would give way and let him fall through the platform and into deep space. He was mortified when he noticed that the seats were designed for two people, realising with a sudden fit of panic that nobody was going to want to sit next to him, and he would have to face the humiliation of riding the entire journey on his own.

He slumped into the nearest chair and pretended to be very interested in looking out of the window, hoping he would blend into the furniture and disappear.

'Mind if I sit here?' a voice said.

Will jumped and looked up to see a girl standing over him. She flicked her long, chestnut hair from her shoulders and smiled at him, her arms folded nonchalantly as she awaited his response. He recognised the voice as belonging to the person who had saved him from Rudy's mockery.

'Y-yes of course,' Will stammered, caught off guard.

The girl sat down beside him, and swung her handheld luggage onto the floor, resting it safely between her knees. For the first time in his life, Will became acutely aware of his limbs, and wasn't sure where to place them. He was certain that even an accidental brush of his arm against hers would cause his head to explode in a fire of embarrassment, and so positioned himself awkwardly against the wall.

He didn't have much time to worry about how to seat himself however, for no sooner had the girl sat down than Rudy had begun to call out from the back of the compartment where he and a group of his friends were sitting.

'Emily what are you doing?!' he sneered. 'I know there's obviously something wrong with that boy, but you don't have to feel sorry for him. Come and sit with us!'

Emily continued staring forwards as though Rudy had never spoken, her deep blue eyes flashing with contempt.

'Just ignore him,' she told Will. 'He's always like that.'

'Wow!' Rudy continued, ensuring that he was in earshot of everyone around him, 'it must be true love! Good job your mum's a nurse, Emily, I think that one is going to need all the help he can get.'

Rudy's gaggle of followers burst into exaggerated, raucous laughter, though Will didn't find the insult particularly clever or funny.

He looked around to see if any of his peers from Floor One would jump to his defence, but they were all doing an extremely convincing job of pretending not to recognise him. In fact, Lois seemed to find him completely invisible when he attempted to catch her eye. She looked around wildly, terrified that somebody would have seen her with Will on the platform and would expose her for knowing him.

'We used to be tutored together, Rudy and I,' Emily explained calmly, as though this situation was a regular occurrence for her. 'He always seemed to think that we were friends. I don't know why. I never liked him. I was hoping that going to school would mean I could get away from him and make a fresh start.'

'I can relate to that,' Will replied, throwing a cursory glance towards Spencer, Alasdair and the rest of the tutor group.

A wave of silence suddenly fell across the compartment. Will looked around in confusion, unsure what was going on.

It took him a few seconds to notice the boy from the ragged looking family he had seen earlier, frozen in the doorway of the shuttle, aware that every face inside was turned towards him. He was holding on to his patchy bag so tightly that his knuckles were turning white. Sitting down on the empty front seat, he turned his back on all his spectators and positioned himself as motionless as a statue.

Before a single word could be uttered, Miss Fortem appeared, her presence alone stifling any taunts or nasty remarks that might have been aimed his way. Will saw his shoulders sag with relief as Miss Fortem began to speak, distracting everybody's attention towards her.

'Okay, first-years,' she began, 'the shuttle is about to take off at any moment. Please make sure you have arranged yourselves as two to a seat. There are protective seat belts located to the left of each person, however they will not be needed unless we experience any difficulties-'

Will swallowed hard. He wasn't entirely sure what 'difficulties' they might encounter flying through space, and nor was he in any hurry to find out.

'If they are required, you will see a flashing red light in the compartment at which point you must immediately take your seat belt and clip it across your waist, securing it firmly in the slot on the right-hand side. I must ask that you do not move around while the shuttle is in motion, unless absolutely necessary. '

Will remembered her soothing words in front of the parents about approaching her on the journey, and was suddenly convinced that anyone seeking her help would find more peril going to her than they would ever encounter in outer space.

'The journey takes roughly fifteen minutes,' she continued. 'When we arrive at the Academy, we will enter into the Gathering Hall where you will attend your first assembly. You will be addressed by the Headmaster who you are to refer to as 'Admiral Allance'. After that, you will be assigned into three classes and further instructions will be given to you. Does everybody understand?'

There were a few nods and noises of compliance.

'Good, then. Without further ado, I must ask that we prepare for take-off.'

Miss Fortem sat down at the front next to the ragged boy. He turned his body sideways, shrinking into the window and resting his face against the glass as he stared blankly at the back wall of the platform.

At that moment, everybody in the compartment began leaning backwards and forward, stretching their bodies as high as they could manage so as to see onto the platform, attempting to get one last glimpse of their families before they launched.

Will caught sight of his mother moving through the crowd, pushing her way right to the front so that she was almost touching the shuttle. She blew kisses to him with both hands and waved furiously. Will grinned and waved back, bemused to see his mother so expressive.

The engines beneath them whirred into life, shaking the entire ship with the force of their activation.

They lifted into the air, Will's mother and the other parents pushed backwards by a sudden surge of energy that pulsated out from under them as they took off. They hovered towards the ceiling, floating higher and higher until the people below began to resemble toys in a dollhouse.

Will kept his eyes on his mother, even as she became minuscule, fixated upon her figure until the metal roof of the platform snapped shut and they found themselves in an enclosed capsule. As one roof closed, a second one above their heads opened, providing their exit into space. They ascended through it, sitting suspended for a moment as they hung still in the infinite black sky.

Will felt Emily stiffen beside him as they waited in the silence, full of bewilderment and fear. The moment lasted only a few seconds before there was a sudden jolt, flinging them forward as the shuttle began hurtling through the air.

'This is it!' Emily said.

'This is it,' Will repeated, taking a deep breath.

4

THE SPACE ACADEMY

Emily peered out of the window, straining her neck to see past Will, who had pressed his face upon the glass in awe. There was something wonderful and yet equally terrifying about being in the depths of space as they travelled to the school, the stars blurring into a silvery haze as the speed of the shuttle increased.

Emily felt a deep sense of discomfort as she gazed at the Universe around her, realising how small and insignificant she was in comparison to its sheer size. Suddenly, Will turned to her with a concerned expression on his face, breaking the silence and rescuing her from her thoughts.

'What do you think it's like at the school?' he asked her, his eyes wide and eager.

'My brother's in third-year and he's told me a few things. We get to study real-life aliens and fly our own rockets through space,' she replied, making a conscious effort to keep her tone cool and indifferent in order to impress him.

'Wow' he said after a moment. 'Are you sure he isn't winding you up?'

'He does enjoy winding me up,' she acknowledged. 'But no, I don't think he is this time. He knows how excited I am about starting at the Academy. It's the only way I get to escape from our dad. He and I don't get on.'

The words ran off her tongue before she could stop them and she flushed crimson with embarrassment, internally berating herself for having shared such personal information with a stranger. She braced herself for the awkward, stuttered reply she was customary to receiving after bringing up her relationship with her father.

'That's a shame,' Will said with sincerity. 'But at least you have a dad. Mine died before I was born.'

'I'm sorry to hear that,' she told him, surprised by how truly sad she felt at the thought of him suffering such a loss. He smiled with gratitude and the two of them exchanged a moment of understanding, each one trusting the other with what they had revealed.

'What do you think you'd like to be, then?' Will asked her. 'When we get to Novum. I mean that's the whole point of the school, isn't it? To train us up and make us useful!'

Emily laughed, but was momentarily thrown by the question. No one had ever asked her what she wanted to be. There had been so much emphasis by her parents on getting into the Space Academy, like her brother, that no one had ever considered what would happen afterwards.

'I haven't really thought about it,' Emily mused. 'I like technology. I think I want to be something to do with that. My dad wouldn't like it, though. He doesn't think subjects like that are suitable for girls.'

Will raised his eyebrows.

'Well, I suppose you'll have to prove him wrong, then, won't you?' he grinned.

'Yes,' Emily agreed. 'I suppose I will.'

As the journey progressed, their conversation flowed easily, and Emily couldn't help but hope that their friendship would continue once they had arrived at the school.

After a while, an excited wave of voices went up in the seats around them. Emily and Will returned their attention to the window to discover what had caused the ruckus, and were quick to lay eyes on the culprit.

Looming out of the darkness just in front of them was the Space Academy. The school itself was encased in a huge transparent dome that was floating graciously in mid-air. Through the surface, a grand building could be seen, set in the centre of the grounds and rising to the height of at least a hundred feet or more.

A colossal, white tower lurched out of the floor to the left of the school, reaching almost to the top of the protective dome. A smattering of buildings filled the rest of the campus, most notable among them a silver observatory, glittering as it caught the light from the stars above it.

'Wow,' Emily breathed as they drew closer to the school, circling around the edge until they reached a round, metal door in its casing- just big enough for the shuttle to fit through. It sprung open as they approached, revealing a hidden room designed for spacecrafts to land in, and providing just enough room for them to begin their descent.

The door sealed shut immediately behind them as they juddered into landing and oxygen was pumped noisily around them through a ventilation system. Despite this, Emily felt as though all the air had disappeared from her surroundings and her head swam with anticipation as the engines cut, immersing the first-year students into a sharp and sudden silence.

Miss Fortem leapt straight into action, jumping out of her chair and twisting around to face everybody in the same, swift movement.

'Okay, boys and girls,' she said. 'We are about to get off the shuttle, but before we do, it's important that we listen and that we all understand exactly what needs to happen.'

She pursed her lips and tilted her head down, widening her eyes to emphasise the importance of the point she was making. She waited until she had personally ensured that every individual student was listening.

'First of all, I need everyone to check that they have all their belongings. Most of you will have bags stowed in the luggage compartments as well. That luggage will be taken for you and unloaded into your new rooms.'

A hum of excited whispers sounded at the mention of new rooms. Miss Fortem cleared her throat loudly.

'Secondly,' she continued, 'I want you all to have a look at the person sitting next to you.'

Emily and Will glanced at each other, before hastily looking back at Miss Fortem.

'This person is going to be your partner on our walk up to the school. Unfortunately, we have had incidences in the past where pupils have become over excited and wandered off, only to be found somewhere in the grounds hours later. As you may have noticed, our school campus is rather big, so it is extremely important that you do not make any detours. You are each responsible for ensuring that your partner stays with you for the entire walk. Are we all clear?'

There was a mild murmur of understanding.

'Yes, Miss Fortem,' she demanded.

'Yes, Miss Fortem,' the compartment repeated.

'Okay, we are now going to get off the shuttle, so please stand up with your partners.'

There was a flurry of movement as everyone scuffled to their feet, hauling rucksacks and holdalls off the floor and out of the overhead bins. Emily bent down to grab her bag from the floor, catching sight of Miss Fortem gently putting her hand on the arm of the scruffy looking boy as she stood up.

'You can walk with me,' she told him. He nodded dejectedly, without making eye contact.

Miss Fortem scanned her thumb against the touch pad on the door and it opened with a puff of air. The scruffy boy by her side, she began to lead all the passengers out of the shuttle in their pairs. Emily and Will waited patiently for a chance to leave their seats and join in the queue.

At least a dozen students had passed them on the way out, when Rudy drew up alongside them.

'Are you two love birds going to stay here forever?' he taunted, his eyes full of malice.

'Give it a rest, Rudy,' Emily sighed, folding her arms.

'Please,' he said sarcastically. 'Go in front of me. I would hate to be the one responsible for delaying the beautiful journey you two are about to embark on.'

Glowering at him, Emily took the place he had gestured to, dragging Will by the arm and causing Rudy to snort loudly. Together, they filtered down the middle of the compartment, listening to the gasps of the people ahead of them as they made their way outside. They reached the door, a wave of cool air washing over their faces, providing pleasant relief from the warmth of standing too close to so many bodies in a confined space.

Disembarking the shuttle, they exited the room they had landed in and headed into the school grounds, finding themselves at the foot of the Ivory Tower. So impressive was its size, that it had to have its own shuttle ship waiting at the base, ready to fly students to the classrooms high above.

'This building is where Alien Studies is taught,' Miss Fortem explained when the last of the first-years had joined in the gathering. 'The height of the tower provides extra security should any of the aliens that are held there try and escape.'

'Still think my brother was winding me up?' Emily smirked at Will, whose eyes had widened in bewilderment.

'Okay, I take it back,' he conceded.

Feeling satisfied, Emily tore her eyes away from the tower and began to scan the rest of the grounds, trying to take it all in. Even though it was technically daytime, there was no sunlight-fake or otherwise- to be found here. The grounds were mainly lit by lamp posts, placed strategically alongside the interconnecting pathways that wove their way around the school.

Miss Fortem led them all to the front entrance, which proved to be two colossal navy doors fitted into the front of a small dome, attached to the main school building. They were without a doubt the biggest doors that Emily had ever seen. She glanced to the side and saw the same look of amazement reflected in Will's face.

'What do you think that means?' he asked her, pointing to a golden sphere that was fixed above the doors, a small model rocket positioned in mid-flight next to it.

'It's the school's logo,' Emily explained, pleased to have superior knowledge to him on the subject. 'I've seen it on the school uniform. I think the planet in the middle is meant to be Novum, and the rocket represents *The Mayflower*.'

'You seem to know a lot about this already,' Will replied. 'I'll have to stick around with you,'

Emily felt a wave of happiness spreading across her body and tried hard to stifle it, fearful that her pleasure at the sound of his words was visible.

'Welcome to the Space Academy,' Miss Fortem smiled, interrupting their conversation as she addressed them all.

'These are the main doors as you can most probably see. Above them is a 3-D representation of our school logo. The sphere signifies the planet Novum, and the rocket, of course, stands for our journey towards it. You will become very familiar with this image during your time here.'

'Well done,' Will whispered to Emily. She smiled with pride and glanced up at the logo again, the figure of Novum looming over her head and casting her face into shadow.

'Now, we are about to enter the school,' Miss Fortem informed them. 'Once we are inside, I will take you straight into the Gathering Hall. You may sit beside whoever you want, as long as you sit in the first row.'

Before anybody had a chance to process this, Miss Fortem turned on her heel and began knocking on the front doors with efficiency. They swung open on her command, moving backwards at the same speed, as though being pulled by synchronised strings.

Following Miss Fortem, who had promptly made her way inside, the children passed through a set of security scanners and found themselves in the school's Reception Hall.

The floor was made entirely of white tile, polished to such a dazzling hue that the students could see their reflections shimmering across the surface. In the centre of the hall was a bronze statue of a man, at least three times the size of any real human being, standing regally on a large platform, a tiny planet balancing in his outstretched palm. His pupil-less eyes stared forwards, seeing into a future that nobody else could view.

Behind the statue, flanking each side of the hall, were two glass lifts in the shape of bullets. The walls were decorated in banners of navy and gold, and were covered in framed photographs that documented the Academy's proudest achievements thus far- including a victory against the rocket racing team for Weltraumschule, the German version of the school.

A trophy case stood proudly on the left-hand side of the room, drawing immediate attention to itself upon entry. From where she stood, Emily was able to read the inscription for a prize given to the Academic Decathlon team, who had won the competition in 2110, an accompanying video replaying the moment of victory from a small screen inside the case. Beside it, was a large collage containing photographs of all the members of staff at the school, each one beaming out from behind the frame.

Overhead, a great glass roof revealed a magnificently clear view of the stars above, a holographic projection of the current solar system they were travelling through spinning in mid-air underneath it.

To the left of the Reception Hall was a door marked 'Gathering Hall' in important gold lettering, with a second marked 'Dining Hall' on the right. The smell of piping hot food began to waft from the latter, causing Emily's stomach to growl, as she suddenly realised how long it had been since breakfast. To her disappointment, Miss Fortem ushered the children towards the Gathering Hall and away from the delicious odour of the lunch she so yearned for.

They entered a large rectangular room, congregating at the front under Miss Fortem's instruction. Emily craned her neck to look at the seating behind them, which rose up in staggered levels to the back of the hall, giving her an impression of the large number of students at the school. Directly in front of them was a huge stage set in front of a glass wall, which boasted an impressive view of the school grounds.

While gazing through it, Emily noticed an artificial lake she hadn't yet seen, its surface glinting and glistening in the starlight. She was just imagining how it would feel to take a dip in its cool, clear waters, when a booming voice shook her from her thoughts.

'Good afternoon, new students!'.

Emily turned to see a tall and broad looking man striding across the stage, his arms outstretched in welcome. He wore a deep blue suit that seemed to accentuate the silvery-grey hue of his hair and eyes. His thick, bushy eyebrows were drawn together, and his slanted mouth set in what resembled a permanent frown, despite the fact he was trying his utmost to attempt a smile. His footsteps crashed across the smooth stage, reverberating all around the room, as though a stampede of wild aliens were heading towards them.

'Miss Fortem,' he grunted, as he addressed the gaggle of students. 'You have brought us a fine, young bunch of children yet again. How lovely.'

He regarded them all with a strained look of delight.

'My name is Admiral Allance,' he nodded curtly, his hands folded neatly behind his back. 'Welcome to the Space Academy.'

ALDERIN CLASS

Standing shoulder to shoulder among the crowd of anxious first-years, Will waited with bated breath for Admiral Allance to speak, certain that he had never laid eyes on a man who could command so much attention simply by being present. His mannerisms and general stature gave the distinct impression that he was someone to be taken seriously, and Will made a mental note to himself never to fall into the Allance's bad books if he could help it.

'Now as you may be aware,' Allance continued, 'I am your Headmaster here at the school.'

There was a brief silence as he allowed this information to sink in. Will wondered if he expected some sort of applause or congratulations for the announcement.

'It is with great warmth that I welcome you all here. It's our pleasure to receive such bright and wonderful students every year, all finely selected from the most suitable of backgrounds.'

He paused to stare at the ragged boy, who looked as though he wanted to jump through the glass wall and run away as fast as he could.

'I will now ask you to take your seats,' Allance requested, not taking his eyes off the boy. 'In your first year, you must always sit in the front row. Our start of year assembly will be commencing shortly, in which further information will be given to you about the school. Please, be seated.'

Obediently, the first-years trouped over to the midnight blue seats, shuffling around on the soft, spongy material as they got into a comfortable position. Will tried very hard to keep his expression neutral as Emily came to sit beside him, and stared forwards to conceal his pleasure. His efforts proved to be in vain, however, when Rudy wolf-whistled from further down the row, as soon as Emily's body made contact with the chair.

Once everyone had settled, the older students began pouring into the Gathering Hall from opposite sides, flowing smoothly into the rows behind Will and the other first-years. All the students were wearing the same uniform; a navy jumper emblazoned with a yellow emblem of the school logo and a pair of plain black trousers.

Will drew his legs under his chair sharply as the fifth years passed him, making their way to their seats without giving the first-years a single cursory glance. He felt very small compared to some of them, and his mind was abruptly filled with worrying visions of being trampled to death during the panicked rush between classes.

'Hey, sis,' came a cheerful voice from behind them.

Will and Emily both turned to see an older boy with messy, brown hair grinning jubilantly at them. His cheeks were rosy with happiness and his familiar blue eyes glinted with mischief. He had a smattering of freckles across his nose, which protruded slightly against his otherwise delicate features. Will recognised him immediately as Emily's older brother, the resemblance between them unmistakeable.

'Hello, Charlie,' she beamed at him. 'This is my friend, Will.'

She pointed towards Will, who grinned, pleased to have been introduced as a friend.

'Nice to meet you, Will,' Charlie said with genuine enthusiasm. 'You two better brace yourselves. The first day here is a bit mind blowing.'

'Will thought you were winding me up about the aliens.' Emily laughed, then added uncertainly, 'it was all true, what you told me, wasn't it?'

'Yeah,' Charlie replied ecstatically, 'and there's so much more that I can't even explain. Just you wait!'

He rubbed his hands together with glee, unable to control himself. Will was distracted by a procession of stern-looking teachers entering the hall, but was soon forced to turn his attention back to Admiral Allance, who had raised his hand in the air pointedly. Slowly, the students began to copy his action and the excited racket of chatter died down from a buzz into a hum before falling silent.

'Welcome, welcome all!' the Headmaster bellowed. 'I do hope you have all enjoyed your holidays, and are now fully prepared to put your thinking caps on and study hard for another year.'

Every word he spoke was enunciated with expert care, his voice travelling around the hall with ease. He walked across the stage as he spoke, looking students directly in the eye to capture their attention, his overwhelming presence spreading to every corner of the room.

'Now, tradition dictates I must begin the welcome assembly by addressing our wonderful new first-years. Let me start by saying that we hope you will be very happy and well looked after here. The Space Academy strives to provide each and every student with the best academic experience we can muster, but in order for you to properly thrive, I must explain a few things about our school that will help you to understand both what our aims are, and what we have achieved thus far.

'This will be the thirteenth year that the Space Academy has been up and running, and we hope that it will be our best and most successful year to date. Our school was built at the same time as *The Mayflower* and was sent into space a few days after the Split, latching on to *The Mayflower's* gravitational field and orbiting from a safe distance. I won't bore you too much with the physics though, as I must say I don't really understand it myself.'

He laughed a booming laugh. There were a few titters of courtesy from across the hall.

'What will we find when we reach Novum?' Allance asked rhetorically. Some of the students looked at each other in confusion, unsure whether they were expected to raise their hands and answer.

'We cannot answer that question,' Allance clarified, 'because nobody knows. What we do know, however, is that we will need to rebuild a civilisation from scratch. Here at the school, we intend to give you the skills you will need to help us rebirth humanity from the ashes. Of course, we also wish to share our knowledge with you about the many exciting things we discovered during our last years on Earth. From the mind-blowing technologies to the in-depth study of aliens, we provide a curriculum that is as thrilling as it is comprehensive.

'We offer many exciting extra-curricular activities here as well. Although we do not study literature, we have a large selection of downloadable I-Books in our library. We also have a virtual reality club, a camping club - which takes place in the Resources Biodome- an Earth appreciation society and a rocket racing team that students can try out for once they have their personal licence.'

Will's whole body reverberated with excitement as he pictured himself as the next Pablo Pianthus, telling interviewers with delight that his successful career began when he joined the rocket racing team at the Space Academy.

'Now onto the boring part,' Admiral Allance continued. 'Of course, it goes without saying that there are rules here. These rules have been put into place not for our benefit, but for your protection. Therefore, I must ask that you listen carefully and heed what I am about to tell you. Firstly, no student must ever leave the school grounds without a chaperone. I must remind you of this, older students, for as you may recall we have had some rather grizzly incidents involving rocket hijacking,'

'Two boys stole rockets and flew to the nearest moon,' Charlie whispered, sticking his head between Emily and Will. 'They caught some weird space sickness and turned purple. They've been in the Medic Ward on *The Mayflower* ever since.'

'Secondly- 'Admiral Allance boomed. 'Students must not leave their bedrooms after curfew. The reason for this being that our Alien Studies teacher, Mr Krecher,' he gestured to a shabby, stout man who was dressed head to toe in tweed, 'takes some of the creatures out of the Alienary at night for exercise and hunting purposes. Though I can assure you that none of these aliens hunt students, it would be very unwise and foolish to cross paths with them during their one daily glimpse of freedom.'

'The third and final most important rule is that no student

enters the Resources biodome without a teacher, unless they are part of an authorised event. This rule has been created due to a very nasty situation in which a student entered the biodome without proper guidance and has been lost in one of its unlimited terrains ever since. '

'There's all these different settings,' Charlie explained in a hushed voice. 'Rainforest, desert, tundra, etc, etc. There are millions. They keep shuffling through them, hoping they'll find him, but no luck so far.'

'That's awful,' Will whispered back.

'Yeah,' Charlie agreed. 'I mean, there'll be enough food and stuff for him to survive, but could you imagine the boredom? There's no technology in there. It'd be just him and ... nature.' He shuddered.

'Now that the serious part is out of the way, I am pleased to announce that it is finally time for the long-awaited back to school lunch,' Admiral Allance projected.

A few of the older students cheered.

'Yes, yes,' he continued. 'Our cooks have gone out of their way to once again produce a delicious meal to welcome you all back. I believe the menu is traditional shepherd's pie, with sticky toffee pudding for dessert.'

An excited chorus of 'yes!' echoed around the hall.

'I must add that there will, of course, be vegetarian and vegan options for those that need them, although whether they will be as spectacular, I personally could not say.'

'Typical,' Emily rolled her eyes. 'I'm a vegetarian. We always get left out.'

'That said, I will not delay you from your taste-bud Heaven any longer,' Admiral Allance proclaimed. 'First-years. if you would like to stand up and make your way towards the Dining Hall,' he gestured towards the door.

Will leapt to his feet with avid enthusiasm, and followed the trail of first-years out of the Gathering Hall and back into the Reception Hall. They bounded past the eye-less statue with haste, the prospect of food bringing a new spring to their step as they rushed to sample the much-anticipated meal.

They entered the Dining Hall, which was laid out like any normal canteen, with gleaming, silver picnic tables lined up in rows across the wide space. There was a serving station that spanned the length of the entire front wall, manned by shiny white robots that whirred into life upon their entry, and began rapidly producing plates full of sumptuous food from shutters behind them. When Will and Emily reached the station, the robots provided them with two steaming hot plates of shepherd's pie and vegetables, the delightful aroma of the food causing Will's stomach to gargle as he suddenly realised how hungry he was.

'Please enjoy your meal,' the robots said in unison.

'Hmm,' Emily said under her breath. 'How do I get it to give me the vegetarian option?'

'I don't know,' Will shrugged. 'Try speaking to it?'

'EXCUSE ME!' he yelled at the robot. 'SHE'S A VEGETARIAN!'

Emily burst into a fit of laughter.

'You don't have to shout at it, Will, it can understand you,' she said with amusement.

'Is there a problem, Miss?' one of the robots asked her, regarding her with empty, grey eyes.

'I'd like the vegetarian meal please,' Emily replied.

The robot removed the plate of shepherd's pie, putting it back in the shutter. There was a click, and the robot swiftly produced a plate of cheese pasta.

'Thank you,' Emily said graciously.

'You are welcome, Miss. Please enjoy your meal,' the robot replied.

'You won't have to ask them to change it every time, will you?' Will asked her, glancing with concern at the build-up in the queue they had caused with their interruption to the serving.

'No,' she answered confidently. 'They would have scanned my image and committed it to memory. They'll recognise me now, and will remember.'

Will blinked.

'How do you know that?' he asked her in awe.

'It's very basic technology,' she assured him, though Will was not convinced.

Together, they carried their meals towards one of the drinks machines at the end of the service station.

'Right then, technical whizz,' Will teased Emily, 'how does this one work?'

She regarded the machine for a minute, rubbing her fingers under her chin as she considered its appearance.

'It's just a touch screen,' she shrugged, tapping on it and producing two ice-cold glasses of apple juice. They placed the drinks on their lunch trays and made their way over to the nearest free table, sitting down and tucking into their food ravenously.

A few minutes into their meals, a pair of older students approached them, carrying a box full of peculiar looking devices that Will had never seen before.

'Welcome, fellow students!' exclaimed the boy on the right, waving his hands in the air in an exaggerated fashion. Emily jumped, spilling some of her juice into her lap.

'My name is Ant,' he announced, 'and this is Sam.'

He gestured to the boy next to him, who was carrying the heavy box, balancing it on his knee and struggling not to show the strain of carrying its weight.

'We are two of your school prefects, and we are here to deliver you your SPs,' Ant continued, pausing to await their reaction. They stared back at him blankly.

'It stands for Student Planners,' Sam explained, heaving the box onto the table and puffing through red cheeks. 'They were going to name it the 'Space Academy Device,' but abbreviating the name to 'SAD' created far too many jokes about the students in the Technology Club who created it.'

Sam and Ant exchanged a brief smirk, causing Will to strongly suspect that they were responsible for the origin of said jokes.

'Here you are,' said Ant, pressing a device firmly into Will's hands, while Sam passed one to Emily.

Will looked at the oblong object with curiosity. It was a similar size to his personal device, but felt much heavier to hold, its thick, silver casing making it look far older than the technology he was used to on *The Mayflower*. At the centre of its face, sat a rectangular black screen that was currently blank and empty. Will turned it over in his hands, in search of an 'on' button.

'To turn it on, just press your finger into the middle of the screen,' Ant instructed him, noticing his confusion. He did as they told him, and the screen blinked and flickered into life, an hourglass icon appearing as it attempted to load its functions.

'This reminds me of the computers I've seen in the Museum on *The Mayflower*,' Emily laughed.

'Oh, give it a chance!' Ant replied with mock indignation. 'The Tech Club spent almost an entire school year working on them, you know.'

'As if they'd let anyone forget,' Sam rolled his eyes.

A moment later, a holographic projection sprung out of the screen, suspending the image of a piece of paper in front of them, the image so realistic that Will was sure he could reach out and touch it.

'Wow,' Emily said, poking her fingers through the hologram.

'Not bad, is it?' said Ant.

'I didn't expect that,' Emily admitted.

'The image you're seeing in front of you is your timetable. It'll give you all the information you need about your lessons as well as tell you which class you're in. Anything you need to know about the school will be on this device. Keep it with you at all times,' Sam instructed them.

'Anyway, we'd better be going, we've got to hand these out to all the newbies,' said Ant. 'Good luck with your first week.'

With that, the pair of them headed off, leaving Emily and Will to inspect their timetables in peace. Will read the top of the piece of the paper carefully.

'It says I'm in a class called 'Alderin,"' he told Emily, stumbling over the pronunciation of the word.

'I'm in that class too!' Emily replied. The two of them beamed at each other for a moment, unable to supress their happiness, then looked away quickly.

Will scanned down the page to follow the timetable. He

located Monday and let out a loud groan as he read the name of the day's first lesson.

'We have Arithmetic first thing on a Monday,' he informed Emily begrudgingly. 'I didn't think we'd have to study Maths here! I hated it when I was tutored.'

'I quite like Maths,' Emily admitted. 'We probably have to study it because it's the same no matter what planet you're on. It's like the Universal language.'

'Well, you can help me with the homework then,' Will replied with deflation, miffed that such a mundane subject had made it into the Space Academy's famed curriculum.

He continued reading his timetable, in hopes of finding more exciting subjects to learn. After Arithmetic was break, followed by Civilisations, followed by Technology, and then a break for lunch.

Will's heart leapt when he read the section for Monday afternoon, which was filled up by double Rocket Control lessons. He could hardly believe his luck that his first day at the Academy would involve rockets, and he began wolfing the remainder of his food down at record pace. He was just in the middle of wondering whether they'd be allowed to fly in their first lesson, when a shrill voice interrupted his pleasant thoughts.

'Alderin,' the voice squawked across the hall. 'Alderin first-years here please.'

By now, the second and third years had begun to filter their way into the Dining Hall, making it hard to locate the whereabouts of the speaker. Thankfully, Emily noticed the familiar faces of some of their peers who were weaving their way through the crowds of older students. The pair of them followed onto the trail and found the small gathering of their new classmates congregating nervously around a female prefect.

She was a severe-looking girl, her tight bob groomed to absolute perfection, without a single hair daring to fall even slightly out of place. Her strong jaw was set into a firm position, and her face projected an expression of deep contempt upon seeing the first-years gathered around her. Will noticed that she was wearing a light blue fitted jacket with a golden 'P' embroidered on the left breast. He supposed that the 'P' stood for 'Prefect,' but a quick scan around the hall confirmed that she was the only one wearing it.

He wondered, in a moment of genuine depression, if she had gone to the trouble of fashioning it for herself, just so she could appear more important. He watched as she adjusted the jacket sleeves so they were exactly same length on both arms, and felt as though his question had been answered.

'My name is May Parsons and I am the Head Prefect here at the Space Academy,' the girl announced.

'No-such-thing,' coughed Ant, as he walked past her to exit the Dining Hall. There was a murmur of giggles among the group, which was soon silenced by May's cold stare.

'I am here to escort you to your first lesson, since it appears that none of you can be trusted to find your way around without making pests of yourselves,' she sneered. Will felt a shudder of dislike pulsate around the entire class.

'Follow me,' she demanded, swivelling on her heel and sticking her nose into the air as she sauntered towards the exit. Will and Emily raised an eyebrow at one another, and then proceeded to follow the throng of students that would become their class for the rest of the year.

As he scanned the faces around him, Will was ashamed to feel a surge of relief that Spencer and the other boys from his old tutor group were not present. Though they had never wronged him in any way, he looked forward to being able to have his own ideas and interests without their snide comments and scathing opinions to put him down. He did, however, notice Lois among the group, looking remarkably out of place without her Floor One counterparts.

They walked across the Reception Hall, careful not to obstruct the smattering of older students that were beginning to mingle around the school, some of them heading to the Dining Hall, and others making their way jovially to their first lessons, using shortcuts they had memorised long ago. Will caught snippets of their conversations as they lined up to use one of the lifts, subtly eavesdropping with the aim to find out more about the Academy.

'I heard Mr Krecher nearly got sacked last year for letting a Runhorn loose in his class! My brother was there, and he said half the students nearly got impaled,' he heard one boy ecstatically tell his friend.

'No way,' his friend replied, waving his hand dismissively. 'Allance didn't even sack Ms. Dido for leaving the Resources biodome unlocked the night Riley Fitch got lost. He'd never get rid of Krecher.'

'You reckon they'll ever find Riley?' Will heard the boy ask, before the pair moved out of earshot.

When the lift arrived, Alderin class piled in, finding it to be deceptively spacious. They rode to the top floor where they disembarked, following May down a long corridor. TV screens mounted the steel walls on either side, displaying the school's internal temperature, the current time and a countdown to when the first lessons were due to begin.

At the end of the corridor, there was an interactive map of the grounds that was several metres long. It displayed every building in satellite view, featuring multicoloured dotted lines that demonstrated the quickest way to get from one to another.

A group of students were standing in a cluster around the far end of the map, pressing on the image of what Will assumed was the Resources biodome, and enlarging it to reveal a series of notices relating to the subject.

'Awesome!' a boy said upon reading the information. 'Resources Club starts again on Friday.'

He began typing with speed into his Student Planner, which informed him in an electronic voice that a reminder had been set. Will was eager to search for details on rocket racing try-outs, but May had become impatient with the younger student's fascination with the school map.

'Yes, yes, it's all very interesting,' she snapped. 'But we can't stand here all day. I have classes to get to as well, you know.'

May turned on her heels and the first-years followed her into the next corridor, which featured gigantic hangings of inspirational quotes printed onto great blue plaques. The words passed in a blur as Will walked beneath them, but he managed to discern one memorable phrase along the way, making out the words; 'A journey of a thousand miles begins with a single step'.

Eventually, they reached their destination, with May coming to such an abrupt halt that several of Will's classmates bumped into each other with shock.

'For those of you whose reading ability exceeds that of a five-year-old's, you will see that we are at the Launch Bay,' May sniffed, gesturing impatiently to the tall lettering that labelled the door above her.

'This is where all your Rocket Control lessons will take place. Never enter the Launch Bay without proper authorisation, and never attempt to fly any rocket outside of class without holding a proper licence. Now, as terribly sad as it is, I must leave you and get to my own lesson. Mr Zeppler will be out shortly to collect you.'

She made to leave, and then turned back, adding as an after thought;

'Try not to make too much of a nuisance of yourselves.'

The moment she was out of sight, the entire class erupted into a buzz of excited conversation, unable to contain themselves with the anticipation of their first official lesson at the Academy. Will, however, was too agitated to speak to anyone, ignoring even Emily, who was forced to talk instead to a pair of giggling girls. He rubbed his fingers together repetitively as he twitched with impatience, watching the door so intently that his vision began to blur.

Just when he was beginning to feel that he may burst if he had to wait another moment, a clicking noise from beyond the door commanded silence over the babbling students, and they turned in unison towards the source of the noise.

The doors swung open, revealing a young man with long auburn hair that swung down to his waist. He smiled coyly; his hands casually placed on his hips as he took in the awed face of the class that stood before him.

'Well then,' he grinned. 'Who's ready to fly some rockets?'

THE RAGGED BOY

Finley was going to be late. He ran down the corridors, his breath coming out in wheezes as he willed his legs to carry him faster. He cursed himself for allowing this to happen. He had been desperate for his first day to go well- and that meant attracting as little attention as possible. So far, it hadn't gone to plan. It seemed the more he tried to blend in, the more people seemed to notice him.

At lunch, he had tried his hardest to ignore all the whispers that were buzzing around his ears like angry flies. He had been confused by the robots at the serving station and was rather alarmed when one of them started speaking to him in a loud, monotone voice. It had taken every ounce of restraint he had to stop him jumping back in shock and embarrassing himself irreparably.

Once he had taken his meal, he had found he was unable to use the fancy drinks machine, which was much more advanced than anything he had at home. The idea of asking another student for help and revealing himself to be more of an alien than they already thought him to be was unthinkable, and so he had loitered about as inconspicuously as possible until he understood how it worked.

By the time he had sat down to eat, most of the other

first-years had finished their meals and were beginning to head out of the Dining Hall.

He shovelled his food into his mouth, burning his tongue as he tried desperately not to be left behind. He might have caught up in time, had he not been further delayed by a pair of prefects, who came to his table to give him a device they called a 'Student Planner'. They did their best to keep their attitude friendly and their tone light, but Finley could still feel their eyes burning with curiosity as they scrutinised him between sentences, wondering, just like everybody else, what the boy from Floor Seven was doing here.

It took him several minutes to locate his timetable on the somewhat mesmerising Student Planner, which informed him that he was in 'Alderin' class. He looked up and discovered that the Dining Hall had filled with older students, and he was unable to see anybody that he recognised from the shuttle.

Panic rose in his throat as he leapt to his feet, crashing into the table and searching the hall for a familiar face. Eventually, he gave up, realising he had no choice but to ask the two prefects for help.

'Excuse me,' he called as he approached them. 'My timetable says I have Rocket Control next, but I don't know where I'm supposed to go.'

'No problem, mate,' replied the taller, dark-haired boy. 'I can download a map onto your Student Planner if you want?'

He flashed a helpful smile, but it wasn't enough to disguise the surprise he felt at hearing Finley speak. Finley wouldn't have been surprised if most of the students at the Academy had grown up thinking that people from the lower floors spoke a different language or could only communicate through the medium of interpretive dance.

'Don't worry about downloading anything,' Finley said urgently. 'Could you just give me directions?'

The prefect looked at him strangely.

'I suppose so,' he shrugged. 'Are you sure you'll remember, though?'

Finley nodded. When he was a small boy, his father had been forced to take him to work while his mother worked shifts as a maid on Floor One. His father was as a maintenance man, and had taken Finley to work with him in the depths below *The Mayflower*.

The service tunnels were a complicated labyrinth, snaking their way around the entire bottom deck of the vast spaceship. Without knowing how to get around, it would be possible to become lost for days - or even weeks. His father had helped him to memorise his way back to safety, sitting with him for what felt like hours, until he was certain he could recite the directions back to him. Finley felt certain that navigating his way around the school would be extremely easy in comparison.

The prefect gave him the instructions and he set off, repeating the word silently in his head. He rode the lift up to the correct floor and then departed at a brisk run, turning the heads of students and teachers alike as he passed.

He had been at the school for less than two hours and he had already failed at managing to blend in. He could only hope that his lateness wouldn't be a mark against him academically, as he was certain that his education was all he had now, all his hopes of making friends at the Academy now squashed.

His legs carried him forward at a quicker pace than he had thought possible, allowing him to reach the Launch Bay just as the last members of his class were disappearing inside.

Taking a few seconds to catch his breath, he smoothed his trousers down and tucked his shirt in to hide its fraying edges. Once he felt he had made his appearance as satisfactory as could be, he straightened up, stretching himself as tall as he could before he walked into the class.

For one brief and magical moment, Finley forgot himself completely as he took in the room around him with awe.

He had entered into a giant hangar, filled from corner to corner with spacecrafts of every shape, size and design imaginable. The entire back wall was covered by a large window of re-enforced glass that perfectly showcased the millions of stars that surrounded them in deep space.

He sidled up to the back of his class, who had congregated around the long-haired teacher. He was standing next to a small two-seater rocket, which only reached the height of his waist.

Despite its size, the rocket boasted an incredible appearance. Its body was dazzling white and sleek, its wings painted in a deep crimson and set at a perfectly perpendicular angle. Across the dashboard, just behind the steering wheel, was an intricate control panel, designed to regulate hundreds of different functions.

Finley had never been interested in rockets, but he had to admit this one was something to admire. Directly behind it, was the entrance to a large tunnel, which fed through the floor and, judging by the numerous amounts of 'caution' signs that were plastered all over it, into space beyond.

'Good afternoon,' the teacher spoke, his voice light and cheery. 'My name is Mr Zeppler, and as you may have guessed, I teach Rocket Control here at the Space Academy. Who can tell me why they think it's important for the students here to learn how to fly rockets?'

There was a moment's silence and some shuffling, before a few hesitant hands reached into the air.

'Yes,' Mr Zeppler nodded towards a tall, gangly boy at the front.

'Because it's awesome?' he suggested. The class erupted into a giggle.

'That may be so,' Mr Zeppler smiled, 'but being able to fly rockets can have many uses. Does anyone else have an idea?'

Before he could help himself, Finley raised his hand.

'Yes, you at the back there,' said Mr Zeppler, gesturing in his direction.

Finley cleared his throat nervously as he felt every single pair of eyes in the room burn into his person.

'Well, we might need to use them when we reach Novum,' he explained. 'In case we have to transport things or... travel to other planets...' he trailed off, dropping his gaze to the floor as his classmates continued to watch him.

'Correct!' exclaimed Mr Zeppler with great enthusiasm. 'When we reach Novum, it will be essential that we are able to use rockets to help us build our new civilisation. They can be used for both transporting goods and for exploration. What is your name, young man?'

'Finley.'

'Well, Finley, would you like to come and join me at the front of the class? I'll be needing a volunteer.'

Mr Zeppler had posed the offer to him as a question, but Finley knew he had no choice in the matter.

The class parted in the middle, and he headed towards the

front, feeling as though he were back on *The Mayflower* on death row, marching towards his execution.

Once he had reached Mr Zeppler, he turned to face his audience. He was relieved and more than a little surprised to see that most of the thirty-odd faces looking his way were wearing expressions of blank intrigue. Only two of the class members seemed to be sneering at him in disgust. One was a ginger-haired boy with pale, amber eyes and a crooked smile. The other was a girl with dark hair and sallow skin, her black eyes outlined with dark circles that gave her a rather unhealthy appearance. They stood side by side, united in their telepathic hatred for him. He tried not to be intimidated, but there was something about them that made him extremely uncomfortable.

'Okay,' Mr Zeppler smiled. 'Since you gave such a good answer, Finley, you now have the privilege of being the first in the class to sit inside one of our rockets.'

There was an audible 'oh!' of disappointment as Finley's classmates failed to conceal their jealousy.

'Don't worry,' Mr Zeppler assured them, 'a few more of you will be getting a chance throughout the lesson. Now, Finley! If you could please do the honours and step inside the rocket to my left.'

Finley did as he was told. He stood on the footstall that had been placed beside the rocket and clambered inside its open-topped body. The chair was leather and rigid, designed with expertise to provide maximum comfort for the driver, and dyed to match the precise shade of red that covered the rocket's wings.

The moment his body touched the seat, a thick steel bar descended over his head and secured him tightly into position.

He looked down at the control panel in front of him. It featured more buttons, knobs and confusing looking levers than Finley had ever seen in his life, including on the complicated systems his dad had used while performing maintenance on *The Mayflower*. He was completely bewildered, and hoped he wouldn't have to do anything other than sit in the rocket and not touch anything.

'Okay,' Mr Zeppler addressed the rest of the class. 'As keen as I'm sure you all are to experience flying a rocket, for obvious reasons in our lesson today we will mainly be focusing on safety and procedures. Some of you may have noticed a metal bar coming down across Finley's seat. This function is motion activated, so will automatically occur whenever anyone enters the rocket. However, there are also seatbelts that must be applied manually to secure the driver. Once all of this has been put into place, there's still something very important we need to do before we can fly. Who can tell me why I shouldn't just send Finley into space right now?'

There was a long silence, and Finley wondered whether anyone was going to answer, or if they were all in favour of him being blasted off into space and never seen again.

'He can't go into space like that. He'd die,' a boy answered at last.

'And why is that?' Mr Zeppler pressed him.

'Well, the rocket is open-topped, and he hasn't got any special gear on,' the boy replied. 'He wouldn't be able to breathe.'

'Correct!' Mr Zeppler exclaimed. 'What is your name, son?'

'Will,' the boy answered.

Finley craned his neck to get a glimpse of him, and recognised him immediately as the boy he had seen walking with the Captain on the platform earlier that morning.

'Excellent, Will, you can be my next volunteer,' Mr Zeppler beamed. He hurried off towards a second small rocket with blue tipped wings and began typing on its control pad at an impressive speed. A moment later, it hummed into life, moving at a meticulously slow pace across metal tracks on the floor, until it stopped a short distance behind Finley's rocket.

'Okay, Will, if you wait there...' Mr Zeppler said, pointing beside the rocket. Will followed his instructions with haste, scrambling to stand beside the spacecraft.

'Will shall kindly be demonstrating the protective gear every rocket user must wear on any journey into space,' Mr Zeppler explained, heading towards a concealed door in the wall of the hangar, his waist-length hair floating about his back as he moved. He pressed a button, and the disguised door slid back to reveal several spacesuits hanging from a battered, iron rail.

'In this cupboard, you'll find spare suits in various sizes, but it's usually customary for students to purchase one for their lessons. It would be a good idea if you could contact your parents at home and have them send you what you need,' Mr Zeppler informed them, as he pulled a small suit from the rack.

Finley swallowed hard. He wondered if his parents would be able to get him a suit with their current credit status. He considered sneaking back into the Launch Bay after hours and stealing one, desperate to avoid the humiliation of having to borrow one every lesson.

Sitting uncomfortably in the driver's chair, Finley listened, rather than watched, as Will tried on the spacesuit and clambered into the rocket behind him. Mr Zeppler informed the class that the rocket was a 'PR-11' and was the best model for beginners to fly in. He was in the middle of fixing the complicated seatbelt system around Will, when a cold voice interrupted his teaching, causing Finley to startle.

'How do you make the rockets start?' the voice asked. Finley knew immediately that it belonged to the sallow-faced girl, who had unnerved him earlier with her loathsome looks.

'Well, I suppose I could demonstrate,' Mr Zeppler answered, eagerly proceeding to press a series of buttons on the control pad in Will's rocket.

It happened in a flash. Mr Zeppler finished his display and returned to teaching the lesson. In a second, the sallow girl was next to Finley, a strange smirk on her face and a deep look of malice in her eyes. She reached inside his rocket, her fingers moving seamlessly across the controls as she looked at Finley with contempt.

He was completely frozen, paralysed by fear. There was a second's pause. He twisted his body round sharply, his ribs jamming into the metal bar with the force of the movement.

Panic engulfed him as he called out for help. Time seemed to be distorted, passing with an unnatural slowness. His class appeared in a tableau, their looks of confusion turning to horror as they realised what was about to happen.

With one final sneer, the girl pressed the last button that triggered the rocket to activate.

He heard the screams of the class and saw Mr Zeppler reel backwards in alarm as the Launch Bay disappeared before his eyes, his rocket hurtling down the metal tunnel and towards outer space.

Without a helmet on, he would certainly suffocate. A vivid memory flashed into his mind of when his parents had taken him to the Water Park on *The Mayflower* as a small child. It had taken all their credits for the month to get in, but his parents hadn't minded. His father had smiled at him, telling him to enjoy himself and to absorb every minute.

Riding the biggest slide there, Finley had clasped the rubber ring in his tiny hands, exhilaration and fear filling his entire body as he slid down the impossibly large flume. As he hurtled down the tunnel and towards space, he felt a similar sensation of adrenaline and terror pulse through his veins.

He prayed silently to no one in particular, hoping his suffering would be over quickly as the exit grew larger in his vision. He closed his eyes and braced himself for the end.

Several things happened at once. A loud cry pierced the tunnel, echoing horribly across the walls and bouncing back towards the entrance. Finley didn't know whether it had come from him or someone else.

He felt a tight, painful sensation across his neck and shoulders, as though he were being grabbed from behind. A second later, he was flying through the air, independent of the rocket.

He hit the hard floor of the tunnel, a wave of pain shooting down his back and head. At almost the exact same moment, there was the sound of what he could only assume was the exit opening, and a deafening roar filled his ears as he was sucked towards the vacuum of space. A second later, the noise subsided. Everything was still.

Finley opened his eyes slowly and saw the roof of the tunnel above him. The pain in his neck twinged, and he realised there was something lodged uncomfortably beneath him. He propped himself on his elbows and looked around. The object that had been stuck underneath him groaned, and began to stir and Finley realised with a jolt that it was a person.

He looked down to see Will in a full spacesuit, complete with helmet, lying spread-eagled on the floor. He had followed him into the tunnel and saved his life.

'Are you okay, mate?' Will asked dazedly.

'Er... yeah... thank you...' Finley replied, unsure what else to say. He blinked as he tried to comprehend what had happened.

Their stunned silence was interrupted by voices calling out from the other end of the tunnel.

'Will! Finley! Are you alright?' Mr Zeppler shouted with concern.

'We're okay! We're down here!' Will called back.

'Oh, thank the Universe,' Mr Zeppler exclaimed with relief. 'Stay there! I'll come and get you!'

Finley lay back down on the floor next to Will, overwhelmed by both relief and exhaustion now that the adrenaline had stopped pumping through his veins. Will groaned loudly, not attempting to move, let alone get up.

'How did you save me?' Finley asked him after a minute, staring up at the metal ceiling that encased them.

'I followed you in as soon as that creepy girl sent you down. Mr Zeppler tried to stop me, but he wasn't quick enough. Once I caught up with you, I kind of jumped out of my rocket and pulled you out of yours, then both the rockets flew out from underneath us and we hit the floor. I don't know how I actually managed to pull that off,' he laughed in disbelief, 'It's lucky you weren't going very fast. Still, I couldn't exactly just sit there and do nothing.'

Finley didn't answer. He had no idea how to express his gratitude appropriately.

'I can't believe that girl did that to you!' Will continued, unperturbed by Finley's silence. 'Was she trying to kill you? It's insane!'

Their conversation was abruptly ended by the sound of an approaching engine. Mr Zeppler rode towards them on a larger rocket, floating slowly and with perfect control.

Finley glanced towards the door at the end of the tunnel, afraid it would spring open again and pull him out into space without a suit.

'Don't worry,' said Mr Zeppler through his helmet. 'I've disabled it. Get in.'

He extended a hand towards the boys, and the two of them clambered into the backseat of the rocket. Mr Zeppler carefully turned around in the small space and drove them safely back into the classroom.

Everybody applauded as they disembarked. Finley smiled awkwardly, while Will took an exaggerated bow and laughed. Notably not applauding, was the ginger-haired friend of the sallow girl, who herself had disappeared from the class completely.

Almost immediately after their feet had touched the floor, a girl with long, dark hair rushed over to Will, demanding to know whether he was okay. He nodded, and she gave him a hug, which caused him to go redder than a beetroot.

'I'm fine, Emily,' Will re-assured her.

Once she was satisfied that he was, in fact, all in one piece, she approached Finley and squeezed him in a tight embrace.

'I'm glad you're alright, too,' she told him sincerely. 'What that girl did is terrible! She's been taken away now. Hopefully she won't ever come back!'

Finley nodded profusely, still tongue-tied. It was only the second time someone at the Academy had spoken to him out of choice, and he seemed to have become inexplicably mute as a result.

Mr Zeppler regained his control of the class, and wrapped the lesson up by tying the horrible incident to his earlier point about safety, preaching about the importance of taking rocket use seriously, and never engaging in any flying activity without proper experience.

At the end of the lesson, Mr. Zeppler sent everyone down to the Dining Hall, where they would receive instructions on what to do next.

As the students began to file out, chattering chaotically about what they had witnessed, Mr Zeppler called Will and Finley back in to speak to them, Emily waiting by the door.

'You'll probably be sent to speak to Admiral Allance,' he sighed, running his hands through his long hair. 'Nothing like this has ever happened before. There's been accidents at the school, but nothing on that scale. I'm not even entirely sure that it was an accident!'

He rubbed his eyes, suddenly looking exhausted.

'Anyway, I apologise to you both,' he sighed. 'I wanted you to have a first lesson you'd remember, but that's not quite what I had in mind.'

'It's okay, Mr Zeppler, it isn't your fault,' Will re-assured him.

'I shouldn't have been so keen to show off how to start up the rockets,' he frowned, returning his hands to his hips and standing jauntily. 'Just for future reference, though boys, if that ever were to happen again, there is an 'emergency seal' button, which will contain about fifteen minutes of oxygen inside the rocket. I'll cover it properly next lesson – just in case.'

'Is this likely to happen again?' Finley asked him dubiously.

'Of course not! In all my years of teaching, I've never witnessed something as appalling as that,' Mr Zeppler shook his head. 'Anyway, you boys better get going. Nothing more to do around here except clean up the scene of the crime.'

He winced at his choice of words.

'Just an expression,' he added sheepishly.

Finley smiled to show that he hadn't taken offence, and followed after Will as he made to exit the Launch Bay.

'I don't know about you,' Will said to Emily, as he strolled over to where she was waiting for him, 'but I could really do with a good cup of tea after that.'

'Agreed,' Emily laughed, and the pair began to walk off together. Just before they left the room, Will stopped and turned back.

'Are you coming, Finley?' he asked.

Finley glanced at Emily, who smiled with encouragement.

'Yeah, that'd be great,' he replied, catching up to walk in step beside them, a huge grin spreading uncontrollably across his face.

ROOM 211

It was safe to say that Emily's first day at the Space Academy had been eventful. As she slid into the bed in her new room for the very first time, she let her mind drift into a sleepy state, her weary body grateful for the luxury of rest. The bed was extremely comfortable, more so than her one at home, and she burrowed into its warm depths.

The inexplicably comforting smell of fresh laundry rose around her, as she swathed herself in the thick duvet adorned with stars, feeling as though she were wrapping herself up in the night sky itself. She soothed her aching feet against the soft cotton of the bedsheet and resisted the strong urge she felt to drift into a sound sleep, clinging onto consciousness so that she could revisit the afternoon's events in her head.

After the drama of their first Rocket Control lesson, Emily and Will headed down to the Dining Hall with Finley to have hot drinks and discuss what had happened in detail. Upon their arrival, however, it became clear that Will had become some sort of mini-celebrity after the event, and a mob of students both from Alderin class and the other two classes in their year group, Armstrong and Gagarin, had descended upon them with a flurry of questions.

Will had thoroughly enjoyed recounting the tale, and those

present at the gathering of his new fan club had listened with delight, as he explained how he had flown down the tunnel at maximum speed and leapt fearlessly from his rocket, pulling Finley to safety seconds before they hurtled into space.

It seemed like everyone in first year was ecstatic over Will's heroics - everyone that is, except Rudy, who skulked about in the background. Will's tutor group from Floor One, who he pointed out as they sat haughtily at their own table, also refused to acknowledge the hum of excitement around them. Even the Captain's daughter, who Will had been seen with on the platform, didn't come over to congratulate him, or ask whether he was okay.

Emily had rolled her eyes as some of the older students started to drift over, catching wind of the story and shaking Will's hand as they shared their admiration for what he had done. Some of them clapped a bemused Finley on the back as they walked past, but none of them stopped to say much to him, perhaps uncertain of how to behave towards him.

'How is it fair that I'm the one who nearly died, but Will's the one getting all the glory?' Finley laughed, as yet another student they didn't know came over to congratulate Will.

'He's getting all the glory because he's milking it for all it's worth!' Emily replied.

'I am not!' Will insisted, before flashing them both a grin.

The three of them enjoyed hot chocolates with whipped cream, mixed to perfection by the drinks machine. They chatted happily among each other, the seriousness of what could have come to pass overshadowed by the extraordinary way things had turned out.

Halfway through their conversation, their Student Planners

beeped to inform them that first-years would now have some free time before dinner to explore the school and do as they please. Not wanting to pass up the opportunity, the three of them leapt to their feet and headed off into the Academy.

They rushed through the Reception Hall, passing the statue of the no-eyed man as they did so, and headed to the first floor via the lift. They traipsed around the identical looking corridors, not managing to discover anything of interest as they passed by the endless rows of bathrooms, teacher's offices and classrooms.

They were just about to give up on their adventures, when they overheard a group of students discussing their intention to visit the library. Silently, they exchanged a look of excitement, and began following the group in unison.

Keeping a safe and calculated distance, they walked just far enough behind the older students to remain unnoticed. Emily, Finley and Will listened as they discussed how crowded the lifts were at the start of term, opting instead to take the stairs.

After clambering up five staircases, Emily was ready to turn to the boys and demand through ragged breath that they find the nearest lift immediately, when a set of double doors labelled 'Library' appeared just ahead of them.

'The pot of gold at the end of the rainbow!' Will huffed, his face rosy and glistening with sweat.

'The what?' Emily asked, glancing over at Finley, who looked back at her with an equally befuddled expression.

'It's just something my mum says. I think it's some old Earth expression,' he blushed.

'I like it,' said Emily, despite having no idea what the saying meant. 'To the pot of gold!' She cringed at her over-enthusiasm, but Will smiled at her with gratitude.

They entered the library, immediately realising the hike to reach it had been worthwhile. Of all the things Emily had seen at the school that day, this was by far the most impressive.

Standing strikingly tall, at least twenty rows of silver shelf-units spanned the length of the room in pairs, their tops touching the high ceiling. Each individual unit featured thousands of cubby holes, cradling small sticks of downloadable book files.

Robotic machines were whizzing around the shelves, retrieving the sticks that were unreachable to the human hand, and bringing them down to the ground. In the centre of the room, were several circular, white tables where groups of dedicated students were already beginning to gather to start their work for the year.

The librarian's desk was situated on the right-hand side of the room, and was currently being manned by an older boy with dishevelled brown hair and thick, black glasses. Upon seeing the three of them standing motionless, he strode over, kindly asking if he could be of any assistance.

'This place is huge,' Will informed him, as though he somehow hadn't noticed. The librarian laughed.

'Yes, we do have the biggest collection of titles anywhere since the Split,' he informed them.

'It's amazing,' Emily replied, and he smiled brightly as though she had paid him a personal compliment.

'I'm Martyn, by the way,' he said, offering Emily his hand to shake. She took it and blushed, conscious of the eyes of Will and Finley burning upon her.

'I'm Emily,' she told him.

Will cleared his throat loudly.

'And this is Will and Finley,' she added.

'Good to meet you,' Martyn nodded.

'What are those things?' Finley asked, pointing towards the data sticks.

'They're the sticks you use to download books,' Martyn replied, confused by the question. 'They're called I-Books? Have you not heard of them?'

'Oh, we don't have I-Books at home,' Finley explained. 'We still use I-Readers.'

Emily glanced at Will, who looked back at her with the same expression of surprise. Her family had donated all their I-Readers to charity several years ago, when they had been made obsolete by the flurry of new technology that was constantly being developed on *The Mayflower*.

'Yes, well the I-Books are a new invention, created, of course, by the Interactive-Tech company. It's taken them long enough to develop. The technology of books and reading has always taken a backseat to the production of new gadgets,' Martyn sighed, momentarily lost in anguish.

'Allow me to explain how the library works,' he said, regaining himself.

He walked them to the nearest storage unit, and demonstrated how to browse through all the different titles it offered by using a touch screen fixed into its side. Once a title had been selected, it was retrieved by one of the robots, and passed carefully to its new temporary owner.

'The I-Books can be used with any device; you simply point and click the button in the middle, and the data will be transferred across. It works with Student Planners, tablets, any T.V screen or even laptops,' Martyn informed them with passion.

'Laptops?' Will repeated with confusion. 'Does anyone still use them?'

'They have proven to be quite popular here at the Academy. Students seem to find something satisfying in typing on a real keyboard. It's quite therapeutic, actually,' Martyn replied, adjusting the buttons on the light brown blazer he had donned over his school uniform.

'Retro,' Will nodded. 'You'll feel right at home then, Finley!'

Their conversation with Martyn was cut short by a loud, beeping sound, which Will and Finley discovered was erupting from each of their Student Planners.

'Uh-oh,' Will said after checking the screen.

'What is it?' Emily asked, attempting to peer over his shoulder.

'A video message from Miss Fortem,' Will swallowed, pressing play.

'William James, please report to the admiral's office immediately,' Miss Fortem said in the recording, her facial expression and tone of voice giving no indication as to what the nature of the meeting would be.

Finley played his message to find that he had received the exact same summons. The two boys exchanged a look of mutual fear and panic.

'Do you think we're in trouble?' Finley asked Will, his eyes wide with worry.

'You can't be. You didn't do anything wrong,' Emily assured him.

'Well, I did nearly fly a rocket into space without a licence and without permission from a teacher,' Will pointed out.

'You were saving Finley. If you hadn't intervened, who knows what would have happened,' Emily argued.

'We don't even know where Allance's office is,' Finley fretted.

'I was just about to finish my shift here, so I can show you if you like,' Martyn offered. The two boys accepted and headed out of the library, alongside their new guide.

Emily standing still for a moment after they left. It was the first time since she'd entered the Academy that she had been alone, and she was unsure what to do with herself.

After a moment of deliberating, she decided to make her way back down to the Dining Hall, hoping the boys would return there after their meeting. To ensure she didn't get lost, she adopted the tactic of climbing down every staircase she came across, until eventually she reached a lift and was able to descend into the Reception Hall.

Veering right, she was surprised to find the Dining Hall packed to almost full capacity, with a hungry pack of students already swarming the serving station. She scanned the tables, seeking out any first-years she recognised.

To her relief, she caught sight of Cara and Matina, who she had spoken to briefly before Rocket Control. They were sitting with a boy she hadn't yet met, but she made her way over nonetheless, sitting down confidently and hoping there would be no objections to her intrusion.

She needn't have worried, however, as the three of them seemed all too keen to discuss the details of Finley's earlier ordeal

'Alasdair doesn't believe what happened in Rocket Control class,' Cara told Emily with indignation, after she had seated herself midway through their discussion of the event.

'Weren't you there?' Emily asked him.

'I'm not in Alderin class,' he told her with a hint of disgust. 'I'm in Gagarin with all of the other Floor One pupils.'

'Except Will and the Captain's daughter,' Emily reminded him. 'They're in Alderin class too.'

'Yes, well, Lois is very displeased with her class placement. As for Will, he seems to have forgotten where he comes from already,' Alasdair replied. Emily raised her eyebrows.

'Tell Alasdair what happened,' Cara encouraged her.

Emily paused for a moment, choosing her words carefully.

'A horrible girl in our class took a disliking to Finley for no reason whatsoever and decided to try and launch him into space without any oxygen. If Will hadn't gone after him, he could have died,' she explained.

'Will was so brave,' said Matina dreamily, resting her face in her hands and staring towards the ceiling. For a moment, Emily felt extremely resentful of her pretty features, noting with envy her big, round doe-eyes, her jet-black hair and small, pink mouth. She quickly dismissed her thoughts and turned her attention back to Alasdair, who unfortunately had decided to speak again.

'You've got to feel sorry for Finley,' he sighed, though Emily was unable to detect any real sympathy in his voice. 'It was such a mistake for him to come here. You know his mother is one of our family maids? It's just embarrassing. Cruel to let him into the Academy if you ask me.'

'Except, I don't think anybody did ask you, did they, Alasdair?' Emily shot back at him, unable to control the fire that was building inside her with his every word.

'I can see my opinions aren't welcome here,' he said coolly. 'Perhaps I should find somebody from Gagarin class to sit with.'

Emily said nothing, her glare informing him that she agreed with his notion of leaving.

Affronted, he got to his feet, his chair scraping noisily against the floor. With a scathing look in Emily's direction, he turned on his heels and sauntered off to find the rest of his Floor One friends.

'Sorry about him,' said Cara, once he was out of earshot. 'We didn't know who he was, he just started talking to us.'

'It's okay,' said Emily. 'It isn't your fault. He was obviously just being nosey about Finley.'

'What's he like, anyway?' Cara asked. 'Finley, I mean?'

'He's just a normal boy,' Emily replied, confused by the question.

The intrigue surrounding Finley's enrolment at the school was a mystery to Emily. He had passed the entrance exams, the same as everybody else, and as far as Emily was aware, there was no rule which specified that only the children from higher floors could attend the Space Academy. In her mind, Finley had more of a right to be there than pupils like Alasdair and his smug friends, whose parents had no doubt used their influence and credits to get their children a place at the school.

Cara and Matina seemed to sense Emily's reluctance to discuss the topic any further, and promptly changed the subject, chatting happily about what they had learnt so far at the Space Academy.

Following that, the girls launched into an in-depth conversation about how handsome they found Mr Zeppler. They were just in the middle of arguing over whether 'Cara Zeppler' or 'Matina Zeppler' sounded better, when Will and Finley came to join them at the table, each one full of energy and exuberance.

'How did it go?' Emily asked them the moment they arrived. Finley glanced towards the other two girls at the table, hesitant to answer in their company.

'It's okay,' Emily re-assured him. 'This is Cara and this is Matina. They're on your side about the whole thing.'

The girls looked at her with gratitude and leaned in, readily awaiting the private conversation they were being let in on.

'It went well,' Finley grinned. 'The girl has been expelled. Her name was Josie Jones. Apparently, she kept insisting that what she did was only a prank and that she just wanted to scare me, but Allance said there could be no excuses and sent her home.'

'Yeah,' Will chimed in, impatient to tell his part of the story. 'I got told off for flying a rocket without a licence, but I was also commended for my bravery.' He puffed his chest out with pride.

'The only bad thing is, Allance decided to tell our parents,' Finley frowned.

'My mum's going to be beside herself,' Will sighed.

'I've already spoken to my mum and dad,' Finley said. 'They wanted me to come home, but I said 'no'. I'm not going to let anything spoil my chance to be here.'

'So that's it, then? It's all over?' Emily asked with relief.

'It's all over,' Will confirmed.

'We were offered follow up care with Miss Fortem in case the event had traumatised us, but we turned it down,' Finley added.

'I'd be more traumatised spending one-on-one time with her than I would being blasted into space!' Will exclaimed. 'She's terrifying!'.

Cara and Matina burst into high-pitched, exaggerated

laughter. Emily stood up sharply, ushering the boys over to the serving station and insisting she was suddenly ravenous.

The three of them collected their dinners from the helpful robots and moved around the hall, until they found an empty table they could sit at where they wouldn't be disturbed.

They ate with enthusiasm, returning to collect second helpings and stuffing themselves until they were sleepy and satisfied.

Their conversation was light and full of laughter, with all of them basking in the knowledge that the day's drama was over, and they could now continue their academic lives as normal students, united in their conviction that nothing bad would ever happen to them again for the entirety of the five years they would spend at the Space Academy.

After they had finished their meals, the first-years were gathered together in the Reception Hall by Miss Fortem, where it was announced that their belongings had been sorted through, and they would now be shown to their new rooms. The excitement was uncontainable, and the students spent the whole march across the school grounds buzzing with anticipation.

They were led to a mini-complex of buildings, each one varying in size and shape, but all of them coated in the same light grey material. Miss Fortem stopped outside the closest of the small cluster, and touched the sensor pad beside the door, allowing the first-years and their prefect escorts inside.

They entered a small foyer, carpeted in the same shade of navy blue as the material used for the school jumpers. The room was dimly lit by rectangular lights that buzzed and flickered with the effort of staying on. Four tall plants in wide terracotta vases flanked the corners of the foyer, wilting with neglect and lack of UV light.

The walls were decorated with paintings of cats, birds and enough other species of animals from Earth to make up an entire menagerie. An old, wooden desk stood in the corner, its surface worn and stained with age.

Behind the desk stood a dowdy woman, her grey hair pulled into a scraggy bun, strands of hair escaping around her face and tangling around her thick horn-rimmed glasses. She was wearing a long blue dress embellished with the images of yellow flowers, their green stalks weaving and intertwining to form a swirling pattern across the fabric that was somewhat harsh upon the eyes.

Upon their entrance, she shuffled towards them, the slight stoop of her posture dwarfing her in contrast to Miss Fortem.

'Boys and girls, allow me to introduce Ms. Everly,' Miss Fortem began. 'She is in charge of running your rooms and making sure that our service bots keep them clean and tidy. She also patrols the corridors at night to make sure that nobody is out of bed past the ten o'clock curfew. If you need Ms. Everly's assistance during school hours, you will find her in the foyer, which she decorated herself.'

There was a silent moment of understanding among the first-years as they compared Ms. Everly to the decor.

'She'll be here for most of the day, so if you have any questions, please feel free to ask,' Miss Fortem continued.

'I have a question,' called Rudy from the back of the group.

'Yes, what is it?' snapped Miss Fortem.

'Did Ms. Everly design all of our rooms too?' he asked, attempting for the question to sound innocent, though its true meaning was thinly veiled.

'Oh no, dear,' laughed Ms. Everly. 'All the student's rooms

were designed by a proper architect. Something Hullington I think his name was.'

'Spencer's dad,' Will said under his breath with disdain. Emily was wholly relieved that their bedrooms would not be following the decorative theme of the foyer, and wondered if Ms. Everly needed stronger glasses so that she could see the proper outcome of her work.

'Thank you, Rudy, for that interesting, yet highly unnecessary question,' said Miss Fortem, turning her attention back to the task at hand.

'Now,' she continued, 'as you may have seen, behind me there are three lifts which can be used by students at any time of the day. Of course, I will remind you again that nobody should be out of bed after curfew, which is ten p.m. sharp. If there is an emergency after this hour, you must use your Student Planners to contact a member of staff. In the event of a fire, you will hear an alarm ring out, after which you may use the lift if necessary,' Miss Fortem explained.

"If necessary'," muttered Will in disbelief.

'There are three floors of rooms above us. We are currently on the ground floor. I will now ask Ms. Everly to send your room numbers through to your Student Planners. Once you have received these, one of our prefects will show you the way,' Miss Fortem concluded.

Ms. Everly moved back to her desk at a painfully slow pace. Emily was desperate to find out where her room would be, and, more importantly, who she would become neighbours with. When Ms. Everly reached the desk, she produced a battered tablet from its depths and began squinting at its screen, stabbing it extremely hard with one finger, before retracting it again, as though she were afraid the tablet would bite her.

Several agonising minutes passed before the message was sent, the foyer erupting in the sound of beeping as everybody scrambled to check their planners. Emily huddled next to Will and Finley, eager to find out how close to each other they would be.

'I'm in 311!' announced Will, as the number appeared on his screen.

'211,' Emily replied. 'We're not on the same floor.'

'No, but you're right underneath me,' Will grinned.

'No late-night dance parties then, please,' Emily teased.

'Only on a Tuesday,' Will retorted.

Finley cleared his throat.

'Which room are you in, Finley?' Will asked him hastily.

'101,' he responded.

'Oh, I hoped we'd all be near each other,' Emily sighed.

'Don't worry, I'm used to being on a low floor,' Finley said with a weak smile.

Emily frowned, but she had no chance to console him before Miss Fortem began ordering them to be taken to their rooms. They were divided into three groups, one for each floor, and called over to their designated prefect. Emily was pleased to see that her group was being led by Sam, and not by the loathsome May, who had taken them to their Rocket Control class.

Her relief was cut short, however, by the sight of Rudy strutting over to join them, surrounded by his entourage of faceless cronies. When he noticed her, attempting to shrink into the back of the huddle, he strode over and placed his arm tightly around her shoulders.

'Hey, Em,' he smirked. 'Take it you're on the second

floor too?'

'Unfortunately, yes,' Emily replied through gritted teeth, removing his arm from around her.

'It'll be just like old times,' he laughed, nudging her a little bit too hard with his elbow.

She groaned, unable to think of anything worse than having to endure Rudy's presence on a daily basis. She silently cursed her own bad luck that she had been the only girl from her tutor group to get into the Space Academy, meaning that Rudy and his insufferable gang of followers were the only familiar faces she had from home.

Desperate to escape, she weaved her way to the front of the group, cramming herself among the more eager students who were all staring at Sam, awaiting his instructions.

He led them to the lift in the middle of the foyer and they followed him in, comfortably able to fit inside the spacious interior. The ride to the second floor was smooth and swift, lasting only a matter of seconds.

Once they had come to a standstill, Sam escorted them out into the corridor, decorated in a fashionable silver tile that was buffed and polished to perfection, as though it had never had a spot of dirt on it. Thick blue doors lined the walls, each one displaying a number in the school's favoured gold labelling.

With a helpful point in the right direction from Sam, Emily made her way towards her room, which was at the very end of the corridor.

After a brief walk, she came face to face with her door, the number '211' emblazoned across the middle. She pushed gently, and the door swung back on its hinges, having been left unlocked for her access. She took a deep breath and stepped over the threshold, taking in the sight of what would become her home for the next year.

A Queen-sized bed stood to the left of the door, tucked up snugly in the corner and dressed in fresh bedding that had never been slept in. Against the back wall, stood a triple-fronted, black wardrobe with a matching dresser beside it. There was a desk, complete with a large touch screen, a set of shelves for storage and a comfortable looking sofa. A mini drinks machine stood between two chutes that fed into the wall, marked 'laundry' and 'rubbish'.

A small white door led into her en-suite bathroom, which featured an I-Bath, shower, toilet, washbasin and a round mirror. She walked across the room and gazed at the view of the school grounds that could be seen through her window, pausing to watch the artificial lake, as the starlight from the sky above twinkled upon its surface like a million dancing fairies.

Facing back into the room, she decided to call Will on her personal device to see what his bedroom on the top floor was like. He gave her a virtual tour, and she saw that it was much larger than hers, with significantly more furnishings. His room was light and airy, and all of his décor was painted in matching shades of white and beige to give the space the illusion of brightness.

'It's almost twice the size of mine!' Emily complained.

'That'll be Spencer's dad's doing,' Will said, rolling his eyes. 'Can't resist making the higher floors better than the lower.'

The two of them continued to chat while they unpacked the belongings that had been left for them at the end of their beds. Half-way through the conversation, they remembered Finley and added him to a group call, getting a tour of his own, much smaller, room. Will spent the remainder of the call informing them of which gadgets he was going to ask his mum to send from home- including his virtual reality headset, his television screens and a snack vendor.

There was some speculation about their new subjects, particularly about which one would be the most exciting. Emily was outnumbered two-to-one on her notion that it would be Technology, while Will and Finley both voted for Alien Studies.

After a while, they all became tired, the events of the first day taking their toll. They said goodnight and Emily got ready for bed, sliding into the warm covers where she now lay.

After re-living the past twelve hours in her mind, she finally felt ready for sleep, and rolled over to burrow into her pillow.

As she drifted into unconsciousness, she found herself wondering with a feverish delight what the future held in store for her and her new friends. Hardly able to contain her anticipation, she fell into a peaceful sleep, dreaming of what new excitement her second day at the Space Academy would hold.

THE STUDY OF ALIENS

Kurt Krecher woke at six a.m. sharp on the morning of his first day back at work and rose straight from his bed to make a cup of strong, black coffee. Still wearing the threadbare dressing gown his wife had bought him for Christmas many years ago, he went to sit at his desk and open his laptop – an old souvenir he had kept from Earth.

As was customary, he downloaded the files of information Admiral Allance had sent him regarding their new students, and -though he suspected he was the only teacher to do so- read through the details carefully so he could get to know his new class.

Scrolling down the list of names and birth dates, it struck him that this was the first class to ever attend the Space Academy that had never set foot on Earth. It gave him a strange feeling to comprehend the thought of them being born on *The Mayflower*, never knowing any other life outside its unyielding, titanium walls.

As he continued to scroll, he was surprised to find one of the pupils was listed as being from Floor Seven. He had heard rumours that a boy from the lower floors was being admitted to the Space Academy, but had never believed that it could be true. He had always advocated for the school to open its doors to all of the children on *The Mayflower* that were of the right age to attend, but Admiral Allance had vehemently rejected the idea on several occasions.

He wondered what, or indeed who, had convinced him to allow this new student in, suspecting a hefty increase in budget from the governors may have changed Allance's mind.

A note in the boy's file informed him that there had already been an incident with another pupil in his first Rocket Control lesson, in which he had narrowly escaped being launched into space without oxygen.

A hard lump of disgust formed in his throat that turned the taste of his coffee sour. It troubled him that the rife inequality between the social classes had followed them from Earth onto *The Mayflower*, and would no doubt be transferred to Novum.

They had been promised a better world before the Split, but the longer time went on, the less Kurt was able to believe in such a dream. No doubt the same suffering that had occurred in the last days of Earth would follow humanity wherever it went. There was no escaping it in his opinion. In all his years of studying and teaching, he had never come across an alien race that was able to inflict as much cruelty onto their own kind as human beings were.

Sighing, he made a note of the poor boy's name - 'Finley Campbell'- and committed it to memory. If he couldn't fight for social justice on a wider scale, he would certainly ensure it was practised in his own classroom.

He took another deep swig of his coffee and continued to read about the new students through bleary, bloodshot eyes. His heart fluttered in a funny sort of way when the image of a strangely familiar face appeared on his screen.

The picture was of a boy from Alderin class, the name 'William James' attached to his file. It took him a moment to place him, his brain desperately searching through the memories of the hundreds of students he had taught over the years.

As soon as he remembered, he wondered, with a slight twang of panic, how he ever could have forgotten. The boy was the son of two of the most memorable people he had ever met, and his inability to immediately recognise him served as confirmation that his mind was softening with age.

He got up and strode over to the window, looking out pensively as he finished his warm drink. For a moment, he had forgotten where he was, expecting to see the sunrise bathing the horizon in its glorious shades of red, orange and pink.

He imagined he could see rolling green hills, running into each other as they peaked and fell, creating a sea of brown and green in the distance. He pictured wispy clouds and tall trees, and houses with thatched rooves with black birds flying overhead. He hoped with all his heart that he might see such views again one day, but for now, there was only the infinite black of space.

As he dressed himself in his patched brown suit and silk waistcoat, his mind began to wander. Thinking about William James' parents had triggered an involuntary trip down memory lane, and he became immersed in a powerful recollection of the past.

The time in which he had first encountered William's mother, Elsie, and his father, Austin, had been a dire time on Earth. The population was at its lowest ebb, having fallen to around twenty percent of what it had originally been, and the conflict for Earth's limited resources had been rife and violent as ever.

Kurt was a professor at one of only a hundred existing colleges around the country, and by a stroke of luck, had managed to find himself a haven.

The college was situated in North Wales and was aptly named 'College Snowdonia' after its magnificent view of the Welsh mountains. The Split had not long been announced, and as a result, everyone with the slightest bit of intelligence was desperately trying to improve their skills and make themselves worthy enough to gain passage on *The Mayflower*. Due to the sudden boom of enthusiasm in education, the government had taken it upon themselves to ensure every college received enough food, water and power to sustain itself, with security installed to protect the various campuses.

The small city where College Snowdonia was based had been almost completely deserted, and so the teaching staff and students had taken their pick of the empty houses. Kurt and his wife had discovered an old farmhouse in the city's surrounding countryside and had spent all their free time renovating it, until they had created themselves a beautiful, rustic home.

They herded animals from the fields around them and were able to live off the land, being successful enough in their farming to donate some of their produce to the other local residents. It had been an oasis of peace in a desert of atrocities. Over time, everybody associated with the college came together to form a tight-knit community, and, as the days and nights rolled on, it was almost possible to forget that the Earth was slowly dying around them.

He hadn't known William's parents well at first, for his mother had studied Psychology and his father Navigation. However, he often saw them about the stone corridors of the college building, looking like love's young dream, their awkward friend Alfie bumbling after them, always in their shadow.

No one ever would have guessed he would become Captain of *The Mayflower*, beating out the other thousands of hopeful Navigation students across the country. Kurt had strongly suspected Alfie's mother's influential position in society had a lot more to do with him getting the job than his skills, though he had been careful not to voice this opinion to anyone.

It wasn't until their final year that Kurt had come into contact with the three, when they had unexpectedly signed up to do a module in Alien Studies. They all claimed to have been struck by a sudden interest in the topic, but Kurt was always suspicious of their true motives.

The real reason for their joining his class, however, had been far stranger and more twisted than he could ever have imagined. To even think of it now made the hairs on the back of his neck stand on end and gave him the distinct feeling he was being watched.

Shuddering, Kurt shook the memory from his mind and left his apartment, walking briskly across the school grounds. The cool air filtered around the enclosed bubble of the school, causing him to shiver and hug his jacket tighter about his person.

When he reached the main school building, he stepped quickly through the entrance, glancing up at the oppressively large representation of Novum as he did so. Every time he passed under it, he was afraid it would somehow come unattached and fall, crushing him like a bug beneath a boot. On this occasion, however, he had managed to survive, and so he headed into the Dining Hall, intending to reward himself with a second cup of coffee.

He grunted at the robot at the serving station to give him his usual, and sat down at the nearest table, chewing unenthusiastically on a limp piece of toast. They had tried their hardest to replicate the Earth's food at the Space Academy, but the results of their labour could simply not compare to the taste of his wife's freshly baked bread, warm from the Aga. Still, he had no choice but to make do.

The hall was quiet, with only a few members of the teaching staff milling about, as they prepared to start their day. Kurt responded to their obligatory greetings with mumbled 'mornings', as they passed him to gather in a gaggle on the other side of the room. He tried to block out the noise of their chatter as he read over his lesson plans on the tablet that he kept in his inner jacket pocket.

Once he had filled himself sufficiently with food, he got up and left the hall, his hands shaking from the amount of caffeine he had already consumed that morning. He walked back out of the main entrance and turned left, heading down the asphalt path that led to the Ivory Tower, where his lessons took place.

He reached the tower's base and climbed into the open-topped shuttle rocket stationed beside it. The tower had no stairs, and was designed to prevent the alien subjects he kept inside it from escaping. Therefore, the only way for Kurt to access his office and classroom was by flight. He had always hated flying, finding the whole experience entirely unnatural, and he clung tightly to the metal bar around his waist as the rocket took off.

The driver, Jeff, was a friendly man with a relentlessly positive attitude, despite the fact he spent his days ferrying Kurt and his students back and forth on the same monotonous journey. He was a similar age to Kurt, his hair grey and thinning, and his hands wrinkled and battered from a lifetime of hard work. For that reason, Kurt felt a strange sort of affinity with him, and was willing to indulge his inane conversations, which usually centred around his grandchildren back on *The Mayflower* and how proud he was of them for no obvious reason.

When the brief ride was over, Jeff parked on the small landing pad on the tower's side and Kurt disembarked, thanking him courteously for his service. He walked inside and dropped his things off on his desk, heading straight for the large Alienary located next to his classroom.

The vast storage room was home to dozens of different species, all kept in enclosures that varied in size and design to suit their individual needs. There were cages covered in red dust, with burning lights fixed overhead to represent the scorching planes of far-off desert planets. Others were packed with foliage, filled with soaring trees and wild bushes, thick brown grass growing up from the soil-covered floor and tangling to form a dense hideaway for the aliens within.

There were high tanks, filled to the brim with the swirling multicoloured waters from different worlds, underwater rock formations providing shelter for their inhabitants. Overhead, there were giant swinging cages, attached firmly to the ceiling, their winged occupants waiting impatiently to be allowed into the grounds to fly. It was Kurt's favourite place in existence, and he spent his free period that morning doing his usual rounds, ensuring the alien creatures were comfortable, well-fed and clean.

He had grown increasingly fond of his captives over the years, caring wholeheartedly for the beings, whose intelligence matched only that of the animals which had roamed Earth, making them oblivious to their imprisoned state.

He wandered through the cages, greeting each beast he met with affection. He petted the ten-legged Timor as though it were a domesticated dog, dodging its snapping jaws with expert precision. He crooned at the feral Runhorn, soothing its angry disposition with a helping of raw meat he'd had delivered from the kitchen.

None of the species in the Alienary caused him the slightest bit of unease or fear. In fact, over the years, they had become his only trusted companions, providing him with relief from his otherwise lonely existence.

Noticing the time, Kurt began hurrying to collect the resources he would need for his first lesson. Rushing back to his classroom, he placed an unhatched, yellow egg on each desk, eagerly anticipating the arrival of his students.

The sound of faltering engines and the cheerful hum of chatter outside the door announced it was time for his class to begin. He stood up straight, placing his arms by his side and nodding at the students as they entered his classroom, looking around his classroom with bewilderment and gasping with delight when they noticed the eggs.

Kurt had become so used to the room that he had forgotten how spectacular it was to behold for the first time. The semi-circular walls were covered in small windows that fit together like a jigsaw, allowing an exceptional view of the grounds below. Sick of the constant darkness, Kurt had requested UV lights be installed outside the building to give the impression of sunlight flooding in. Watching the dust particles dancing in the light reminded him of Earth, and provided him with great comfort, inspiring him to start his lesson with a positive attitude in mind.

'Good morning, everyone,' he greeted the class. There was a faint reply of 'good morning,' as the last of the students scrambled to find their seats. Once a small disruption between a brown-haired girl and a tall, smug-looking boy had been settled, Kurt continued.

'My name is Mr Krecher,' he announced, pressing a small button on the control hidden in his hand, causing his name to appear on the interactive board on the back wall.

'As you may have noticed, there is an egg on each of your desks. Does anybody know which species of alien they belong to?' he asked, pacing up and down at the front of the class. His question was met with a resounding silence.

'No? Very well, I shall tell you. What you see before you are the unhatched eggs of a Beakin,' he said, pressing the button again so an image of the small creature appeared on the board. There was a chorus of 'ahh' from the students as they looked upon its small yellow body, enamoured with the sight of its large, round eyes and shiny, beaked mouth.

'Yes, they are rather charming creatures,' he continued. 'They make excellent pets, which is fortunate for you, as your task for the term will be to care for one in the pairs you are now sat in.'

The brown-haired girl from the earlier scuffle shot her hand up in the air with extreme force.

'Yes, er – '

'Emily,' she prompted him.

'Go on,' he said.

'Do we have to work in these pairs? Can we not change?' she asked, her green eyes full of desperation. Kurt glanced at the boy sitting beside her, the confidence draining from his face as everyone in the class stared in their direction.

'I'm afraid it's bad news, Emily. The partner you are with today will remain your partner for the rest of the term,' Kurt answered. 'Teaching the whole year group together can be difficult, so the less discrepancies there are over partners, the easier it will be for me to remember all your names.'

Emily looked nauseated.

'It's not all doom and gloom,' Kurt reassured her. 'Perhaps you will learn something about one another.'

He cast his eyes over the rest of the pairs sat around the room, noticing how the boy from Floor Seven was partnered with William James. Looking at William would almost certainly have sent his mind catapulting into the past again if it wasn't for the eyes of the other eighty-nine students in the room, staring at him expectantly.

'Underneath your desks you will find a drawer with a tablet device inside,' Kurt continued. 'You will use this tablet to send me weekly videos, images and reports on your progress. I will also be checking the health and happiness of your Beakin during our classes, where we will continue to learn about their origins, history and general development.'

'Now, the first thing you must do as new carers is begin hatching your egg. Like most creatures, Beakin eggs require light and heat to hatch. However, their affectionate nature means they also need a demonstration of love to come out of their shells. Desk lights can be collected from the front of class to take care of the former necessity, I shall leave the 'love' part for you to interpret. There will be extra credit for the first pair to hatch their egg during the lesson,' Kurt explained.

There was a small commotion as the class got to their feet to retrieve their lamps. Kurt meandered around the room, which had erupted in a loud discussion of the task, and watched with interest as his pupils showcased their different methods of expressing love.

Some were stroking their eggs, while others hugged them to their chests, inspecting their shells carefully for any cracks on the surface. One boy had taken to kissing his egg with such force and enthusiasm that Kurt couldn't help but feel sorry for any future romantic partner he might have. Unsurprisingly, none of them were successful in hatching their Beakin.

When he approached William and Finley, he hung back, intrigued by the snippets of their conversation he could overhear.

'Do you think it's scared?' William asked Finley, contemplating their egg with concern.

'What do you mean?' asked Finley.

'Well, I reckon if I'd been sat inside an egg all my life and suddenly some strangers were trying to get me to come out, I'd be quite scared,' William replied.

'Yeah, they probably are frightened. I mean, they don't even know that there's anything outside the egg. How do they know they're not destroying their only home for no reason?' Finley reflected.

'Shall we try and comfort it?' William suggested.

'I'm not sure how,' said Finley, chewing his lip in deep thought. There was a moment of silence between the two boys, before Finley spoke again.

'Well... there is something, but it's probably stupid,' he said, looking at the ground with embarrassment.

'What is it?' William encouraged him.

'It's something my mum used to say to me when I was little. You know, when I had nightmares and stuff,' Finley continued.

'Try it,' said William.

'Are you sure?' Finley asked.

'Yeah, go on, it might work.'

Finley picked up the egg and brought it close to his face, glancing around quickly to make sure nobody was watching him. Kurt averted his eyes and pretended to be extremely interested in something he could see out the window. When Finley was certain no one was listening, he spoke to the egg in a voice so gentle, Kurt could hardly hear it over the classroom chatter.

'Don't be scared' Finley told the egg. 'As long as you are loved, you are safe.'

He put the egg down swiftly, as though dropping something red hot, and placed his arms behind his back as his cheeks flushed scarlet. His discomfort only lasted a few seconds however, for almost as soon as the egg had touched the surface of the desk, it began to tremble and shake, splitting open to reveal the infant Beakin inside.

'Excellent work boys!' Kurt exclaimed, rushing over to congratulate them. 'You completed the task in record time.'

'How did they do it?' an irritated boy asked from across the room.

'The Beakins have telepathic abilities,' Kurt explained, 'They are able to read people's genuine intentions, regardless of what they might say out loud. This particular egg knew that William and Finley had its best interests at heart. It felt loved enough to hatch.'

'Well done, mate,' William told Finley, patting him on the back. 'It was all you.'

There was a loud scoffing noise from the desk beside them, as the tall, smug looking boy beside Emily let out a cruel laugh.

'Is something the matter?' Kurt asked him.

'How could Finley know anything about love?' he laughed. 'I'm surprised his parents didn't try to sell him off so they could buy a loaf of bread.'

There were a few titters from around the classroom.

'Why don't you shut your mouth, Rudy?' William shot back at him, stepping towards him in a fit of fury.

'Why don't you make me?' Rudy challenged him.

Before Kurt could react, William was upon him, shoving him hard into the desk behind him and causing several students to jump back in shock, clutching their eggs to their chests to stop them breaking. The boys began to fight, throwing punches at each other blindly and falling about the classroom.

'Enough!' Kurt boomed, using the full volume of his voice. The whole room fell deathly quiet, and the two boys ceased their brawl immediately.

'How dare you disrupt my lesson! Fighting on school grounds is completely unacceptable!' he scolded them, 'You will both see me after class.'

The boys looked down at their feet in shame and made their way sheepishly back to their desks, avoiding the gaze of the other pupils around them.

'Idiot,' Emily whispered to Rudy upon his return. Kurt pretended not to hear.

The rest of the lesson passed smoothly, though the atmosphere in the room was somewhat tense. Kurt advised the rest of the students how to hatch their eggs and sent them away with instructions relating to the Beakin's care. He provided them each with a suitable carry-cage and enough packets of food to last until next lesson and then dismissed them, sending them out to Jeff as they chatted happily about their first lesson, gripping their Beakin's cages with delight.

William and Rudy stayed behind, scuffing their feet on the floor and refusing to look each other in the eye as they awaited their punishment. Kurt sighed and rubbed the bridge of his nose. Discipline was his least favourite part of the job, but he knew it had to be done.

'Rudy, I'll speak to you first,' he announced, leading him through a door to the right of his classroom and into his office.

The room was furnished entirely with antique pieces from Earth, and the smell of old, musty wood filled their nostrils as soon as they walked in. His desk and coffee table were cluttered with papers, and his bookcases were filled with assorted junk that he had failed to organise at the end of the last school year. His eyes darted instinctively to the corner, where a floor-length mirror was hidden by a white sheet draped over its twisted, metal top.

He sat on his favourite patchy blue armchair, a cloud of dust arising from its fabric as he sunk into the cushion, gesturing for Rudy to sit on the faded red chair opposite. He perched on the edge, shifting uncomfortably and causing the chair's heavy, golden feet to creak noisily with the effort of holding his weight.

Kurt launched into an obligatory lecture, reprimanding him for making offensive comments and exhibiting violent behaviour in a classroom environment. He went through all the necessary points, emphasising the importance of proper conduct at school and threatening to involve Admiral Allance if another incident of this nature should occur.

After Rudy had apologised, Kurt nodded his acceptance and dismissed him, instructing him to send William in after him, and then wait for Jeff to take him back to the grounds.

Moments later, William walked in, sitting down in the red armchair without waiting to be asked. Kurt paused for a moment, deciding to change tact for their conversation.

'Now William-'

'It's Will,' he interrupted.

'Will,' Kurt corrected himself. 'I understand you were defending your friend, which is admirable, but you must understand the way you behaved is not appropriate for the classroom. There are better ways to deal with people like Rudy than resorting to violence.'

'I know, sir,' said Will. 'Sorry for disrupting your class."

Kurt regarded him for a moment. He had expected Will to have his mother's disposition, knowing he was raised by her alone, but he could see now that he had much more of his father in him than Kurt had thought possible. He sat back in his chair and exhaled, softening his tone as much as his gruff voice would allow.

'When we left Earth, we were told that inequality would become a thing of the past. Now you and I both know that isn't the case, but this injustice doesn't have to continue. Your generation have the power to change things before we reach Novum. If you wish to help Finley, you need to make others see that he is no different from the rest of us, despite where he comes from. Attacking anyone who insults him will only draw more attention to him, and cause problems in the long-term. The boy needs a friend, not a bodyguard. That is my advice to you.'

Will nodded, a muscle twitching in his jaw as he digested Kurt's words. Not wishing to punish him too much for a display of loyalty, Kurt decided to draw the conversation to a close.

'I must also make it clear that if you are caught fighting again in my class, I will have to inform Admiral Allance. Unfortunately, I also have no choice but to withhold your extra credit for completing today's egg task,' Kurt concluded.

'That's alright,' said Will sincerely. 'You should give my credit to Finley. He's the one who worked out how to hatch it.'

Kurt nodded with satisfaction and dismissed him, his thoughts already on the upcoming lunch hour and which creatures he would visit in his Alienary.

Will excused himself and stood up, making his way towards the door. Just before he reached for the handle, he stopped and froze, rendered immobile by something he could see in front of him on the wall. He turned his head back slightly, as though he were going to speak, but then seemed to think better of it, walking through the door and slamming it behind him.

Kurt stood up and walked over to where Will had stood, searching for a clue as to what he may have seen. When he noticed the offending picture on the wall, his body became momentarily numb. How could he have been so stupid as to forget what was hanging there?

Overwhelmed with guilt, he gazed at the smiling faces of Will's parents staring innocently out from behind the frame, trying to ignore the whispers that were buzzing in his ears. The voices in his head grew louder, until he could no longer shut them out, their harsh tones reminding him with persistent hostility of the secrets he had long hoped to forget.

THE QUEST FOR ANSWERS

Will's first few weeks at the Space Academy had passed in a flash, and before he knew it, he was enjoying the seven-day break given to the students half-way through the term. He had spent the first days of his holidays holed up in his room with Finley and Emily, playing games on his virtual reality machine, the three of them only emerging into the real world for mealtimes and to walk their Beakins around the school grounds.

On the fourth day, Finley began to panic about all the homework they'd been set, and had forced Emily and Will to the library, demanding they start their written assignments. Emily had insisted they begin with their Technology essay, since it was her favourite subject, and had rolled her eyes in an exaggerated fashion when Will and Finley complained of not understanding the title.

''The advancement of technology is a danger to the survival and overall welfare of human beings',' Will read for a second time from his Student Planner. 'Do you agree with this statement? Give reasons for your answer.'

'I'm still not sure what that means,' Finley frowned.

'Me neither,' Will huffed.

'Come on,' sighed Emily. 'You must be aware of the dangers

of technology?'

The boys looked at each other and shrugged. Trying to conjure an answer, Will cast his mind back to the Technology lessons they'd attended so far that term.

Held in the Tech Lab, the class provided the students with access to an array of different gadgets and machines, with hundreds of different functions. From robotics to teleportation systems, there was nothing about the lessons that hadn't completely fascinated them, including their teacher, Mr Mayheim, aptly nicknamed 'Mr Mayhem' by the students.

As ditzy as he was intelligent, Mr Mayhem was an older gentleman, who was rarely seen without his white lab coat on. The students at the school were convinced he never took it off, even when he slept or showered. He was deeply enthusiastic about his subject, so much so that his lessons often included passionate rants about various devices, with Will unconvinced he was aware of the presence of his students.

On his desk, Mr Mayhem kept two large spheres containing trapped electrical energy, sparking and swirling in various shades of blue and yellow. Nobody knew exactly what the spheres were for, but a boy in Will's class, Scott Holmes, was adamant they were responsible for the appearance of Mr Mayhem's long, white hair, which was consistently stuck on end.

'I'm telling you,' Scott had whispered to Will in class one day. 'Why do you think no one's allowed to touch them?'

Mulling the essay title over again in his mind, Will concluded that the only real danger he had ever encountered in Technology was Mr Mayhem himself, who had successfully managed to blow up two ancient computer monitors worth thousands of credits and cause a minor fire in the first week alone. Other than that, he had been completely amazed by everything they had studied so far, and couldn't see how anything which made life easier could possibly be a danger to humanity.

He voiced this opinion to Emily, which proved to be an unwise decision, resulting in a ten-minute lecture about the War on Earth, caused by the rebellion of artificial intelligence after their capabilities had become too highly developed.

Emily finished her essay in less than half an hour, and proceeded to help the boys come up with ideas for their own work that were just varied enough from hers to avoid accusations of copying.

Once they had finished, they took a break, during which they argued over which piece of homework to tackle next. Finley wanted to do their Combat and Weaponry task, which involved researching, drawing and labelling three weapons of their choice. Emily, who currently had custody of her and Rudy's Beakin, ironically named 'Monster' by the latter, wanted to work on their diaries for Alien Studies.

Will disagreed with them both, suggesting they write instructions on how to start and move off in a rocket for Mr Zeppler. Eventually, they agreed to do their Civilisations essay – an exceptionally dull piece on the flaws of the Roman Empire-before moving onto subjects they enjoyed.

'The worst thing about Civilisations,' Will reflected, after attempting to write his opening sentence six or seven times, 'is that it's so boring, but because Miss. Fortem is absolutely terrifying, you can't even zone out and daydream without putting your life at risk.'

'At least we don't have Arithmetic homework,' Emily pointed out, referring to Will's second most hated subject.

'Or Resources,' quipped Finley.

'I like Resources,' Emily countered.

'I did at first,' said Will, 'but how many times can you walk round a forest looking for fruit before it becomes incredibly dull?'

'It would be nice to try some different terrains,' Emily admitted.

'Our exam is in the forest, though,' Finley reminded them.

'Oh yeah,' Will remembered. 'I think it'll be quite fun being left in a forest all day and having to fend for ourselves.'

''Fun' or highly irresponsible of the school?' Emily laughed.

'At least Ms. Dido will be in the biodome with us the whole time,' Finley replied. 'I can't imagine her letting anything go wrong after Riley Fitch.'

'That's true,' Emily concurred. 'If there's anything dangerous in there, she will definitely scare it off.'

Will nodded in silent agreement. Ms. Dido was, without a doubt, the most impressive woman Will had ever seen, her height dwarfing anyone that stood beside her. Every inch of her body was defined with taught muscle, her clothes stretching and straining as they struggled to cover her wide frame. Even her hair, which she wore in two tight braids on the side of her head, exuded the impression of strength.

When Will had described her appearance to his mother during one of their calls, she had told him the polite way of describing her was 'Amazonian', but Will had no idea what this meant.

After sitting for several hours among a sprawled mass of laptops, tablets and I-Books, Emily, Will and Finley decided they had enough, and headed into the Dining Hall for their evening meal.

They were joined at their table by Cara and Matina, which seemed to send Emily into a bad mood, though Will couldn't understand why. He had always found the two girls very pleasant. They wolfed down their spaghetti and meatballs, discussing their holiday so far and comparing notes on the homework they'd completed. Emily sighed loudly, watching them chew their dinners in disgust, while picking at her own mushroom risotto.

'I don't know how you eat that stuff,' said Will, gesturing to her food. 'I couldn't live without meat. Especially bacon. It'd kill me off.'

'I'm sure you'd survive,' replied Emily drily. 'Meat isn't good for you.'

'Did you know that back on Earth, they used to raise animals for slaughter,' said Cara darkly. 'Food wasn't made in labs like it is now.'

'How do you know that?' Will asked.

'Matina and I joined the Earth Appreciation Society. We've actually found out some really interesting things.'

As Cara and Matina launched into a gruesome fact-file about Earth, Will glanced up and noticed Kyan Smith, the unsettling former best friend of Josie Jones, staring at him from his seat across the room. When they made eye contact, he didn't look away as Will had expected, but continued to watch him menacingly for a few seconds.

The uncomfortable moment was interrupted by Charlie, who walked over to the table and blocked Will's view of Kyan. By the time he had moved from Will's line of sight, Kyan had disappeared.

'Hey, little sis,' Charlie grinned at Emily, taking a seat opposite her and sending Cara and Matina into a flutter.

'Hi, Charlie,' replied Emily. 'To what do we owe the pleasure of your company.'

'Now, now that's no way to talk to your big brother,' Charlie teased. 'Especially when he's come to invite you to a party.'

'A party?' Cara repeated with excitement.

'Yeah, in my room. It'll be after curfew, when all the teachers go to bed,' Charlie replied.

'Your room is in the third-year dorms,' Emily frowned. 'We can't be caught in the grounds after curfew. We'd get in so much trouble.'

'That's the beauty of it,' Charlie beamed, leaning in and speaking in a hushed voice. 'I overheard Miss Fortem talking to Admiral Allance in the library earlier. It turns out that Mr Mayhem is trying to invent some inter-planetary teleportation device that keeps going wrong. Miss Fortem was telling Allance that all the teachers need to be on guard tonight, because apparently Mayhem blew all the cameras out with a massive power surge! None of them are working! There's no surveillance at all.'

He leant back in his chair triumphantly, watching his audience's reaction to the tale with his tongue pressed in his cheek.

'But, Charlie...' Emily said after a moment, 'if all the teachers are on guard, we'll still get caught.'

'I didn't tell you the best part,' Charlie responded. 'Allance told Miss Fortem that as long as none of the students know about the broken cameras, there's no need to stand guard. He told her just to keep it hush and then none of them have to go on patrolling duty.'

'Seems a bit risky,' Will mused, wondering how the

Headmaster could be so nonchalant about a possible breach in security, especially when Mr Krecher took his aliens out to roam the grounds at night. Charlie rolled his eyes, a cornerstone trait of the Pannell family.

'Who cares?!' he exclaimed. 'The point is, are you coming or not?'

'If it means that much to you,' Emily sighed.

'Great, see you there,' Charlie beamed.

'Can we come?' Cara and Matina asked in unison.

'Sure, the more the merrier,' Charlie shrugged, excusing himself from the table with a wink.

After dinner, Emily retreated to her room to get ready, Cara and Matina following behind her and giggling as they discussed various choices of outfit. Will and Finley went to collect their Beakin - named 'Beaky' - and took him for a walk around the school grounds, a small pink leash tied around his neck.

As they strolled around the Resources biodome, listening to the sound of the torrential rain inside it, Will broke the news to Finley that he wouldn't be attending the party that evening.

'Oh, come on Will, I need you there,' Finley pleaded. 'The older students still look at me like I'm an alien with three heads.'

Will apologised, appeasing him off with a weak excuse about being tired from all the homework and wanting to use his personal device to call his mum.

'Anyway,' he reminded Finley, 'you don't need me around when you've got Emily to protect you. She's far scarier than I am.'

Finley accepted his point and the two of them returned to the dorms, where they parted ways, promising to meet for breakfast so Will could be filled in on all the details from the party.

Once Finley had gone, Will rode the lift to the third floor and walked briskly to his room, closing the door behind him as the relief of being alone flooded through his body.

He walked into the bathroom and undressed, stepping into his large shower. The hot water cascaded over his body and relaxed his mind, his thoughts drifting lazily back to his first Alien Studies lesson.

It had become customary for him to think about it whenever he was alone, and the niggling memory of what he had seen when he'd been called into Krecher's office after his fight with Rudy rarely gave him a minute's peace. When he had stepped into the room, he had noticed a series of framed photographs hanging on Krecher's wall. He had taken no notice, until one of them had caught his eye as he made to leave, stopping him dead in his tracks.

Standing in the photo with Krecher was Will's mother, her face fuller and brighter with youth but unmistakeable, none-theless. Among the gathering of students was a young man, his sandy-blonde hair, tanned skin and height making him stand out sharply from the rest of the group.

Will had studied the man's features carefully, taking in his blue, shining eyes, strong jaw and pronounced nose. He knew those features. He saw them every morning when he looked in the bathroom mirror. They were his own. This man was his father.

He must have only been standing still for a few seconds, but he had sensed Krecher's eyes burning into the back of his head. In a fit of adrenaline, he had left, resolving not to tell his friends about what he had seen. He wasn't sure how he felt about it yet, and he hadn't wanted them asking questions. Instead, he had brooded over his discovery in secret, the complicated emotions it had brought up bubbling away just under the surface.

In all the Alien Studies lessons that followed, Will had stared at Krecher whenever he wasn't looking, as though he might find the answers he was seeking written on the back of his head. He spent the hours in the Ivory Tower with his brow knitted together, trying to put the pieces of this strange jigsaw puzzle together as he wondered what the connection was between his parents and his teacher.

Will could not understand why, if the memory of teaching his mother and father was so precious to Krecher that he kept a framed photograph of them, he had never decided to mention that he knew them. Will had never heard his mother so much as utter Krecher's name. He had the strong inclination that something was being kept from him, and he was determined to find out what.

Occasionally, Krecher had caught Will's eye in class, and each time his face had clouded with what Will could only describe as an expression of guilt. This behaviour served only to enflame Will's curiosity further, and he had promptly begun plotting a way to find out the truth.

He knew, by the strength of gut instinct, that the information he sought would be found in Krecher's office. He also knew that Krecher took his aliens out at precisely half past ten every night, having watched him through the window for several weeks.

By carefully studying the interactive school map in stolen moments between classes, he had discovered the fastest way to reach the Ivory Tower from the first-year dormitories. The only obstacle that had been standing in his way were the security cameras that were dotted around the grounds. The moment Charlie had announced they were broken, he had made his decision: tonight would be the night he put his plan into action.

At quarter past ten, he got up from his bed, ending the mind-numbing task of staring absentmindedly at the patterns on his ceiling. He walked purposefully over the wardrobe and pushed his school uniform to the side, rifling through the clothes he had brought from home to find the darkest possible items he owned. After successfully locating a black hoody and a pair of matching trousers, he dressed and went to the window, waiting for his cue to leave.

A few minutes later, the faint pinprick of yellow light appeared in the distance, signalling that Krecher had left the Ivory Tower and was walking through the darkened grounds by torchlight.

Will made for the door and headed down the hallway without hesitation, keeping up a quick pace as he moved. He faltered as he was greeted by the unexpected sight of Lois ahead of him, standing in her bedroom doorway and gossiping with a group of the Floor One girls that were gathered in the corridor.

He cursed himself for not preparing for the possibility of bumping into anyone. After all, there were no cameras in the student dorms, with it apparently being considered 'unethical' by the school board, and so the only form of security the first-years had to contend with was the achingly slow patrol Ms. Everly conducted each night. Once she had gone, the dorms were available for free roaming, which many of the students regularly took advantage of.

Will ducked into the lift as discreetly as possible and

descended to the ground floor. He hurried through the foyer and out the doors without stopping, allowing the thrill of his mission to carry him forward into the night.

Without the lamps on, the Space Academy was swathed in an almost impenetrable darkness, which only enabled Will to see for a few feet in front of him. He found his route from memory, using his feet to feel out where the paths bent and twisted beneath him as he snuck his way around the back of the campus.

Buildings loomed out of the shadows as he passed them, menacing in the gloom. He strained to recognize their exteriors, which were strikingly different in the deep darkness. Hoping to be comforted by a familiar sight, he glanced up at the blanket of stars that hung above him.

In the black of night, he could see the glinting edge of the dome that encased the school. Gazing upon it made him feel claustrophobic, as if he were trapped inside one of the novelty snow-globes that his mother had purchased from the Earth souvenirs shop on *The Mayflower*. He looked away, focussing his mind on the task in hand, hoping he would find the key to unlock the strange mystery he had been presented with. Something in Krecher's behaviour had convinced him that simply asking his teacher or his mother how they knew each other would be pointless, and perhaps even get him into trouble. He knew this was the only option he had, and so he continued trudging through the grounds, convincing himself his dangerous mission would prove worthwhile.

After what felt like an eternity, he saw the Ivory Tower in the distance; a shiny white beacon of hope among the black. He raced in its direction, his eagerness to reach it and fulfil his task growing with every step.

The sound of aliens screeching in the distance informed him that Krecher was still outside. There was still time. He approached the foot of the tower and stopped short, taking deep a breath as he paused to collect himself. He knew the next stage of his plan would be the most difficult to execute, and he took a moment to gather his thoughts, reciting the next steps to himself until he was certain he knew them by heart.

With a quick scope of his surroundings, Will clambered into Jeff's shuttle, fastening himself carefully into the driver's seat. After much pestering during the journey to Alien Studies, Will had managed to get Jeff to confess that he programmed the shuttle to autopilot, meaning a simple flick of a switch would activate its flight path.

Will had promised not to tell anyone in exchange for a demonstration from Jeff, who quickly showed him how the system worked while the other students were distracted. Little did he know how vital the information was for the success of Will's plan. Praying he wouldn't be seen or heard, Will turned the switch on, ducking down to conceal himself from potential onlookers as the rocket made its ascent.

When he reached the docking bay, he exited the ship and made his way silently into the classroom beyond. He passed through the dark room with haste, the eerie quiet filling him with unease, and reached the door to Krecher's office. He was relieved-and rather surprised-to find it was unlocked and pushed on the handle gently to enter.

The room was cast into shadow, and Will struggled to make sense of his surroundings, his eyes adjusting slowly to the lack of light. He took a step forward and crashed into Mr

Krecher's desk, cursing loudly as his leg painfully caught on the wooden corner.

Rubbing the swollen bruise, he tapped his personal device on his wristband and selected the torch feature, shining the bright light around the room as he searched for clues.

His first thought was to examine the photograph that had drawn him to the office in the first place. He shone his light on the back wall where the collection of framed pictures hung, trawling over each image slowly until he located the right one.

It didn't take long for him to recognise the photo, hanging innocently between Krecher's graduation picture and a snap of a smiling blonde woman. Moving closer, he noticed for the first time that Captain Alfie was also in the photograph, standing between Will's mother and Krecher, his arms folded behind his back and a sombre expression on his face. Will bent down to read the plaque at the base of the frame, wondering if he would recognise any more names.

'Alien Studies class, College Snowdonia 2098,' it read, 'Taught by K. Krecher (middle). Students: Joel Emmett, Zaia Ibrahim, Charlotte Mazur, Austin De Havilland, Elsie James, Alfie Sommers...'

The list continued, but Will had stopped reading. He had always known that his mother had given him her surname, but she had never told him what his father's name had been, and after many years of trying. Will had finally given up asking questions. Seeing the name etched in fine print before him sent Will's mind into overdrive. For a moment, he was lost in a daydream in which he was William De Havilland, a normal boy from a normal family, and not William James - the boy who grew up without a father.

He tore himself away from the photo and searched the rest of the room, raiding Krecher's drawers that were filled with piles of unorganised papers and heavy, bound journals covered in dust. At the bottom of the pile was a thick green notebook, secured by a weighty padlock.

Will picked up the book and turned it over in his hands. It was rough and dog-eared, creases forming over its cover from where it had been opened and closed so many times. Peering down at the thick mass of pages, he saw that some of them had been torn out, leaving a jagged edge where they once had been.

A small white sticker on the sleeve read 'September 2097-June 2098'. Will knew his father had died before the Split in 2100; the year Will was born. That meant Krecher had known his mum and dad just two short years before the tragic event had happened. Something during this time period was significant enough for him to keep a framed photograph of the class and a padlocked journal. Will had a strong feeling about the importance of whatever was inside the locked notebook, and urgently began to search for the key.

After hunting for several minutes with no avail, Will began to feel defeated. He slumped into Krecher's armchair, contemplating whether to abandon his mission altogether. Just as he was about to abandon all hope, the most peculiar sight manifested before his eyes.

The mirror in the corner of Krecher's office had suddenly sprouted a handle, as if by magic. Will stared at the mysterious object, the new handle on its surface shiny, round and inviting. Though he could not understand it, a voice in his head urged him to touch it, and so he did, reaching out and turning the silver knob. Immediately, the mirror swung back on itself, opening as a doorway to something strange and black behind it.

Will dithered for a moment, hesitating between investigating further and leaving the office altogether. His heart was pounding as he contemplated the abyss before him, it's nothingness both terrifying and tantalising. He battled inside his own head, logic urging him to turn and run the other way, while his heart longed for him to step inside.

His mind was made up for him when the sound of approaching footsteps from the classroom outside echoed through the door, informing him that he was about to be caught red-handed in a teacher's office after hours.

Without another thought, Will jumped and sprinted forward, running at full pelt through the mirror-turned-door, falling head first into whatever lay beyond.

THE LOOKING GLASS

The sensation of cold air smothered Will's face and body as he realised with a jolt that he was outside. He bent over to catch his breath, disorientation causing his head to spin.

He looked at the solid concrete beneath his feet in disbelief. Just moments ago, he had been at the top of the Ivory Tower, miles and miles from the ground. There was no way he could have survived a fall from that height. It was impossible, and yet, there he was, all in one piece.

Will turned around, searching wildly for the mirror he had run through, but it had disappeared completely. He staggered backwards as his surroundings came into focus and the understanding of where he was dawned on him.

He was standing upon a street flanked with red-bricked houses, their tiled rooves forming perfect triangles that pointed into the sky. Cars of various makes and models sat in driveways decorated by flowerpots and protected by thick, metal gates. The road was lit up by a combination of yellow street lamps, and the pale moon shone ghost-like over his head. He had paid enough attention in History to know why the scene was so familiar to him. He was on Earth.

The wind blew coolly around his face, and he hugged himself tightly to shelter from its sharp bite. There was a crisp freshness to the air that he had never experienced before, and he inhaled deeply, his lungs filling gratefully with the clean, unfiltered oxygen.

After a few seconds, his head began to steady itself, and he began seeking a reasonable explanation for what had happened. The mirror must be some kind of teleportation device, he concluded, and Mr Krecher must be making secret trips to Earth without anyone knowing.

He was certain that the footsteps he had heard before he fled belonged to Krecher and knew it wouldn't take him long to realise there had been an intruder in his office. Will could only hope Krecher would put two and two together quickly, rescuing him before he became stranded on the desolate Earth forever.

He glanced around the street, hoping to find himself alone. The people who had been left on Earth after the Split were referred to as 'Forgottens,' and Will had heard enough about their volatile and violent nature to know he would be in danger if he were to encounter anybody in the dark of night.

With a sudden twinge of panic, Will activated his personal device, desperate to call someone for help. To his dismay, he found it completely useless, the batteries having deactivated following his arrival. In an attempt to calm himself, Will tried to picture his mother's face, promising himself it wouldn't be long until he saw her again. He imagined telling her the story of his plight; her horror at his plight turning swiftly to relief that he had made it out unscathed. He kept this in his mind as he walked down the street, assuring himself it wouldn't be long before he was found and brought back to *The Mayflower*.

The sound of footsteps behind him made him jump, and he realised he was no longer alone. A woman had appeared from a side street a few yards in front of him, a thick winter coat and scarf drawn around her body to protect her from the cold. She had her back to him, but Will could see her chestnut brown hair billowing out behind her as she moved.

Something about the woman's way of walking was familiar to Will, and he knew instinctively that she wasn't a threat. Deciding she would be his best chance for help, he pursued her, calling after her as he ran.

'Hello!' he shouted, slowing to a halt as he levelled with her. 'Excuse me!'

The woman did not stop or slow down, continuing to stride forward so quickly that Will could not see her face. Desperate for her attention, he ran in front of her, jogging backwards to keep up with her pace. A gust of wind blew her hood back, and Will froze with shock, realising the face of the woman was the very same face that he had pictured just a few seconds earlier. It was the face of his mother.

'Mum!' Will cried, a mixture of euphoria, confusion and fear convulsing through his body.

Much to his distress, she still did not stop, speeding past him as though she were oblivious to his cries.

'Mum!' Will yelled. 'It's me!'

She walked faster still, his words having no effect on her whatsoever.

'Mum?' he faltered, beginning to fear something was wrong.

He ran after her, reaching out to grab her coat, but his hands slipped through the material as if there was nothing there. He reached out to grasp hold of her arm, but all he felt between his fingers was the cold, night air.

'What's happening?' he asked himself, his voice rising in

terror as his mind began to race.

His mother was here but she was a ghost, or a hologram, unable to see, hear or feel his touch. He was utterly petrified and confused beyond anything he had ever experienced. He began to wonder if he had fallen and hit his head in Krecher's office, falling into a coma-induced dream from which he would soon wake. As he continued to try and make sense of what was happening, he followed his mother, instinct driving him to stay close to her presence despite her inability to see him. Even if he was in a dream, he knew his mother would guide him to safety, and so he kept up with her, glancing every so often at her face to reassure himself that she was really there.

Suddenly, they turned a corner, the suburban road they were descending sharply down a hill, giving way to a magnificent view. Will paused for a moment, his breath taken away by the sight. Glorious mountains rose in the distance, their peaks topped with heavy dustings of white snow, which tumbled down the sturdy rock of their faces until it reached the ground. Spanning between the mountains were rolling hills and plummeting valleys, dotted with sheep and a smattering of small cottages. It was a truly beautiful sight to behold.

Returning to his senses, Will continued tailing his mum as she veered into an alleyway, arriving at a vast body of water on the other side that he recognised from his history books as the sea.

Without hesitation, Elsie made her way towards the water's edge with Will a few paces behind her, stones crunching beneath his feet as he struggled to keep his balance on the strange, new terrain. At the end of the beach, a figure was waiting, his back turned to them as he contemplated the infinite, black surface of the water.

Elsie stopped walking, and for a moment, all was still. Will stood quietly, listening to the soothing sound of waves breaking against the shore. The stars in the sky shone as brightly as they did on *The Mayflower*, and Will was struck by a sudden understanding of what it meant to live on Earth as he stared at the vastness of space before him and began to feel part of something much bigger than he could comprehend. The feel of solid ground beneath his feet was alien to him, and yet something about it felt right somehow. The humanity in him seemed to pulsate and come alive, the connection to his home planet awakening for the first time.

Will's reverie was broken by the sudden movement of the figure before him, who turned around and began to walk in Will's direction, his face becoming clearer as he drew closer. Will recognised the same features he had seen in Mr Krecher's photograph and was struck once again by the similarity of this man to himself. He stared dumbfounded at his father, unable to believe he was truly seeing him in the flesh.

'Elsie, I'm so glad you came,' Austin smiled as he approached her, taking both her hands in his own. There is a tranquillity to his voice that Will finds unnerving, as though he found the end of the world to be a peaceful prospect.

'Of course I came,' Elsie replied. 'Where have you been, Austin? You promised you would come home. It's been two weeks without a word from you. I've been insane with worry."

'All is well, Elsie,' Austin smiled. 'I have found a way for us to escape the Earth. You know the government can't be trusted. We have to save ourselves. We have to leave."

'No, Austin,' Elsie said, shaking her head. 'Please, stop this.'

'Is it really so hard to believe? After all the things we've seen?' Austin asked, his calm demeanour never wavering. "It is time to go, now. Everything will be fine."

Elsie said nothing, her face twisted with despair.

'You're too scared to admit the truth,' Austin sighed, shaking his head. 'You know I'm right. Letting go of this planet will be difficult, I know, but what other choice do we have?'

'Austin, we promised we would forget about the great conspiracy,' Elsie said, her eyes beginning to fill with tears. 'We have to go to Novum. We have to get onto *The Mayflower*. There is no other way to survive."

Austin opened his mouth to protest, but Elsie cut him off, raising her voice louder to make sure she was heard.

'No one is trying to interfere with *The Mayflower*, Austin. Humans ruined the Earth. We are greedy and flawed, and we have destroyed the planet that gave us life. We deserve to be punished, but there is hope. Perhaps we can create a better world. That is what we've been promised. There is some risk in believing it, I know, but if it's all true... Imagine what we could do now we've learnt from our mistakes? It may seem too good to be true, but we have to believe there's a better life out there somewhere. Otherwise, what's the point of it all?'

'I've got something for us,' Austin replied, gesturing down the beach to a large spacecraft parked a few metres away. Will was surprised he hadn't immediately noticed it, its sheer size making it difficult to miss.

'Where did you get that?' Elsie demanded, panic rising in her voice.

'The flying department at the college has very lax security' Austin laughed. 'It was easy to steal. The ship is big enough to accommodate us for several years. We can find our own new planet to live on. We don't need Novum or *The Mayflower*. *This* is the only way.'

'Austin, stop this! You sound insane,' Elsie pleaded with him. 'We need to go home. We need to get away from this place. It's not good for you to be here.'

'I can't do that,' Austin replied.

'Yes, you can!' Elsie argued. 'Come home and apply to *The Mayflower* with me. It's the only hope the three of us have.'

She put her hand on her stomach, drawing Will's attention to her rounded belly. His heart began to pound in his ears as the sickening reality of what he was about to witness dawned upon him.

'We can stand here and argue about it all night,' Austin sighed. 'But the fact of the matter is; *The Mayflower* isn't safe. I've been saying it since college, and I know I'm right. I'm leaving. And you can either come with me, or you can stay here and die with everyone else.'

Elsie jerked her head back as though he had slapped her.

'How can you say that?' she whispered, tears escaping down her cheeks. 'You would really leave us here to die? Do we mean nothing to you?'

Austin was silent, watching in contempt as she continued to sob.

'I'm disappointed you didn't believe in me, Elsie,' he said thickly, his voice beginning to shake with anger. 'And now it has come to this.'

'You can't be serious,' she spluttered. 'You're out of your mind. I don't understand this. This isn't you, Austin. How could you do this?'

'You've given me no choice,' Austin replied coldly.

Elsie sank to her knees, watching as he strode with determination down the beach, her sobs growing louder and more uncontrollable with every step he took.

Will watched with horror as his father left, not stopping once to look back at his mother or the unborn child he was leaving behind.

He tried to reach out to comfort Elsie, but she couldn't feel him. He yelled out in rage against his father, but he couldn't hear. After a moment, he dropped to the floor, sitting beside his mother as he waited for the turmoil to end.

There was a 'whooshing' noise and a powerful gust of air as his father entered the spacecraft and took off, ascending into the sky with furious speed.

Will watched as he flew higher and higher, drifting over the sea directly in front of them.

Suddenly, the spacecraft halted and hovered, floating gently in mid-air. Will's heart leapt with hope for the possibility that his father had changed his mind, despite knowing how the story ended.

His mother's sobs slowed beside him as her eyes too glimmered with the dream that Austin was about to return to her. With a colossal 'bang' that echoed terribly through the night, the spacecraft exploded into a spectacular ball of fire, illuminating the sky in a burst of orange and red.

Will got up and ran, covering his ears so he could not hear the horrible, broken screams that were coming from his mother. He could not bear to look at her, running until the water's edge had filled every corner of his vision.

A glinting light in his peripherals caught his attention, and he turned to see the mirror from Krecher's office materialising beside the shore.

He ran towards it at top speed, not caring if he smashed it into pieces, and threw his body against its surface.

There was a moment of inky blackness before he fell, hitting the floor with a heavy thud. He lay still, refusing to open his eyes in case he should find himself back on the beach, trapped inside the terrible moment forever.

'Had a nice trip did you, boy?' Krecher said, his gruff voice sounding from somewhere close by.

Will opened his eyes and saw, with great relief, that he was in Krecher's office. Krecher himself was sitting on his patchy, blue armchair, sipping coffee from a china mug and watching Will with concern.

'Come and sit down,' he ordered him. Will stood up on shaking legs and did as he was told, moving to sit in the red armchair opposite his teacher.

'Cup of tea?' he asked, and Will nodded, sitting in silence as Krecher rose and made his way over to the drinks machine in the corner, presenting Will with the piping hot beverage before sitting back down in his original position.

Will sipped the tea gratefully, the warm liquid soothing the numbness which had spread all over his body.

'So,' said Krecher. 'I see you found my Looking Glass.'

'Y-your what?' Will stammered.

'The Looking Glass. That's what I call it,' he motioned towards the mirror, standing perfectly in-tact in the corner.

'What is it?' Will asked, staring at its glass surface with terror.

'That's a good question,' Krecher replied. 'One I've spent many years trying to answer. The truth is, I don't know exactly what it is. I discovered it one day, a very long time ago when I was still a professor on Earth, and I have been trying to understand it ever since. It's alien, of course, that much is clear. No human technology could ever match its capabilities. As to how it works, I must confess it's still as much of a mystery to me now as it was on the first day I found it. All I know is, it shows you things; past, present and future, but only if they are important to you. Only if they mean something.'

'I don't understand,' Will shook his head. 'How is that even possible? Just then... I was... It was like I was inside my mum's memories. How could that be?'

'It wasn't memories,' Krecher responded. 'I thought so, too, at first, but then I saw something from the future and realised it could not be so. It makes sense if you think about it. Memories are unreliable. They are altered by time and perception. You can convince yourself of anything if you tell yourself its true. No, this doesn't show memory. It shows you a point in time. It allows you to explore it, to spectate and journey about to your heart's content, but it doesn't let you change anything. The people you can see don't know you're there. Nothing you do has any affect on what happens. I've tried to change the past, to right a few wrongs, but it's impossible. You are helpless, simply watching as events unfold. That is the mirror's curse.'

'I think the curse is being able to see anything at all,' Will swallowed. Krecher looked at him with worry.

'What did you see?' he questioned him. 'If you don't mind me asking?'

'My dad,' Will replied. 'I saw my dad... die.'

Krecher inhaled deeply.

'My boy, I'm so sorry,' he sighed. 'You shouldn't have been

145

put through that.'

He glared at the mirror with fury as though it could understand that he was displeased. Will said nothing, unable to find the words to describe what he had witnessed.

'Well,' Krecher continued. 'Now you know my secret. I trust you will keep it in exchange for me keeping yours.'

'Mine?' Will repeated with confusion.

'Sneaking out after curfew,' Krecher smiled. 'Breaking into my office. I don't need to remind you how Admiral Allance would feel if he knew any of this. I think it's best for both of us if we keep this incident to ourselves.'

'Yes, Mr Krecher' Will said. 'I understand why you're angry. I shouldn't have come here. It was stupid.'

'I'm not angry,' Krecher assured him. 'Truth be told, I feel I'm to blame for the whole thing. It was only natural that you'd come looking for answers after you saw a picture of your mother and father in here. I should have sat you down and spoken to you about it, but I confess it's not a time in my life I enjoy discussing.'

'How did you know them?' Will pressed, seizing his chance to ask the questions that had plagued him since the start of the school term.

'Your parents? I taught them at college,' Krecher answered simply. 'They joined my Alien Studies class, along with the Captain, in their final year. They were my best students. They showed a dedication to the subject that was unprecedented among their peers. I was terribly sad when I heard about what happened to your father. He was a bright young man full of promise, but his obsession with the great conspiracy got the better of him. Terrible waste of a life.'

'I don't understand why my mum didn't tell me any of this,' Will wondered aloud. 'Why hide the truth from me? It's not as if keeping it from me could change any of it.'

'For the same reason that I didn't, I suspect' Krecher sighed. 'She was probably trying to protect you. The truth can be a complicated thing, far less black and white than most people realise. Leaving your father's death a mystery was the kinder option to her. You must try to forgive her, Will. She had your best interests at heart.'

Will nodded, digesting this information slowly.

He thought back to the times he had questioned his mother as a boy, and felt he was beginning to understand why she had struggled to answer him. How could you tell a child about what he had just seen?

Will finished his tea and put his cup down on the small wooden coffee table beside his armchair, his eyes itching with tiredness. He let out a small yawn, his brain exhausted from all the revelations he had been dealt that evening. Krecher noticed his tiredness and rose to his feet, Will doing the same.

'It's probably best that you get yourself to bed now,' he told Will. 'Try not to get caught on the way back.'

Will smiled and made to leave. He was a few centimetres from the door when Krecher called to him again.

'Oh, and Will... try not to get lost in the past again. There are some things there that are best left undiscovered.'

Will left the office quickly, trying hard to ignore the unescapable curiosity that burned fiercely in his mind.

THE CREATURE IN THE HALLWAY

Lois flicked her perfectly coiffed blonde hair over her shoulder and sighed, examining the chipped pink nail varnish on her fingers. Despite her best efforts, contemplating which shade of varnish suited her best was not providing a sufficient distraction from Ms. Dido's lecture, which droned on unbearably in the background. Truthfully, Lois didn't think any of her peers enjoyed being confined to a classroom to learn about Resources, but the entire year group were forced to endure it once a week before their practical session started.

The effort to not look at the time on her personal device was strenuous, and so she let her eyes wander around the class, taking in the mutual boredom of the Alderin, Armstrong and Gagarin students alike.

A pang of envy shot through her as she looked at Penelope and Florence, her best friends from Floor One, sat beside each other and laughing silently at a whispered private joke. Ms. Dido insisted that her pupils were organised alphabetically, which unfortunately meant that Lois was stuck next to Kyan Smith, who spent most of his time smirking to himself and glaring at people in a very off-putting manner. In all her time as his desk partner, she had never once heard him speak, his apparent mutism proving extremely problematic when they were set work to be completed in pairs.

Lois glanced towards the window, hoping to amuse herself with the view of the lamplit school grounds, but was drawn instead to the sight of Will, sitting next to his friend Emily on the far side of the room.

She watched as he bent down to rest his head on the desk, an expression of deep disinterest on his face. It reminded her of the first time she had ever seen Will. He had been standing awkwardly at her mother's funeral, which was held in the Commiserations Hall on *The Mayflower*. Lois had only been five years old, but the memory of that day was still razor sharp in her head, available to replay in super high definition at any time.

'That's Will,' her father had said, bending down to talk softly in her ear. 'He's Elsie's little boy.'

He pointed to Will's mother, who was standing beside him and doing her best to convey the appropriate amount of sadness. Her father's attempt to distract Lois from the fact her mother's coffin had just been launched into space was feeble, and she resented him for even trying.

'I've been hoping you two would meet properly,' her father continued, 'but Elsie and I are always so busy, and you're always with the nanny...' he trailed off awkwardly, as was the custom for discussing the little amount of time he spent with Lois.

She remained silent, watching Will as he took a small toy rocket out of his pocket and began running it along the top of the benches, making 'whooshing' noises as he did so.

'I think it might be good for you to make friends,' Alfie continued, 'You know, what with you losing your mother and his father dying before he was born.'

Lois remained silent. Earlier that morning, she had made a vow to herself that she wouldn't speak for the entire day. Her mother had been the only person who understood her, and if she couldn't talk to her, she resolved that she would remain silent for the rest of her days.

'Go and say hello,' Alfie urged her, nudging Lois forward.

She walked over to Will obligingly, if only to prevent further conversation with her father. Sitting on the bench Will was playing on, she stared at him with her arms folded, scowling darkly to make sure he knew she wasn't happy to be there.

'Hello, Lois,' Elsie smiled sympathetically.

Lois said nothing, continuing to regard Will with her fiery stare.

To her dismay, he was completely unaware of her anger. He continued playing with his toy happily, soaring the rocket above his head. Her desire to bait him into an argument and release some of her fury overwhelmed her, and before she could stop herself, she began to speak.

'Can I have a go?' she asked. She was almost certain that Will would say 'no' given his obvious attachment to the old-fashioned toy, and hoped it would be a valid excuse to start the quarrel she so desperately wanted.

He paused for a moment, chewing his lip as he considered his answer.

'Okay,' he shrugged, handing her the rocket.

Shocked by his response, Lois began to examine the toy, noticing the chipped, red paint on its body and the white scuffs on its wings that indicated how well-loved it was.

In one swift motion, she threw the rocket to the ground and stamped on it as hard as she could. She drove her shiny black shoe into it over and over, until it was completely obliterated, each stamp of her foot releasing part of the overwhelming fury she felt.

When she was finished, Lois looked up at Will, her nose scrunched up in rage and her eyes full of tears. His mouth was hanging open in shock as he gazed forlornly at the remains of the toy. His bottom lip trembled, and he looked to his mother, who placed a firm hand on his shoulders.

'It's okay, Will,' she soothed him. 'We'll go down to the lobby and get you a new one.'

Will considered this for a moment before nodding and taking his mother's hand, squeezing it tightly.

'Thank you, mummy,' he smiled. and Lois felt as though her body was going to burst from hatred.

She hated Will for being happy, and she hated his mother for being alive, and she hated her mother for being dead. Most of all, she hated her father for thinking that this cheerful little boy could possibly understand the magnitude of pain that weighed on her every minute of every day since her mother had gone.

After the funeral, Lois had tried her best to ignore Will, but it had become increasingly difficult after they joined the Space Academy, with him constantly seeming to draw attention to himself. She was sure, however, that she could have successfully continued pretending he didn't exist, had she not personally seen him exhibit a series of odd behaviours over the past few weeks that had begun to intrigue her.

The first strange occurrence had been one night during half-term, when some students from the third year had thrown a party in their dorms. Some of the older girls who had befriended Lois invited her and her friends along. They had been standing in the hallway, ready to leave, when Lois had caught sight of Will, decked head to foot in black clothing, ducking into the lift on his own. Thinking it strange, she had looked for him at the party, but had failed to see him mingling among the guests.

A few days later, Lois had found him standing alone in the corridor, staring transfixed at the school map. She had hung back and watched as he began tracing over pathways with his finger, as though planning a very elaborate journey around the school.

Her curiosity had started to grow, and a result she began to watch Will closely, observing him in the Dining Hall on several occasions. Each time, she had noticed him staring into space and looking uncharacteristically troubled, his face pale with worry.

After piecing everything together, Lois had come to the conclusion that something extremely strange was going on, and she was determined to find out what.

Her thoughts about Will had carried her successfully through Ms. Dido's lecture, and she came back to reality just in time to start the practical segment of the lesson.

She followed the other students out of the classroom and congregated with them around the entrance to the Resources biodome, managing to find Florence and Penelope in the process.

'That was so boring,' Florence complained with a sigh, the other girls murmuring in agreement.

'You two looked like you were laughing about something,' Lois said to Florence and Penelope. They exchanged a knowing look and burst into a fit of giggles.

'Well, what was the joke?' Lois pressed them.

'Oh, you wouldn't understand, Lois,' Florence said. 'It was something that happened in our Rocket Control lesson, but you had to be there.'

Lois sighed and turned her attention to Ms. Dido, who had begun booming her instructions.

'We will shortly be going to the Biodome to practise the skills we discussed in our lesson,' she announced. 'Your task will be to find a suitable drinking source in the forest terrain within an hour. You will each take a flask from me and fill it with whatever water you find. The group who finds the cleanest and freshest water will receive the highest grade. I must remind you, as always, to abide by the rules of the biodome, which means staying firmly in your groups and not wandering off. No one is to leave until a proper headcount has been performed at the end of the class.'

Following her address, she opened the doors to the biodome and let the students into the simulated forest.

Despite the fact the forest wasn't real, Lois enjoyed the experience of the 'outdoors' nonetheless; a concept which had been alien to her during a lifetime spent on *The Mayflower*. Often, she would ignore the tasks Ms. Dido had set, focussing instead on the feel of earth and crunching leaves beneath her feet, as the sound of birdsong floated overhead.

Sometimes, Lois would imagine that she was walking through a forest on Earth, fancying herself as the daughter of a baker or a blacksmith; a scenario pulled straight from one of Earth's old fairy tales. In her daydreams, nobody knew her name or stopped to look at her as she passed by. She had a loving and kind father, whose eyes glistened with humour, and a sweet mother with blonde hair and rosy cheeks who always smiled.

As the first-years roamed the biodome that morning, searching for the damp ground and green vegetation that would signal a water source nearby, Lois found she couldn't focus. Even listening to Florence and Penelope as they gossiped and giggled was proving more of a challenge than usual. She hung back a few paces, trailing after them as they weaved around the trees in deep conversation.

Suddenly, she was distracted by the sound of a familiar voice carrying from behind some bushes and shrubbery. Ducking under the cover of a nearby tree, she paused to eavesdrop.

'We won't get in trouble, I'm telling you,' she heard Will insist from out of sight. 'I've studied a route that can get us from our dorms to the Ivory Tower in a matter of five minutes. We're not going to get caught.'

'I don't know,' Emily replied. 'I don't understand why we have to sneak out after curfew. What's in Krecher's office that's so important?'

'I can't explain it. I just need to show you,' Will answered.

'Well, I'm in,' she heard another boy say.

'Finley!' Emily exclaimed. 'You don't even know what you're agreeing to. Will hasn't told us anything.'

'I trust him,' Finley replied.

'Thank you,' Will said triumphantly.

'Fine,' Emily hissed. 'I'll come. But if we get caught- '

'Then I give you express permission to be angry at me for the rest of our natural lives,' Will interrupted her. 'Just meet me outside my room at half-past ten tonight. I promise you, you won't regret it.'

Lois lost her footing and slipped, snapping a twig loudly as her foot skidded across the ground.

The noise seemed to startle Will and his friends, and Lois heard them move off quickly into the clearing. Not wanting to be caught spying, she hastily ran to catch up with Florence and Penelope and joined in with their conversation enthusiastically, pretending she had been investigating a potential river.

Eventually, the girls found a freshwater stream, bending down on its bank to collect a sample in their flasks. Having completed their requirement for the lesson, they followed the trail back to the biodome's entrance, handing their findings into Ms. Dido.

Lois turned her face towards the roof on the way back, letting the UV light warm her skin. Overhearing Will's conversation had made her feel as though she had been let in on a special secret, and her mind was racing with endless possibilities of what she could do with the information she had learned.

The thrill of her secret knowledge carried her happily through the rest of the afternoon and into dinner, where she sat around the table with the Floor One gang, laughing at Spencer's jokes and listening to Alasdair explain his views on the corruption of the Roman Empire, which they had been learning about in Civilisations.

Lois couldn't help but indulge herself with daydreams of dinner the following night, where she would captivate them all with her tale of how she had followed Will and his two friends and uncovered whatever banned activity they were participating in after dark.

She held back from telling any of them her plans, fearing the embarrassment she would face if they came to nothing. Worse still was the possibility of her friends deciding to show up and share in her glory. Lois was determined that she alone would be responsible for the invaluable piece of gossip, which would undoubtedly make her hero among her Floor One peers.

After dinner, she made her way to her room as usual. Arriving inside, she changed out of her school uniform, hanging the navy jumper in her wardrobe and folding the black trousers neatly over the back of her chair.

Once she had changed and prepared her things for the following morning, she curled up on top of her bed and turned on the large television set her father had sent her from home. After browsing for several minutes, she finally settled on the classic films channel, the 3D projection turning into a 2D picture before her eyes.

Watching old films reminded her greatly of her mother, who had spent many Sunday afternoons encouraging Lois to appreciate the century-old art form. She felt pulled under by the familiar stinging sadness she felt whenever her mother entered her mind.

This pain carried her through the evening, and by the time Lois checked her personal device, it was already twenty-five past ten, giving her only five minutes to catch Will and the others unawares. Leaping across the room, she made the distance to her bedroom door in five seconds flat, opening it slowly and peering into the corridor to make sure Ms. Everly was nowhere to be seen.

Seeing the coast was clear, she moved into the hallway, immediately stopped in her tracks by the realisation that something wasn't right. All the lights in the corridor had been switched off, except for one at the end, which had been smashed and was flickering on and off intermittently.

Lois' heart raced as she crept down the hallway, keeping her back close to the wall in case she encountered whoever was responsible for the damaged light. Her hands felt their way across the tile, bumping over the bedroom doors as she passed them.

As she neared the elevator, her hand snagged on something sharp and she drew it back sharply, feeling the hot sting of blood trickle across her palm. She looked around to check where the injury had come from and saw through the flashing light that the door in question had been slashed in three places, causing it to splinter and break.

Fear closed around her throat, and she began to run towards Will's room. She didn't know whether she intended to warn him or to accuse him, but she was certain that being in his company would be better than being alone in this terrifying scenario.

As she got closer, she began to hear voices coming from outside Will's door and, losing her nerve, she dived into the shadows and waited, straining her ears to listen to the conversation.

'Seriously, Will get out here,' she heard Emily hiss, knocking persistently on his door. 'Something weird is going on!'

'I'm just coming!' came Will's muffled reply from inside.

'Do you think this has anything to do with what he wants to show us?' Finley asked Emily.

'I don't know,' Emily answered. 'But I'm starting to get scared. Why are all the lights off?'

'Maybe somebody knows we're out here,' Finley swallowed.

'Don't say that!' Emily scolded him. 'I've got the creeps as it is.'

There was the sound of hinges creaking as Will opened his door and came outside, shining the torch on his personal device at his surroundings.

'Woah,' he said. 'What happened out here?'

'I was about to ask you the same question!' Emily replied. 'Are you trying to play a trick on us or something? Because it's not funny!'

'Calm down, this wasn't me,' Will defended himself.

'Shine your light down there, see if you can see anything,' Emily instructed him.

Lois panicked, realising her hiding place was about to be discovered. Unsure what to do and unwilling to be caught standing silently in the hallway, she stepped forward, revealing herself in the torchlight. Emily, Will and Finley screamed, jumping backwards and grabbing each other in fear.

'Lois?' Will said incredulously when he saw her. 'What are you doing here?'

'I... er...' Lois trailed off, unable to come up with a convincing excuse for being outside Will's bedroom in the middle of the night.

'Were you spying on us?' Emily snapped.

'Well... not exactly,' Lois replied.

''Not exactly?'' Emily repeated. 'What does that mean?'

'I overheard you talking in Resources,' Lois confessed. 'I knew you were planning to sneak out tonight, and I wanted to find out what was going on.'

'So, you *were* spying on us,' Emily concluded.

'Why did you turn all the lights off? Were you trying to scare us?' Will frowned.

'No, that wasn't me. I came out of my room and it was

pitch dark. I thought you might know what was going on,' Lois replied.

'Lois…' said Will, his body suddenly tense and stiffer than a statue. 'Who else knew that you were coming?'

'No one,' Lois replied with confusion. 'I didn't tell anybody.'

'Then,' Will swallowed, raising a shaking hand to point to the corridor behind her, 'who's that?'

Lois whipped her head around in the direction he was pointing it, her blood freezing in her body as she saw what was behind her.

Standing in the hallway, just a few feet away from them, was the silhouette of a man, so unnaturally tall that the top of his head was brushing the ceiling.

'Who's there?' Emily called towards the figure. He did not reply, continuing to stand motionless.

Lois started to back away, able to see, as her eyes adjusted to the darkness, that the silhouette didn't belong to a man at all. The head was far too big and misshapen to be human, the creature's body elongated and spindly.

'I hate to say this,' Finley said as Lois reached the group, 'but I don't think that's a person.'

A hideous noise emitted from the creature's mouth, which sounded like a scream mixed with a roar, and the four of them covered their ears from the deafening noise. As Will moved his arm, the torch from his personal device illuminated the monster before them, allowing them to see clearly its grotesque and terrifying appearance.

The creature's skin was white and sallow, hanging loosely from its bones as though its skeleton was too small for its body. Its head was bulbous, the top half twice the width of the bottom, giving it the look of having been mutilated at birth. Its fingers had been replaced by claws, steely, sharp and menacing, their length ensuring they could kill someone with a single blow.

The most horrifying thing of all, however, was the creature's face. Its mouth was a dark void, six pointed teeth protruding from its depths, with spittle dripping uncontrollably from each one. Its nose was an ugly slit in the centre of its head, and its eyes were gaping black holes.

In all her life, Lois had never seen an alien like it. The thing resembled evil itself. As she stared in its direction, she found she could not move, her breath taken from her body by the sight of the creature alone. As she remained frozen, time seemed to stand still around her, as though it too was immobilised by fear of this unnatural being.

Feeling utterly powerless, Lois awaited her demise, certain the creature would come for her at any moment. It was only when Will tugged on her arm and shouted in her ear that the numbness in her body subsided, causing her to jolt back into life.

'Run!' he yelled.

The four of them tore into his room as fast as their legs would carry them, crashing into safety as Finley slammed the door shut behind them and threw his weight against it, desperate to keep the creature from entering behind them.

'Will, help me move the bed!' Emily shouted, and the two of them lifted the bedframe, heaving it in front of the door to act as a barricade.

Once they had blocked the door, they stepped back, gasping as they tried to catch their breath.

'What *was* that thing?' Emily cried.

'I don't know. I've never seen anything like it,' Lois said with horror.

'What if it's still out there?' Will whispered, his voice shaking.

The four of them stood in silence, listening for any sounds outside the doorway.

'I can't hear anything,' Finley breathed, too afraid to speak in case it should hear them.

'Did anyone see it move? Did it chase us?' Lois asked.

'I'm not sure,' Finley swallowed.

'We can't just stand here!' Emily hissed. 'We need to check if it's gone.'

'Who's going to do it?' Lois gulped.

They looked at one another, each hoping that somebody else would volunteer.

'I'll do it,' Finley declared.

'No,' Will shook his head. 'You don't know why it's out there. What if someone sent it to find you?'

'Why would anyone do that?' Lois exclaimed, disgusted at the thought.

'Don't you remember our first Rocket Control lesson? Not everyone is happy about Finley being at the Space Academy,' Will reminded her bluntly.

'What about your Floor One friends?' Emily scowled at her. 'I know exactly what they think about Finley being here.'

'They may not like him being here, but do you really think they would send an alien monster to murder him?' Lois protested. 'They're not evil.'

'How do we know you weren't involved in this?' Emily demanded, her fear turning to suspicion. 'It's a bit strange that you just happened to be outside Will's room at the exact same time that that *thing* showed up.'

'It is a bit of a co-incidence, Lois,' Will frowned.

'I had nothing to do with it' Lois objected, her voice rising in panic. 'Can't you see I'm just as scared as you are?'

'Alright, everyone calm down,' Finley interjected, raising his hands to quiet them. 'Let's be reasonable. I don't think a thirteen-year-old student would be capable of doing something so horrible. If Lois says she had nothing to do with it, then we should believe her. The longer we spend arguing, the longer that thing has to decide what it's going to do next.'

'You're right, Fin,' Will nodded. 'I'm going to see if it's still out there.'

'Be careful,' Emily fretted, watching with wide eyes as Will slid the bed away from the door, pausing for a moment before opening it a crack.

Lois held her breath as he looked down the corridor, withdrawing and shutting the door after a few seconds.

'It's not there,' he announced with relief.

'So, what do we do now?' Emily asked them.

'Let's just try and figure this out,' Will said, clapping his hands together and pacing the width of his bedroom. 'Supposing it wasn't deliberate, is there any way that creature could have come here by accident?'

'What do you mean?' Emily asked him.

'Well, Krecher takes his aliens out in the grounds around this time of night. Maybe one of them escaped?' Will suggested.

'No,' Finley shook his head. 'It doesn't make sense. Krecher told us all his aliens are completely under his control, and that they act like pets. I wouldn't consider whatever that was to be a 'pet'. There's no way he could control that.'

'My brother Charlie did tell me that other aliens sometimes visit the school,' Emily suggested. 'Apparently, only the older years get to learn about them because the younger pupils get frightened. Do you think it could be one of them?'

'I think the best thing to do is go to Krecher tomorrow and ask him directly,' Will concluded.

'Won't we get in trouble?' Finley frowned. 'We were out after curfew. I fought so hard to get into this school. I don't want to risk losing my place.'

'I trust Krecher,' Will assured him. 'Besides, we have to tell someone. If that things on the loose, who knows what it'll do.'

The four of them shuddered at the thought.'

'Should we go now?' Emily asked.

'Do you really think it's wise to go back out there?' Will replied. 'If its's out in the grounds, hopefully one of the teachers will see it. This whole thing could be sorted by morning.'

'Can we all stay in here tonight?' Lois pleaded. 'I can't go back to my room on my own. It's too scary.'

'Of course,' Finley replied before anyone could argue. 'We're all in this together now.'

He looked pointedly at Emily, who crossed her arms and frowned.

Lois sank down onto Will's bed, attempting to calm her heart rate as the realisation of what they had seen began to set in. Finley sat beside her, sharing in her trauma as they sat in silence, each one trying to process the terrible sight they had just witnessed...

'Thank you,' Lois said, once she had found her ability to speak.

'For what?' Finley asked her, startled by her sudden speech.
'For sticking up for me..'

'That's alright' Finley shrugged. 'I know none of this has anything to do with you.'

'How?' Lois asked him, hanging her head with shame. 'You don't even know me. My friends are so cruel to you, I wouldn't blame you if you thought I was involved.'

'You're not like your friends,' Finley replied. 'I know we don't know each other, but I can tell you're different. You can do better than them. They don't know the real meaning of friendship.'

He smiled at her shyly and she grinned back, the two of them smiling giddily at each other until they are interrupted by Will, their moment ended as he handed them each a cup of tea. When their eyes reddened with tiredness, they put their cups down, yawning and stretching as they looked about Will's room for a place to lay their heads.

'I suppose we should try and sleep now,' Will confirmed. 'You three could take the settees, they're quite comfortable.'

Lois, Emily and Finley trudged over to the sofas, taking one each to settle on for the night.

As Lois lay in the dark, her eyelids began to grow heavy, the adrenaline that had coursed through her body at the sight of the creature diminishing, allowing her eyes and fall into a dreamless sleep.

What felt like a few seconds later, she awoke to the sound of Will's alarm ringing out across the room. She rolled over and sat up groggily, trying to focus on her surroundings through the pain that panged inside her head.

'What time do you call this?' Emily grumbled, shoving the

pillow over her ears to block out the noise of the alarm clock.

'Sorry,' Will croaked from his bed. 'I thought we should get up early so you could all get back to your rooms. Ms. Everly will be doing her rounds soon.'

'Shall we go and find Krecher?' Finley asked as he got up, his hair sticking on end from a night of tossing and turning.

Before any of them could respond, their personal devices bleeped loudly, signalling they had all received a message.

'Admiral Allance will be holding an emergency assembly before breakfast,' Will read aloud. 'All students must get dressed and report to the Gathering Hall immediately.'

They stared at each other, their faces reflecting the terror they all felt.

'Do you think this has to do with last night?' Finley gulped.

'I don't know,' Will grimaced. 'We'd better get dressed and go down.'

Lois raced to her room and pulled her uniform on, dressing in record time before hurrying into the lift to meet the others in the foyer.

Side by side, the four of them walked to the main school building, traipsing into the Gathering Hall, taking a seat in the front row. They waited impatiently as the rest of the students filed in, rubbing their eyes and complaining about the early hour as they found their seats.

Lois' heart sank when she saw Florence, Penelope, Alasdair and the rest of the Floor One clique striding in, staring at her with astonishment as they saw where she was sitting.

'Lois?' Florence said as she approached her. 'What in the Universe are you doing? Come and sit with us. We're going to the back row.'

'No, that's okay,' Lois replied, her face flushing beetroot.

'What's going on?' Alasdair asked, coming to stand beside Florence.

'Lois seems to have lost her mind,' Florence reported, staring at her friend as though she had turned purple from the space sickness.

'Don't tell me she's actually sitting there by choice?' Alasdair said incredulously.

'Actually, I am,' Lois told him calmly, hoping he couldn't hear her pounding heart.

'But, *why?*' he demanded, looking from Will to Finley with disgust.

'I don't have to explain myself,' Lois said firmly. 'I want to sit here.'

For the first time since she had known them, Florence and Alasdair were speechless. Their mouths opened and closed silently with indignation, until Alasdair recovered himself and found his voice again.

'I don't know what's happened to you two' Alasdair sniffed, pointing to Lois and Will. 'But mixing with such… commonness…' He paused, attempting to articulate his indignation. 'Well, it's simply beneath you.'

'Oh, give it a rest, Alasdair,' Will sighed. 'There's no law that says you can't be friends with someone from a different floor.'

'Maybe there should be,' he sneered.

'That's enough,' Lois said pointedly. 'My father is the Captain, and if you don't leave us alone, I'll be telling him about this. He has the power to demote your families to one of these so-called 'common' floors, you know. Perhaps then you'd have a little bit more understanding.'

Their faces draining of colour, the two of them sauntered away, turning their noses up in the air for good measure as they went.

'That was awesome!' Finley laughed, as Will burst into a fit of giggles.

'Seems like you might have lost your friends though,' Emily frowned.

'They weren't my friends,' Lois replied, looking directly at Finley. 'Not really.'

Their conversation was interrupted by a loud crash, as the rear door in the hall bounced open and Admiral Allance strode in, taking his place on the stage with a series of heavy footsteps. He turned to address his audience with a sombre expression, his thick, silvery eyebrows knitted together with anger. His mouth was set into a deeper frown than usual, and his body was stiff, giving him an even more intimidating stance than normal. Nobody in the hall dared to breathe as they awaited his speech.

'It has come to my attention,' he boomed, 'that there was a serious case of vandalism in the first-year dormitory last night.'

Lois, Finley, Will and Emily gaped at each other in shock.

'This morning, it was reported to me by Ms. Everly that there had been significant damage to one of the doors, as well as one of the light fixtures on the top floor. The power in the building had also been tampered with overnight. This is entirely unacceptable.'

He paused to stare with fury at the faces of his pupils, his eyes seeming to accuse each one of them individually.

'All students know they must not leave their bedrooms after curfew, which is ten o'clock sharp. The fact there are no surveillance cameras in your dormitories is a privilege, giving you the privacy and respect we at the school thought you deserved. This trust and act of goodwill has been betrayed, and in hindsight, the school board will now be reviewing whether it would be beneficial to install cameras in the hallways.

'I am sorely disappointed that any student here at the Space Academy would be capable of disregarding our rules in such a manner. As a result, any student found to have been out of bed last night after curfew will be expelled immediately without trial.'

Lois shifted uncomfortably in her seat, her heart racing at a million beats per minute. She tried her best to act normal, frightened that the look of guilt on her face would somehow betray her.

'I would also urge my staff to report any information that they have to me immediately. Needless to say, it would be more than their job's worth to conceal any knowledge of students wandering the grounds after curfew from me.'

Admiral Allance finished his speech and stormed from the stage, his fury lingering in the Gathering Hall for several minutes following his departure. After a while, the students stood up and began, the chatter among them building from a whisper to a roar of speculation, as they discussed the events of the previous night among themselves.

Using the cover of the crowd, Lois, Will, Finley and Emily got up and exited the hall, speaking just loud enough for each other to hear.

'I suppose going to Krecher is no longer an option?' Finley asked Will, once they had reached the safety of the Reception Hall.

'We can't go to him now,' Will sighed. 'I don't want to be

responsible for him getting fired.'

'What are we going to do, then?' Emily fretted. 'That thing could still be out there.'

'If they're adding more cameras across the grounds, they might catch it themselves,' Finley suggested hopefully. 'We might not have to say anything.'

'If Allance finds out we were out of bed, we're done for,' Emily whispered, glancing around to make sure no one could overhear.

'I've got an idea,' Lois announced, struck by a sudden moment of inspiration.

'What is it?' Will urged her.

'Well, it's the Hallowed Eve holidays soon, isn't it?' she asked.

'Yeah…' Will replied uncertainly.

'My dad has a database in his office. It has a list of every single alien ever discovered by humans. If you all come over to my apartment, we can use it to find out what that thing is, and whether or not it's dangerous. Once we know what we're dealing with, we can decide what to do,' Lois suggested.

'It does make sense,' Finley nodded.

'I don't see what other option we have,' Lois replied. 'As scary as that creature was, I don't want to be expelled.'

'Me neither,' Emily agreed. 'My dad would kill me.'

'Okay, it's settled then. We'll all meet at Lois' on the day after Hallowed Eve. The Captain should be back at work by then, right?' Will concluded.

'He has to resume his duty immediately,' Lois nodded.

'So it's agreed, then. In the meantime, we all need to watch our backs,' Will warned them.

'And definitely stay in our bedrooms after curfew,'

Emily concurred.

'What if we see that thing again?' Finley asked, his eyes wide with concern. 'What do we do then?'

'The only thing we can do,' Will shrugged. 'We run.'

THE DREADED CONVERSATION

It was the first day of the school holidays and Elsie was on the platform, unable to contain her excitement as she leant from side to side, desperate to catch a glimpse of her son.

It had been several minutes since the shuttle had docked, clanking loudly as it landed in the loading deck, but to Elsie it felt like hours. She could hardly wait to see Will, who was sure to have grown several inches since he left for school, and she had spent the past few days making special preparations for his return. The fridge had been stocked with his favourite food, his bed had been stripped and freshly made, and she had insisted that a reluctant Derek clean the entire apartment from top to bottom to ensure everything was perfect when he finally came home.

After what felt like an eternity, Elsie caught sight of Will, disembarking from the shuttle with a pretty-looking brunette girl and a slightly dishevelled, mousy boy. They stood in a huddle a few centimetres from the door, talking intensely among themselves.

A moment later, they were joined by Alfie's daughter Lois, who exchanged a few words with them before nodding her goodbyes. Elsie watched as Will patted the scruffy boy on the shoulder and gave the brown-haired girl an awkward hug, waving sadly to them as he strolled away, his eyes now searching the platform for his mother.

She waved and rushed forward to make her presence known to him, and they embraced in a warm hug, Elsie relishing the feeling of having her child in her arms once again.

'Hi, Mum,' he said once they had pulled away from each other, grinning nonchalantly as if they had only been apart for a few days.

'Hello, darling,' she replied. 'Derek's bringing your luggage.'

They walked side by side, manoeuvring their way through the crowds on the platform until they had safely made their way out of the loading deck, Derek trailing moodily behind them as he dragged Will's suitcase behind him.

'I've cleared my schedule for the day,' Elsie told Will with enthusiasm. 'I thought we could go into the lobby and get some lunch. You can tell me all about your first term.'

'Will your clients be alright without you?' Will frowned. 'I thought you said Hallowed Eve was a hard time for them.'

'It can be,' Elsie replied. 'A lot of the people I counsel have had a hard time adjusting after Earth, so naturally the celebration of the Split brings out some difficult emotions. It's been even harder since the Captain imposed the new law that says Forgottens can no longer be mentioned by name. His intention was to stop people dwelling on the past, but it seems to have had the opposite effect. Still, I'm sure they'll be fine for one day. You're more important!'

Will smiled but said no more on the subject. They walked in silence, travelling down the hallways of *The Mayflower* until they eventually reached the lift, squeezing themselves in among the other passengers.

After zooming across the spacecraft to various locations, they reached the lobby and disembarked, Elsie desperately trying to regain the feeling in her legs.

The lobby had been decorated for Hallowed Eve, with replicas of multicoloured planets and glittering paper rockets hanging from every available hook and high place. Luminous stars were stuck in shop windows, glowing invitingly from behind the glass as they walked by. Strings of fairy lights were draped over every available doorway, as cheerful music about Earth's passing blared from the speakers above their heads. In the centre of the lobby floor was a gigantic model of a planet, its multi-coloured surface sparkling as it reflected the light from the ceiling.

Elsie tried to ignore the décor, disturbed by the abundance of drawings of the dead Earth, traditionally handmade by the children of *The Mayflower*. They depicted the planet devastated by fire, with plumes of paper smoke stuck to poorly cut-out circles, clumsily coloured in with shades of green and blue.

Without having to communicate, Elsie and Will made a simultaneous beeline for *'Joe's'*, the coffee shop they habitually visited every time they came into the lobby. Will found them a table by the window and sat down, while Elsie went over to the drinks machine and got them each a hot chocolate with extra cream.

A familiar twinge of guilt knotted in her stomach as she paid for the drinks with a touch of her finger, electronically transferring a small amount of her unlimited credits to the business owner's account. She tried to protest to Alfie for giving her access to such wealth, but he had refused to listen, insisting that she and Will should have everything they need.

Elsie returned to the table and sat opposite Will, handing him his drink and watching as he took his first sips, the cream leaving a small moustache above his upper lip. She smiled as he hastily wiped it away on the back of his sleeve, able to see him once again as his younger self.

'Would you like a slice of carrot cake?' she asked him, bringing up the interactive menu on the tabletop. 'It was always your favourite.'

'I'm okay thanks, Mum,' he replied.

'So, tell me everything, then,' Elsie beamed. 'I want to hear every detail about what you've been up to at school.'

She proceeded to listen intently as Will launched into an enthusiastic explanation of his first term, describing the school grounds, his dormitory and his lessons in vivid detail. When she probed him about his teachers, he paused, his face clouding over as though he were suddenly remembering something unpleasant.

'I have Mr Krecher for Alien Studies,' Will said darkly. 'He's my favourite teacher. Was he yours, too? When he taught you at college?'

For a second. Elsie was rendered speechless, the shock of being confronted by a past she had long buried blocking her ability to speak. Quickly, she regained control, fixing her face into what she hoped was a placid smile.

'Yes,' she said, calmly. 'He was my favourite. I didn't realise he was teaching at the Space Academy now. I had heard he was on *The Mayflower*, but we never crossed paths.'

Will nodded. Elsie could tell from his expression that he knew something was being kept from him, but he didn't press her any further. Feeling relieved, she seized the opportunity to change the subject.

'What about your friends?' she asked. 'I saw you getting off the train with a boy and a girl.'

'Yeah, that's Finley and Emily,' he smiled. 'Finley's the one I rescued at the start of term.'

'You were very brave to go after him,' Elsie praised him. 'But also very foolish. That entire situation could have ended terribly....' She trailed off, unable to bear the thought.

'If I hadn't gone after him, he'd probably be dead," Will shrugged. 'Anyone would have done the same,'

'What about Spencer and the others?' Elsie pressed him, taking a sip of her drink. 'How are they doing?'

'I don't really speak to them anymore,' Will mumbled. 'We kind of... drifted apart.'

Elsie was sure Will expected her to admonish him for no longer talking to his former friends, but she didn't. In fact, she was secretly pleased he had distanced himself from them. She had always known he was different to his Floor One peers and was immeasurably proud of the fact.

'And Lois?' Elsie continued. 'I saw you with her on the platform, too.'

'I suppose we're friends now,' Will confirmed, surprised by his own revelation.

Satisfied with the information she had garnered from him; Elsie asked no more questions of her son. The two of them finished their drinks and left Joe's, wandering about the shops as they once had when he was a boy, desperate to get his hands on the latest rocket gadget or toy.

They left the lobby an hour later with several new purchases under their belt, taking the lift to Floor One and arriving home just as Derek was laying the table for dinner. She had insisted on preparing the meal herself that evening, and had made Will's favourite macaroni and cheese, instructing Derek to put it in the oven just in time for their return.

The two of them sat down to eat, Elsie sipping on her wine as she filled her stomach with the sumptuous meal. Will seemed to become more relaxed with each passing second, his stories growing more animated and vibrant. Elsie laughed heartily as he shared tales of 'Beaky', the pet alien he had been assigned to look after in Krecher's class and smiled warmly as he boasted about being the first person in Resources class to successfully set a fire.

Elsie leant her head on her hand and listened as he described Finley's kindness and Emily's fiery temper and quick wit. She knew by the fondness in his voice when he spoke that he was experiencing the same captivation she had felt at college, the thrill of finally discovering people he truly connected with bringing him a joy he had never yet experienced.

After dinner, Will retreated to his room, talking to his friends on his personal device as he went. Unsure what to do with herself, Elsie went to her bedroom to change into the pair of silk pyjamas she had bought that afternoon, and was somewhat surprised to find Derek had already laid them out on the bed for her, as though he had read her mind.

In such moments, she felt a confusing sensation of gratitude, mixed with the uncomfortable sense of guilt over having her own attendant. She was aware that Will resented Derek's presence in their home, seeing him as more of an intrusion rather than a help, and she was empathetic to her son's feelings. Elsie had never admitted it to Will, but there had been several occasions on which she had considered dismissing Derek, but she found she was never able to find the heart to do it.

Derek had been her assistant since her very first day on *The Mayflower*, when she had been a struggling single mother, weighed down by the unimaginable grief of losing everyone she loved. In those days, she had been completely useless at everything other than caring for Will, and Derek had made sure that she could focus on being a good mother to him without starving herself or the destroying the apartment in the process. Over the years, his presence had become somewhat of a comfort to her, and she could not imagine living on *The Mayflower* without him. Aside from Alfie, there weren't many people around her that Elsie felt she could trust, but Derek was one of them. His unwavering loyalty to her service never went unnoticed, and Elsie decided she should be more grateful for his help, dispelling her negative thoughts from her mind.

Once she had changed into her nightclothes, Elsie went into the living room, sinking into the plush, white sofa and putting her feet on the coffee table as she switched on the television.

She was halfway through the traditional broadcast programme about the The Split, when her personal device started beeping, informing her she had an incoming call.

She accepted, and Alfie's face appeared, projected in perfect definition into the air in front of her.

'Hi, Els',' he greeted her. 'Sorry to bother you in the evening, I would have dropped by in person, but I'm still stuck at work,' he frowned, moving his head slightly to show *The Mayflower's* control room in the background. 'I just wanted to check you're still coming to the Celebration Hall tomorrow. You've never missed my traditional Hallowed Eve party. I would hate for you start now.'

'Of course,' Elsie smiled. 'As soon as Will and I have had our breakfast, we'll come down. It'll be nice for Will to see Lois. They've recently become friends, you know.'

'Have they?' Alfie asked with surprise.

'So I hear,' Elsie responded.

'I haven't had a chance to see Lois yet,' Alfie frowned. 'I sent my mother to pick her up. I hope she didn't mind.'

'I'm sure she didn't,' Elsie reassured him. 'I'd better go and tell Will to get his best clothes ready for tomorrow. Try not to work too hard.'

'I'll do my best,' Alfie grinned, 'Bye Els".

He ended the call, his face vanishing as quickly as it had appeared. Elsie swung her legs off the sofa and padded bare-foot down the corridor, reaching Will's room and knocking on the door.

'Come in,' he said quietly.

Elsie walked in to find Will sitting on his bed, his personal device discarded by his side.

'Sorry to disturb you, sweetheart," she smiled. 'Alfie just called me about his Hallowed Eve party tomorrow. He's worried we're going to miss it. Do you know where your smart trousers and jacket are?' I'll lay them out for you so you don't have to look for them in the morning.'

'They're hanging up in the wardrobe,' Will replied, his eyes cast downward as he refused to meet his mother's gaze.

'Is everything alright?' Elsie questioned him, disturbed by her son's uncharacteristic behaviour.

'Not really,' Will sighed.

'Well, what's the matter?' Elsie pressed him. 'You know you

can tell me anything.'

'I saw him, mum,' Will replied, his face as serious as she had ever seen it.

'Saw who?' she asked him with confusion.

'My dad.'

The word pierced the air like a wailing siren.

'What do you mean; you saw him?' Elsie asked, sitting down slowly on the chair beside his desk, her heart beginning to race with the unease of where this conversation was leading.

'In Mr Krecher's office,' he explained. 'There was a photo of you all when you were students.'

'I see,' Elsie said, unsure how to respond. She waited for Will to continue, bracing herself for the questions that she knew were coming.

'Why did you never tell me what really happened Mum?' he demanded, his eyes bearing into her. 'With dad's death. You never explained the whole story.'

'Your father died in an accident. I've told you that many times,' Elsie defended herself, hoping her change of tone would be enough to deter Will's probing.

'There's more to it than that,' he shook his head. 'I know there is. I'm not a child anymore. I want the truth.'

There was a hardness to his expression that Elsie had never seen before. Realising she could not ply him with vague answers any longer, she took a deep breath, accepting that it was now time to engage in the conversation she had dreaded for the past thirteen years.

'After college, your father and I moved back to where he grew up,' she said, her voice heavy with the weight of the story she was about to share. 'We had a small house in a countryside village. His parents were wealthy and so we managed to stay safe from the violence that was going on in most of the country. We lived in our own world, his parents providing us security and food whenever we needed it. It almost felt like how it was before all the wars started,' she said wistfully.

'One day, I came home from getting supplies to find your father in the strangest mood. He had received a message from an anonymous sender, asking him to go back to Snowdonia to meet with them. Apparently, they had 'invaluable information' that he would find 'extremely useful'.

'You see, while we were in college, your father and I joined a group called 'The Society of the Enlightened,'. Alfie was part of it too, and the three of us became obsessed by its message. The Society believed in what was referred to as the 'Great Conspiracy'; the idea that Split was evil and *The Mayflower* was unsafe. It's all seems very silly now, but we were young. Towards the end of our final year, we all agreed to leave the Society and let go of our beliefs. It had started to destroy us, you see. It was toxic. The only way to survive was to get a ticket onto *The Mayflower*. We knew we had to stop preaching hate against it, or we would never be accepted. Your father was reluctant to relinquish his faith in the Great Conspiracy. It had become an integral part of who he was I think, but Alfie and I managed to persuade him it was all nonsense, or so we believed, anyway.

'The anonymous message your father received all those years later, re-awoke his obsession with the conspiracy. He decided immediately he was going to meet the stranger who had contacted him. I begged him to stay. I was pregnant with you by then, and the thought of him leaving me alone terrified me. He wouldn't listen, though. He was adamant he had to go. He went and gathered enough food and supplies for three days and told me to lock all the doors. He promised he'd be back by the end of the week…and then he left.'

Elsie paused, gathering herself before she continued.

'A week passed, and I still hadn't heard from him. I began to worry that he was dead. Locked up in that house, with no way of knowing where he was or what he was doing was driving me mad. I thought I was going to lose my mind. I paced up and down all day, unable to eat, drink or sleep. I checked my personal device every minute to see if he'd messaged me. Just when I was about to give up all hope, he got in touch with me, begging for me to come and find him. He said he had found out the truth and discovered a way to save us. I got in the car and drove to him as soon as I could. I knew what had happened. I hadn't heard him talk like that since we were part of the Society. It took me nearly ten hours to make the journey. I had to take the scenic route to avoid passing through any major cities or populated area where the gangs and looters had control. When I finally arrived in Snowdonia, your father told me he was on our favourite beach.'

Will bowed his head, seeming to sense what was coming.

'I went down and found him. He was… different. The way he spoke…it was like it wasn't him. There he was, the man I had loved for all those years, but he might as well have been a stranger. He told me he had stolen a ship and wanted us to go into space in it. I couldn't reason with him. I tried. I really did, but no matter what I said, he wouldn't listen. When I wouldn't agree to his plan, he gave me an ultimatum; either go with him or stay on Earth and die.'

She swallowed hard to suppress the lump in her throat.

'I said 'no', and he got in the spaceship anyway and flew away. He had no experience in piloting a craft like that. Something went wrong and it exploded. He was killed instantly.'

She looked away, blinking furiously to stop the burning tears that were welling in her eyes. Will was silent, his hard expression and defiant manner abated by the sincerity of Elsie's story.

'Why did you never just tell me the truth, Mum?' he asked, his round, innocent eyes staring sorrowfully into her own. Elsie reached out and ruffled his hair, overwhelmed by the love she felt for her child.

'I was trying to protect you,' she said honestly. 'I never wanted you to feel the hurt and betrayal that I did. I thought it would be easier for you to have a dead father than one who abandoned you by choice.'

'I suppose that makes sense,' Will said reflectively, after a moment's pause. 'But I didn't know him, Mum. He's a stranger to me. It was you who was really hurt by it. It was you he let down. I could have handled the truth. It would have been better than wondering all my life whether it was my faut that he died.'

'Is that what you thought?' Elsie whispered, a tear rolling down her cheek as she choked on her own words.

'I started to, after the hundredth time you refused to tell me what happened to him,' Will confessed.

'I'm so sorry,' Elsie shook her head. 'I made the wrong choice. I thought I was doing what was best for you.'

'I know,' Will shrugged. 'You always do what you think is best for everyone. But maybe sometimes you should do what you think is best for yourself. You're a human being, Mum. You're allowed to have feelings.'

'When did you get so wise?' Elsie laughed, her heart bursting with pride at the boy she had raised to be so kind.

'I always was,' Will grinned, 'I just hide it well.'

Elsie grinned and stood up, intending to give Will space as he processed all the information she had given him. As she turned to leave, he spoke again, stopping her before she reached his bedroom door.

'There is one thing I don't understand,' Will said.

'What's that, darling?'

'Dad's parents- my grandparents- you said they were wealthy. Why are they not on *The Mayflower*? I thought you said it was possible to buy your way on board,' he frowned.

'That's a question I'm afraid I can't answer,' Elsie sighed. 'After your father died, I lost contact with them. They needed someone to blame, and I suppose was an easy target. They were convinced I could have done more to stop him. It was easier to hate me than to accept what their son had done in his last moments. When I came aboard *The Mayflower*, I looked for them, but they weren't here. I expect they perished on Earth with the rest of the Forgottens.'

Will looked crestfallen, his hopes of having some piece of his father on *The Mayflower* ripped away from him. He attempted to hide his pain from his mother, but she knew it was there, her heart filling with sympathy for the hurt he must be feeling.

'You have me,' Elsie comforted him. 'And that will never change.'

'Promise we'll always stick together?' Will asked her, his face brightening with the feel of his mother's love.

'Always,' she smiled back.

Drained from their conversation, Elsie took the opportunity

to leave, retreating to the solitude of her bedroom, where she could allow her mind to follow the direction it was clamouring to take.

She lay down on top of her covers and watched the ceiling vacantly. Thinking of Austin was never easy, and recounting the events of the worst day of her life had taken its toll. She longed for her thoughts to take her to one of her happy places, which were often filled with fond memories of her parents from her childhood, but her mind would not co-operate, intent that she must dwell on the parts of her past she spent most of her days trying desperately not to think about.

She attempted to fight against it, but she was tired, her heart insistent that she must face up to her agony in light of re-awakening it for her son. She closed her eyes as she was pulled vividly back in time, the scenes she had forcibly erased from her brain returning to haunt her once again.

THE NATURE OF MEMORY

It was September 21st, 2095, and Elsie was sitting in the backseat of Aunt Veronica's self-driving car. Veronica was sitting beside her, legs crossed, scrolling through a fashion download on her I-Reader. Elsie was chewing gum, deliberately making her Aunt jump each time she popped a bubble between her teeth.

'Do you have to do that?' her aunt snapped after the fifth or sixth time, hunching her bony white shoulders with irritation.

'I'm bored,' Elsie complained. 'I wish you had let me drive.'

'Oh, honestly, Elsie. Nobody drives their own cars anymore. Not unless they're poor,' Aunt Veronica retorted.

'Well, then, what was the point of you coming with me?' Elsie argued. 'The car could have driven me here itself.'

'Nonsense,' Aunt Veronica sniffed. 'I made a promise to my brother that I would take care of you, and I have no intention of breaking my word now. Unfortunately for you, that involves me seeing you safely to college.'

'Don't pretend you're doing it for Dad,' Elsie said, rolling her eyes. 'You want to see me go so you can make sure I'm not coming back.'

'Don't be so dramatic,' Aunt Veronica scolded her. 'I know losing your parents has left you with a chip on your shoulder, but you'd do well to remember who has provided for you for the past four years. Some gratitude wouldn't go amiss.'

'Thank you,' Elsie smiled, speaking with as much sarcasm as she could muster. 'You've always made sure I know just how much of a burden I am.'

'You could cheer up a bit,' Aunt Veronica sighed. 'You're lucky to be going to college. Educational institutes are the last safe places in this country. If you study hard enough, you might have a chance of being accepted for *The Mayflower*.'

'You mean *you* might have a chance,' Elsie corrected her. 'I know accepted applicants can bring their immediate family on board. That's what this is really about, isn't it? Getting me skilled enough to get onto *The Mayflower* so you can escape Earth, too. You'd probably stop recognising me the second you stepped through the door.'

'Just try not to mess this up, Elsie,' Veronica said with exasperation, returning to pour over her article. Elsie peered over her shoulder and read the title; 'Which fur coat will make you look the wealthiest?'. She shook her head and looked away, wondering, not for the first time, how she could possibly be related to this woman.

The rest of their journey passed in silence, aside from Aunt Veronica's habitual tutting each time she read something she disapproved of. If there was anything Aunt Veronica loved to do, it was disapproving. Elsie's father used to joke that if Aunt Veronica didn't disapprove of you, you were doing something wrong. She smiled as she remembered the way he used to pull faces behind her back, imitating her snotty-nosed mannerisms as Elsie tried hard not to laugh. She felt the familiar ache in her chest as she thought about her father, wishing it could have been her parents dropping her off at college instead.

When they finally pulled up outside the old, decrepit building that was to be her accommodation for the next year, Elsie was relieved. The sight of the worn bricks and dusty windows was synonymous with her freedom, and she found herself falling in love with the dormitory, which had existed for at least fifty years.

Aunt Veronica sniffed when she saw the building, her mouth an upside-down semi-circle of disgust. Elsie smiled as she looked on; the crumbling block before her among one of the most beautiful things she had ever seen.

'Isn't someone going to come and take your bags?' Aunt Veronica complained, seconds after they had climbed out of the car.

'It doesn't look like it,' Elsie replied, gesturing to the small cluster of other new arrivals, whose families were carrying their bags in by hand.

'Ridiculous,' Aunt Veronica muttered, opening the boot with a snap of her fingers and revealing Elsie's suitcases within.

Between the two of them, they heaved the cases out of the car, dragging them through the open door and across the foyer, where they clambered into the rusty lift. Once inside, they set the luggage down with a heavy thud, catching their breath as they ascended to the top floor, where Elsie's room was located. They trundled along the corridor, cases in tow, until they found the right room, pushing on the unlocked door to enter.

The space was simple and plain, stripped of all decoration and technology to make it as impersonal as it could possibly be. The furniture was shabby, consisting only of the necessities, which proved to be an unsteady looking single bed, a dented wooden wardrobe and an old grey desk that, covered in the graffiti of previous occupants. The carpet was a discoloured brown, the mirror stained with streaks of black and the small white hand basin had grown rust, the tap continuing to drip steadily, despite being switched off.

'It's awful,' Aunt Veronica breathed in horror.

Elsie gazed around, imagining all the different ways she could make the room her own.

'I love it,' she grinned. Aunt Veronica stared at her as if she was a madwoman, but chose not to comment, the imminence of their separation suppressing her argumentative streak. They both knew, without having to say it, that this parting of ways would be a permanent one, and neither party were sure how to address the situation.

'Well…' Aunt Veronica said, after a long and uncomfortable silence, 'I suppose I should leave you to unpack.'

'Yes,' Elsie replied.

Aunt Veronica cleared her throat.

'Good luck, then,' she nodded, turning to leave.

Just before she reached the door, she stopped, wrestling with herself as she struggled to force out the words she felt obligated to say.

'They… would be proud,' she said slowly. 'Your parents.'

'Thanks,' Elsie said, trying not to smirk at the obvious distress her aunt felt at having to be nice to her.

Veronica flashed a thin smile and left the room. Elsie imagined her punching the air and doing cartwheels in the corridor, unable to contain herself with the joy of knowing her duty to her dead brother was finally over. Now she was free to return to whatever dreary, lonely life she had had before becoming Elsie's guardian.

The feeling of relief was mutual, and Elsie felt weightless as she began to unpack her things, placing her collection of framed photographs carefully on her desk and trying not to think about how many of the people in them were now dead.

She gave the photographic version of her parents an affectionate smile. She knew that Aunt Veronica had only been saying what she felt was necessary, but Elsie was sure her parents would be extremely proud if they had been able to see her start college.

Overcome by a powerful wave of emotion, Elsie made a promise to herself that this would be a fresh start for her; the chance to finally step away from the crippling pain of her childhood and find out for the first time who she truly was. Everyone her age wanted to go to college and live as they would have lived, had there been no wars and no tragedies, and for that reason, she was intent on making the most of the opportunity.

Snapping into action, she busied herself by emptying her suitcases onto the floor, surrounding her with the treasured possessions she had brought with her from her aunt's house. It had been challenging, packing up the belongings that reminded her of the happy years she had had before her parent's death, but she couldn't bear the thought of leaving the mementos with Aunt Veronica. She gathered the things together, stashing her collection of scribbled pictures in her desk, and tossing Ellie the Elephant, who was beginning to look rather worse for wear, onto her bed.

At the bottom of the pile, was her most cherished possession of all; a scribbled note from her mum left out on the side, informing her she had popped out to get supplies. In the bottom corner, she had scrawled the words 'love you' in blue biro, completely unaware of how important this hastily scribbled sentiment would become to her daughter. Elsie hugged the note to her chest; the closest she could come to feeling her mother's love. After a moment, she put it down, slotting it under her pillow in case she should need to see it again.

She resumed her unpacking, until a loud knocking noise disturbed her, causing her to leap up from among a pile of clothes, kicking socks and shoes across the room as she went to answer.

She opened the door to see two young men, not much older than herself, standing in the corridor, a cluster of leaflets clutched in both their hands.

'Welcome, fresher!' exclaimed the one on the right, flicking his long fringe out of his face as he spoke. 'My name is Dylan.'

'And I'm Toby,' his shorter-haired companion beamed.

'I'm Elsie,' she replied with amusement, feeling as though she was watching a badly rehearsed double-act on a children's television show.

'We're your student mentors,' Dylan explained. 'Which basically means we're here to tell you about all the safest places to go drinking.'

'As well as giving you essential tips for surviving your first year,' Toby added.

'So, what are you studying here, Elsie?' Dylan asked her.

'Psychology,' she answered. They raised their eyebrows.

'Unusual choice these days,' Toby noted.

'I want to be a counsellor,' Elsie explained. 'I want to help the people that have suffered... people who have lost someone they care about.'

'So… everyone then?' Dylan joked. 'At least you'll never be short of clients.'

'What do you two study?' Elsie asked, desperate to change the subject.

'Navigation,' Dylan answered, proudly, puffing out his chest. 'I'm in my second year. I want to work in the control room on *The Mayflower* when it sets off. Maybe even apply for the captaincy.'

'You've got to dream big,' Toby laughed. 'I study Alien Studies. I'm in my third year. If you get a chance, take a module in the subject. You won't regret it.'

'Professor Krecher is his hero,' Dylan rolled his eyes. 'He teaches the course. You'll probably see him around campus. He farms as well as professing. He sometimes gives his students free apples in exchange for a good grade.'

'He's got apples?' Elsie said with disbelief. She couldn't remember the last time she'd seen one.

'Oh yeah,' Toby replied. 'He's not one of your typical farmers either. As Dylan was saying, he gives all his stuff away, no charge. Even to the locals.'

'Sounds like an interesting man,' Elsie mused.

'He is. Anyway, believe it or not, we did come for a reason,' Toby smiled.

'And what reason was that?' Elsie smiled, amused by their goofy enthusiasm.

'To give you these,' Dylan answered, handing her a few leaflets from his large collection. 'You'll find everything you need to know on there. There's a map of the town and the campus, and a few advertisements for places to eat and drink.'

'There's two restaurants in the town!" Toby exclaimed. "I

think most of their produce comes from Krecher, but still. They've got to be among the last ones left in the country. You definitely have to check them out when you get a chance.'

'Thank you, I will,' Elsie said, putting the flyers down on the desk beside her.

'We were going to create downloads for everyone's personal devices, but we thought leaflets would be more impressive. They've still got a computer and printer on the college campus from the old days. The thing is so slow, it's unbelievable. But still, pretty cool, right? Like stepping back into history,' Toby grinned.

'We also came to let you know there's a mixer this evening for the people living in this building,' Dylan interjected. 'There'll be free alcohol, otherwise no one comes. It starts at seven p.m. in the foyer. It's a great opportunity for you to meet the people you'll be living with for the next year.'

'I'll be there,' Elsie promised them.

Satisfied with her answer, Toby and Dylan departed, leaving Elsie alone to finish her unpacking. Once everything was in order, she inspected her handiwork, deciding with satisfaction that her room was beginning to look more like a home, and less like a prison.

As she made plans with herself to visit the market town in the morning, she absentmindedly wandered to the window, admiring her new view of high sycamore trees and far away mountains. She felt as though she had fallen straight into the pages of the book of fairy-tales her mother used to read to her as a girl, lost in an enchanted kingdom where the perils of the outside world could not hurt her.

At that moment, her attention was drawn to the gravel car

park below where armed guards in full defensive uniform had begun their patrol, their huge weapons cradled in their arms as though they were precious children. Elsie raised her eyebrows at the sight, her fairy-tale fantasy coming to abrupt end as she realised the need for protection was still prevalent, the government doing all they can to protect the education system in preparation for the Split.

Seven o'clock rolled around, and before Elsie knew it, it was time to head down to the foyer and meet whichever lucky strangers had also made it to the Utopia that was College Snowdonia. She had dressed well for the event, choosing her best pair of black trousers with a dark blue top and high heels.

She had never had an occasion to dress up properly before, but she was sure that she had read in one of her aunt's fashion downloads that wearing all dark colours gave the most flattering impression. To add colour to the bleakness, she wore a gold chain around her neck, stolen from the depths of Aunt Veronica's closet, and painted bright, red lipstick on her lips. She arranged her hair in an up-do, the way she had seen her mother do as a child, and paused in the mirror to admire her reflection. The young girl she had used to see staring back at her was gone, replaced by a woman she was excited to meet.

Once she was ready, Elsie made her way downstairs, her heels clacking on the stone steps as she descended to the foyer below. She reached her destination, astonished by its transformation as she struggled to comprehend how this could be the same desolate space she had walked through just hours earlier.

The first thing that caught her eye was a huge, holographic banner, projected into the centre of the room, the words 'welcome freshers' displayed across it in giant, multicoloured lettering. Several machines had been carefully attached to the faded, yellow walls beside it, their functions varying from periodically spitting out confetti to blowing a constant stream of bubbles into the room. Between them, were several television screens, each displaying 3-D images of people dancing in time to the beat of loud music, which was blaring out from an enormous sound system, operated by an ecstatic Toby.

The foyer floor was crowded, the people mingling around it seeming to have already formed exclusive friendship groups. Attracting the most attention was a sandy-haired boy, who was standing in the middle of a group of girls, their faces bright with admiration as they hung on his every word.

Feeling intimidated by everybody's pre-existing relationships, Elsie moved discreetly over to the corner of the room, where a drinks table had been set up. It was lined with dozens of plastic cups, filled by a choice of red or a yellow liquid. The cups were handed out and refilled by a sleek white robot, the letters 'CS' and the mountainous logo for College Snowdonia emblazoned across its chest.

Elsie approached the table with confidence. Drinking was something she had some experience in, mostly due to her aunt's enthusiasm for alcohol, which had grown steadily stronger the worse things had become on Earth.

'What may I get you, Miss?' the robot asked her in a polite voice.

'What are these?' Elsie asked, looking dubiously at the plastic cups.

'I only know this one is 'red', and one is 'yellow', Miss,' the robot replied, its voice emitting from a speaker inside its spherical head.

'I'll have a yellow one, then,' Elsie said. The robot picked up a cup in its curved hand and passed it to her effortlessly.

'Thank you,' she smiled.

'You are welcome, Miss,' the robot replied.

'So, are you owned by the College?' Elsie asked him, desperate to speak to someone, even if they were made of metal.

'I was programmed by the Interactive Tech company, commonly referred to as I-Tech' the robot informed her. 'I was purchased by the College in the year 2090. Tonight, I am in the service of Mr Toby Wyatt and Mr Dylan Martinez. Does this answer your question, Miss?'

'Yes, thank you,' Elsie nodded, hastily walking away and she realised it was impossible to make small talk with a robot.

Feeling defeated, she scanned the foyer around her, wondering if it would be better to retreat to the safety of her bedroom, the humiliation of standing alone at the gathering too much to handle.

She was just about to leave, when she saw a tall boy with dark hair shrinking into a wall in the corner. Seeing him as her only opportunity to socialise, Elsie walked over to him, assured by his timid posture that he wouldn't be difficult to approach.

'I'm glad I'm not the only one who feels like hiding in the corner,' Elsie remarked with a smile as she reached him. 'This is all a bit overwhelming, isn't it?'

'It is,' the boy replied shyly. 'Everyone seems to know each other.'

'I noticed that,' Elsie frowned. 'It's like they've all had a secret meeting without us. Maybe we missed the memo.'

It was a phrase she had heard on an American television show, and she wasn't entirely sure what it meant, but, thankfully, this boy seemed to understand, tipping his head back and laughing musically at the comment.

'What are you drinking?' he asked her, pointing to her plastic cup.

'Honestly, I have no idea,' she admitted.

'You chose yellow,' the boy observed, peering over her shoulder. 'I was too frightened by the smell. I've got what I think is supposed to be red wine, but it tastes like vinegar.'

'I don't think much of the budget for this evening was spent on the drinks,' Elsie noted, glancing again at all the garish decoration in the foyer.

'You might be right,' the boy agreed. 'I suppose people don't really have much to celebrate anymore. It looks like whoever organised this might have got a little bit carried away.'

'You can say that again,' Elsie asserted. Realising that she hadn't introduced herself, she extended her hand.

'I'm Elsie by the way, Elsie James.'

'Alfie,' the boy grinned in response, taking her hand and shaking it.

'Just Alfie?' Elsie replied. 'How diva of you.'

'Alfie Sommers,' he corrected himself, his face turning red.

'Nice to meet you, Alfie Sommers,' Elsie smiled.

'You too,' he grinned.

'Look at them," Elsie noted, gesturing at all the happy faces around them. 'You'd never know the world was ending.'

'My mother said it's the way of the British,' Alfie smirked. 'She said this country would fight wars with tea and wine if they could.'

'I suppose that's true,' Elsie laughed. 'I guess it just shows how resilient human beings are. Everything we know may be coming to an end, but if the chance for a bit of normality arises, we take it with both hands, not thinking about what happens when it ends.'

Alfie cocked his head and looked at her curiously, his mouth opening as he formulated his response. At that moment, however, their conversation was interrupted by the sound of approaching engines. They searched for the source of the noise, which proves to be a group of shiny black cars adorned with the university logo. They pulled up noisily in the gravel car park, sending the patrolling guards rushing over to investigate. Once the cars were given the all clear, they returned to their duties, leaving Alfie and Elsie to wonder what the purpose of the vehicles were.

'Are people going out?' Elsie asked Alfie. 'Is it safe?'

'It must be,' Alfie shrugged. 'It is quite remote out here. I suppose all the real danger is in the cities.'

'Who called the cars?' Toby shouted over the music.

'Guilty,' the boy with sandy-blonde hair laughed from among his group of fans, holding his hands up in mock surrender. 'A few of us thought we'd head out and see what the town's like. We've never been out at night before. Can't waste the opportunity, now, can we?'

Toby frowned, but even he could not argue with the boy's obvious charm.

'Just be careful,' he said darkly.

'I always am,' the boy grinned.

The gaggle of girls swanned their way into the cars first, but the boy hung back, looking around to double check he hadn't left anyone behind. It was at this moment that Elsie realised how good looking he was, immediately understanding the girls' embarrassing fascination with him.

There didn't seem to be a single flaw on his perfectly chiselled face. His eyes, noticeably green, even from across the room, shone brilliantly, setting them apart from all his other features. His sand blonde-hair was dishevelled, giving him a careless appearance that only added to his appeal. He was tall and strong, the muscles in his arms visible from underneath the lilac blazer he was wearing, the sleeves slightly rolled up to reveal his biceps. He noticed Elsie looking at him, and grinned impishly, bemused by her attention, though she was sure he knew exactly how charming he was.

Her heart began to race as the boy strolled towards her, his confidence filling every corner of the room. He stopped in front of her, ignoring Alfie's presence and staring at Elsie with an intensity that made her blush.

'Hi,' he said, extending his hand for her to shake. 'I'm Austin.'

Back in the present, Elsie sat bolt upright, cursing herself as a searing pain tugged across her chest. She had foolishly let her mind wander into such painful territory, and now she would certainly pay the price.

It took every ounce of strength she had not to revisit the happy days of her early relationship with Austin. She could not bear to think of the blissful five years she had experienced with him, before he so cruelly destroyed everything she thought she knew.

Deciding she would not sleep otherwise, Elsie retrieved a bottle of sleeping pills from her bedside drawer and took two, allowing them to calm her frantic mind and lull her into drowsiness. As she drifted off to sleep, her mind entering a state of numbness, she could not shake the unsettling feeling that her past was re-awakening, bringing with it a terrible darkness that threatened to swallow her whole.

14

HALLOWED EVE

O n the morning of Hallowed Eve, Emily awoke early. She rushed out of bed and pulled on the purple velvet dress her mother had selected for her to wear the previous evening. She dragged a brush through her thick, dark hair, making sure she removed all the knots and kinks that had formed in it overnight. Once she was satisfied she had made herself presentable, she took a deep breath, steadying the nerves that had been building inside her stomach since she woke up.

'You can do this,' she told her own reflection, hoping it was enough to convince her wobbly legs to strengthen themselves.

Collecting herself, she walked from her bedroom and into the dining room, the smell of pancakes wafting out from the kitchen where Liza, the family assistant, was making their traditional Hallowed Eve breakfast.

Emily's family were already gathered around the long glass table which sat in the centre of the room. Her father was reading news stories from his tablet, grunting with disapproval every so often at the headlines, while her brother, Charlie, tapped furiously on his personal device, sending messages to one of his many friends. Emily's mother was staring at the ceiling, her eyes glazed over and her face pale from the exhaustion of working the night shift on the Medic Ward.

'Good morning,' Emily said when she entered, announcing her presence to the room.

'Morning, sis',' Charlie grinned. 'Happy Hallowed Eve.'

'Morning, sweetheart,' her mother said, flashing her a weak smile. 'Come and sit down.'

Emily did as she was told, sitting in the chair across from her mother and folding her hands in her lap.

'Thank you,' she smiled at Liza, as she placed her plate in front of her, the food steaming hot and fresh from the pan.

'You're welcome, Miss,' Liza replied, continuing to serve the rest of the family. Emily's father sniffed as she put his meal in front of him, refusing to acknowledge her presence as he feigned his engrossment with the news.

'Shouldn't you be at home, Liza?' Charlie asked her., embarrassed by his father's behaviour. 'Nobody's supposed to work on Hallowed Eve.'

'Mr Pannell insisted I work today, sir,' she replied, her voice strained.

'Of course he did,' Charlie grimaced, proceeding to attack his food with his fork.

'Stop talking to the help, Charlie,' Mr Pannell snapped. 'You're distracting her from her job. Go and clear up in the kitchen now, Liza.'

'Yes, Mr Pannell,' Liza nodded, disappearing from sight as quickly as she could muster.

'So, Emily,' her father said, putting his tablet down and crossing his legs as he leant back in his chair. 'I assume you've had a successful first term at the Space Academy?'

'Yes,' she replied bluntly, irritated by the prospect of having to speak with him.

'Your examinations will begin when you return after the holidays,' Mr Pannell continued. 'I hope you plan to spend the rest of your holidays studying.'

'I'm going to my friend Lois' tomorrow to revise with her,' Emily informed him, still desperate to please him despite her resentment. Her father sat up, his ears pricking at the mention of a high-ranking name.

'Lois Sommers?' he pressed her. 'The Captain's daughter?'

'Yes,' Emily nodded, praying the conversation would so be over.

'Excellent,' her father nodded his approval. 'The Captain is a fine man with excellent taste. That much became clear when he recently re-appointed me as Governor of Education for the fifth year running.'

Charlie rolled his eyes in an exaggerated fashion so that only Emily could see. It was the fourth time their father had mentioned his renewal of office since they had returned home for the holidays alone, and they had grown sick of his bragging, the smug expression on his face enough to put them off their breakfast.

'I was wondering,' Mr Pannell continued, clearing his throat, 'has the curriculum at the Academy given you an idea about what you want to do when we reach Novum? Only Space Academy students are given the opportunity to take up important positions, you know.'

'Yes, I know, father. You told me every day when I was studying for the entrance exams,' Emily replied. 'Anyway, I think I'd like to do something in technology. It's always been my favourite subject.'

There was a moment of silence, as Charlie and Emily's

mother froze with surprise. Her father had voiced strong opinions about women working in such areas over the years, and until this point, Emily had never been brave enough to reveal her true ambitions to him.

He chewed over her words for a minute, calculating his response.

'Jarvis Holt, the CEO of I-Tech is an acquaintance of mine,' he boasted. 'He's a fine gentleman. He's gone an excellent head for business. His negotiations made I-Tech the only company on Earth to be granted permission to operate on *The Mayflower*. He's very talented. He only hires the best of the best. If you wanted to work for him, you'd better start studying a lot harder than you do now. I'm not entirely sure you're cut out for it. Perhaps you should consider a gentler profession? Something more suited to the female nature.'

Emily looked down at the white linen napkin she had folded on her lap, concentrating on the pattern of sewing across its hem as she tried to block out the noise of her father.

'Still,' he continued, 'at least you aren't following in your mother's footsteps. To be a nurse in this day and age is absolutely preposterous. The pay is laughable, there's no status in it and with all the medical science and technology we have, there's no need for human involvement in healthcare at all. Who knows? Maybe you'll end up inventing something that will make your mother's 'job' completely obsolete. Wouldn't that be amusing?'

'People need human contact,' Emily's mother said quietly, her voice hardly more than a whisper. 'They wouldn't recover without it.'

'Oh, nonsense!' her father exclaimed, waving his hand in

the air. 'You tell yourself whatever you need to, dear. We both know if it wasn't for me, you'd be down on Floor Seven with the rest of the trash.'

'My friend Finley is from Floor Seven,' Emily said, setting her knife and fork down with a crash, 'and he is probably the nicest person I've ever met- not to mention the most intelligent.'

'What rubbish,' her father replied. 'I still can't believe Allance allowed him into the school. I was one of the Governors that voted against the motion. Such a pity I was overruled. Allance couldn't help but be swayed by the hefty sum of credits he was given by the board for taking a pupil from a disadvantaged background. A waste of a valuable school place if you ask me.'

Emily pushed her plate away, her face flushing red as beet-root as she resisted the urge to take the large jug of water on the table and pour it over her father's head. Her mother noticed her anger, and reached out to squeeze her hand, attempting, as she always did, to distract her from the vileness of her father.

'Aren't you going to eat your breakfast?' she asks gently, attempting to smile through the obvious discomfort painted on her face.

'I've lost my appetite,' Emily said, keeping her head bent low to avoid eye contact.

'Don't be so dramatic, Emily,' her father scolded her. 'I was only pointing out the truth. That friend of yours might be able to live out his little fantasy with the better half now, but as soon as his education is over, it'll be off to the Bureau of Labour where he belongs. By the time we reach Novum, he'll be a faceless man in a crowd of builders, with no higher status than the dogs I used to own back on Earth.'

Emily stood up, knocking into the table with the force of

the action, the glasses clattering as they wobbled dangerously near the edge.

'Sit down, Emily,' her father ordered, spit flying from his mouth as he turned puce with rage.

'No,' Emily replied with defiance, turning to leave the table.

'Sit down, girl' he repeated with force. 'Or I promise your life won't be worth living.'

'I said 'no'!' she yelled; her voice louder than she had ever heard it. Her father recoiled in shock and she seized upon the moment, exiting the room as fast as her legs would carry her.

'Go on, Emily!' Charlie cheered after her,

She reached her bedroom and pulled out her suitcase, packing it with bundles of tangled clothes as she tried to see through the tears that were filling her eyes. She was just about to leave when her mother walked in, stopping her in her tracks.

'Emily, sweetheart, you don't have to go,' she pleaded, her eyes full of sadness.

'How can you let him speak to you like that, Mum?' Emily exclaimed. 'The things he says are awful. I don't understand why you just sit there and do nothing!'

'Your father is very a complicated man,' her mother replied tiredly, repeating the same line she had used throughout Emily's childhood.

'Complicated?!' Emily repeated with disgust. 'He's not complicated, he's an awful human being. Why did you marry him? I can't stand it! I wish he wasn't my father.'

Her mother hung her head in shame and sat down slowly on the bed, sighing deeply as she spoke in a cracked and broken voice.

'The Pannell family were very wealthy,' she admitted,

stunning Emily with her sudden honesty. 'When the Wars broke out on Earth, money was the only way to gain protection. I was young and I was scared. I met your father when I was treating your grandfather for war wounds he later died of. He left everything to his only son. Your father took a shine to me, and I took the opportunity to provide my family with safety.'

'Money,' Emily repeated, unable to believe what she was hearing. 'You married him for money?'

'You don't know what it was like on Earth,' her mother told her, her voice filled with more emotion than Emily had heard in years. 'In the last days it was truly terrible. There were gangs and looters everywhere, and hardly any food. The air was filled with toxic smog. There were freak heatwaves every other day, and floods and fires on the rest. We woke up each morning not knowing if that day was going to be our last. There was danger everywhere. The only instinct I had was to survive, and I was willing to pay any price for it.

When the Split was announced, I had already had your brother, and I was pregnant with you. Thanks to your father, we made it onto *The Mayflower*. If it wasn't for him, we'd all be dead. I made the sacrifices I had to make, and any mother would have done the same.'

'Well you're here now,' Emily pointed out. 'We're on *The Mayflower*. Why don't you just leave him? I'd rather live on Floor Seven in poverty than live on Floor Two in misery.'

'You don't know what you're talking about,' her mother sighed. 'You're too young to understand.'

Emily shook her head pitilessly and turned to leave, hauling her heavy bag onto her shoulder and making for the door.

'I had a brother, you know,' her mother said suddenly,

halting Emily mid-step. 'You're uncle. I never told you. He's a Forgotten. We're not supposed to talk about them anymore but, his name was Bernard. When your father got us a place on *The Mayflower*, there wasn't enough space for him. I had to make a choice. Let my children perish on Earth or leave my brother behind instead. Our parents were gone, and I was all he had. Can you imagine having to make a decision like that?'

Her eyes filled with tears, and for the first time Emily saw how tortured her mother truly was. Though she could not begin to imagine the torment she had endured, she still could not understand how someone could give up everything they knew was right in exchange for a materialistic and comfortable life.

'You left him?' Emily asked her mother, unable to believe what she was hearing. 'You left your own brother to die?'

'I had to,' her mother insisted. 'I chose to protect my children. I still think about him every single day. It destroyed me to leave him there, but I want you to know that things aren't as simple as you think they are. At your age, everything seems so black and white. The choice between good and bad, brave and evil. In real life, things are more complex. People do bad things for good reasons sometimes. Try to understand, Emily. If I left your father now, then everything I did to secure us a decent life here would be for nothing. I'd never be able to forgive myself.'

'You shouldn't be able to forgive yourself' Emily retorted. 'All along I thought Dad was the evil one, but you're both as bad as each other! Wealth and status are more important to you than your own family.'

She picked her bag up and hauled it over her shoulder, making for the door again in spite of her mother's protests.

'Emily, it's Hallowed Eve. Where could you possibly be going?'

'Anywhere is better than here,' Emily muttered, storming out of the room and moving with determination towards the front door. She opened it with force and slammed it behind her, the frame reverberating loudly in her wake.

Without looking back, she made her way to the nearest lift, descending into the empty lobby which had been abandoned in favour of private family celebrations. There was something extremely unsettling about being in a deserted place that was usually full of life, and Emily moved quickly, her footsteps echoing across the marble floor.

She glanced into shop windows as she passed them, taking in the sight of the frightening mannequins that modelled the latest fashions and gadgets. Without the hustle and bustle to distract her from the sight, she was able to fully appreciate the sheer size of the lobby floor, its epic proportions making her feel incredibly small in comparison, her feet echoing eerily as she passed under the gigantic screen hanging in the centre.

Veering to the left, she moved away from the central shopping area and headed towards the entertainment section, passing by doors that led to the Multiplex Cinema, the Holographic Room and the Water Park, until she reached the large entranceway that led to the Celebration Hall.

From inside, she could hear soft music playing, the tinkling of the piano mixing with the sound of glasses clinking together as people toasted one another and chattered in pleasant tones. Immediately, she knew she had successfully found the Captain's Hallowed Eve party, where she would be able to find Will and Lois. The only obstacle standing in her way was a surly looking guard, who stood in a military stance, scoping the area for any signs of danger. When he saw Emily, he fixated on her, trying to distinguish her identity from under his black visor. Realising she had the opportunity to gain entry to the party without confrontation, Emily seized her chance.

Trying her best not to look intimidated, she walked over, doing her utmost to convey the impression that she belonged here. She stuck her nose in the air and swanned forward, shooting the guard the same disapproving glower she had seen her father give Liza many times in the past.

The snivelling attitude seemed to work, and the guard allowed her to pass into the hall without questioning her. Unable to believe her luck, she integrated herself into the party, grateful for the first time that her father had insisted she wear formal attire at home, allowing her to easily blend in with the other black-tie wearing guests.

She searched for Will and Lois, peering over the heads of the many adults that were mingling around the hall, each one speaking with perfect inflection and laughing loudly to show off their pearly, white teeth. She recognised several faces, including Pax Madden, the stoutly, bald man in charge of security on *The Mayflower*, and Wendy Weaver, the smiling blonde who read the daily news bulletins on the big screen in the lobby. She couldn't help but feel smug at the thought of her father's seething jealousy when he found out she had attended such an exclusive event. She could only imagine what he would have given for the chance to schmooze with the elite class, and suspected he was deeply enraged to not have received an invite, despite the renewal of his position as Governor of Education.

Spotting Will and Lois hovering by a buffet table at the

back of the hall, Emily weaved her way towards them, careful not to hit any of the prestigious guests with her overnight bag. They had their backs to her, and were turning to face out of the conspicuously large gold-framed windows that lined the rear wall of the hall.

She cleared her throat to alert them to her presence and they both jumped, spinning round to see who had interrupted their conversation.

'Emily!' Will exclaimed. 'What are you doing here?'

'Sorry to gate crash,' Emily blushed. 'I had to get away from home.'

She gave Will a meaningful look, and he nodded with understanding.

'What's in your bag?' he asked her, eyeing the bulging holdall with curiosity.

'My things. I was hoping I could stay with you until we go back to school,' Emily answered, a look of pleading in her eyes.

'Oh...' Will stuttered, running his hand through the back of his sandy hair. 'You know I'd love to Em', but I don't think my mum would let a girl stay over.'

He turned crimson, suddenly appearing much younger than his fourteen years.

'You can stay with me,' Lois offered. 'We've got plenty of room.'

'Thank you,' Emily replied.

'I'll get someone to take your bag,' Lois smiled.

She shook her shiny blonde hair away from her shoulders, its strands reflected the light from the silver chandeliers above their heads, and raised her hand into the air, clicking to get the attention of one of the many staff that were serving at the party.

In seconds, a male attendant was upon them, balancing a tray of champagne glasses on his palm and nodding subserviently as Lois gave him instructions.

With her bag safely out of the way, Emily felt less likely to attract attention as an intruder. Beginning to relax, she scanned the crowd before her with interest, observing the peculiarly rehearsed manner with which the upper class seemed to interact with each other.

Her eyes were suddenly drawn to the face of Admiral Allance, his silvery hair and eyebrows unmistakeable in the crowd. Wearing the same navy-blue pressed suit he favoured at the Space Academy, he engaged in deep conversation with a dark-haired man in his mid-forties. Between the two of them was a small robot, whizzing in circles as its head spun wildly, its body bouncing from the legs of one man to the other.

After further scrutiny, Emily noticed the words 'I-Tech' inscribed on the robot's chest. With a surge of giddiness, she realised the dark-haired man was none other than Jarvis Holt, the CEO of I-Tech and her hero since she was a little girl.

She nudged Will and pointed, unable to believe she was in proximity to such an exceptional human being.

'That's Jarvis Holt!' she exclaimed. 'He's talking to Admiral Allance!'

'I know,' Will replied. 'He's here every year. He's very nice, actually. I could introduce you if you like?'

Emily was tongue-tied, the thought of conversing with her hero too much for her to comprehend. She stammered and spluttered, attempting to make some sort of refusal under the conviction that she would certainly embarrass herself beyond repair, but Will had already made his way over to Jarvis, interrupting his conversation with the affronted Allance.

After a moment, Will beckoned Emily and Lois over to join them. Lois strode towards them with confidence, leaving Emily to drag herself on heavy legs, feeling as though she were wading through cement as she advanced towards the group.

'Mr Holt, this is Emily,' Will said, introducing her upon her arrival.

'Nice to meet you, Emily,' Jarvis grinned, extending his hand, which she accepted into her own shaky one. 'Are you a student at the Space Academy?'

'Yes, I am,' Emily replied, cursing herself for not being more eloquent or interesting.

'That's right,' Admiral Allance interjected. 'Emily is among our most gifted and talented pupils at the school.'

Emily smiled at him gratefully, though she was certain he had no idea who she was.

'Excellent,' Jarvis nodded. 'I have just been discussing your fantastic curriculum with Admiral Allance. He has asked me to send him a sample of the projects I-Tech are currently working on so he can showcase them to you in your Technology lessons.'

'Emily's amazing at Technology,' Will boasted. 'She's easily the best in our class. There's nothing technical she doesn't understand.'

'Is that so?' Jarvis said, raising his eyebrows.

'It's my favourite subject,' Emily replied with mortification. 'I hope to work in the field when I'm older.'

'That is encouraging to hear. We're always looking for sharp, young minds to join our company. Perhaps we could arrange some work experience for you over your school holidays? If that's something you'd be interested in?' Jarvis offered.

Emily's ability to speak was momentarily lost as she struggled to stay upright, blown over by the proposition to fulfil her lifelong dream.

'I think Emily would be very interested, Mr Holt,' Will smirked.

'Great!' Jarvis replied. 'I'll send the arrangements to your mother, Will. She can forward them to you so you can pass them on to Emily.'

'Thanks, Mr Holt,' Will smiled.

'Well,' Admiral Allance announced, 'now that's all been settled, why don't you children run along so Mr Holt and I can get back to talking business.'

Emily, Will and Lois excused themselves, retreating to the safety of the buffet table, which had been replenished with several new plates of food in their brief absence. Will helped himself to a selection of snacks, grumbling about missing the school robots as he piled up his plate by hand.

'I can't believe that just happened!' Emily gushed. 'Am I really going to be working at I-Tech Headquarters?'

'Seems that way,' Will replied, grinning through a mouthful of cheese cracker.

'I can't wait! Thank you so much, Will,' Emily grinned, hugging him tightly.

'Don't mention it,' he blushed.

'I'm happy for you, Emily,' Lois said with sincerity. 'It'll be a great opportunity. My dad says there won't be a single piece of technology I-Tech won't provide by the time we get to Novum.'

'When you work for them, you should tell them to make more serving robots,' Will instructed her. 'If they make them stupid enough, I'm sure they won't rebel this time.'

'Thanks for your suggestion, Will,' Emily laughed.

'No problem' he shrugged. 'See if they can make robot butlers, too. I'd love for my mum to finally get rid of Derek.'

'I don't think I-Tech is interested in making robot servants at the moment,' Lois informed them. 'I overheard my dad talking to the head of security last night. Apparently, the company is in the process of developing experimental weaponry in case we meet hostile forces on the way to Novum.'

'Little do they know the hostile forces might already be here,' Emily frowned, images of the creature from the hallway floating uninvited into her mind.

'We don't know that yet,' Will reminded her. 'Let's wait and see what we find out on the Captain's database.'

'About that,' Lois sighed. 'We're going to have to wait even longer for our answers. My dad has decided to take an extra day off work so we can have some 'quality family time'. We're going to have to put it off until the day after tomorrow.'

'That's alright,' Will re-assured her. 'At least we get another day of normality before we have to deal with finding out what that thing was.'

'We don't know anything for sure yet,' Lois reminded them.

'I know,' Emily said darkly. 'But I don't have a good feeling about any of this, do you?'

The three of them stared at each other in silence, unsettled by the terrifying instinct that what they were about to face was far more dangerous than any of them could anticipate. Not wishing to vocalise their fears out loud in case it made them real, they kept silent, avoiding each other's eye while they attempted to supress their individual panic. Unable to contain herself any longer, Emily broke their impromptu pact, clearing her throat and asking with a quiver in her voice;

'Please tell me you two are as petrified as I am?'

'Yes,' Lois said immediately. 'I've had nightmares every time I've fallen asleep. I want to know the truth but I'm afraid of what we're going to find.'

'Me too,' Will confessed. 'But there's one important thing we have to remember.'

'What is it?' Emily asked with impatience, desperate to be comforted in any way possible.

'We have each other. The only thing worse than facing this would be to face it alone,' Will said, placing a comforting arm around Emily and Lois' shoulder.

'You're right,' Lois nodded. 'We stick together now.'

'No matter what,' Emily added.

'No matter what,' the other two agreed.

15

THE ROCKET RACE

The day after Hallowed Eve came around faster than anticipated, and Finley was hardly able to contain his excitement. As he packed for his stay at Will's apartment, he checked his bag for the second time that morning, making sure he had packed everything he needed for his holiday on Floor One. Once he was certain he had remembered everything, he swung the heavy bag onto his arm and left the bedroom he shared with his brother, Justin. He entered the living room, where his family were gathered around their electric fire.

'Have you got everything you need, love?' his mum asked, the moment he walked into the room.

'Yes, Mum,' he smiled.

'Now remember, I'll be on Floor One cleaning at the Bartholomew's apartment if you need me,' she told him, her eyes wide with motherly concern.

'I know, Mum. You've told me three times already. I'll be fine,' he assured her.

'Be careful, won't you, love?' his mum fretted, touching his cheek.

'Yes. Mum,' he laughed. 'I promise I'll come back in one piece. Stop worrying! It's not good for you.'

His mum nodded and attempted to smile, but Finley could

216

see the unease that lingered in her eyes. He was about to comfort her further, when Justin snorted loudly from one of the armchairs, interrupting their conversation.

'Who would ever have thought it, eh?' he scoffed, addressing their sister Jess, who was sitting in the corner sewing. 'Our little brother Finley off to Floor One. First the Space Academy and now this. He'll be one of *them* before we know it.'

'Stop it, Justin,' their mother scolded him. 'You and Jess have been nothing but unkind to your brother since he came home from school. You should be happy for him. It's good for Finley to make new friends.'

'Oh, we are happy for him, Mum,' Jess sneered. 'We're so happy that he's off galivanting at a floating school in the middle of space while we're stuck here going to the schools for poor people, slaving away to learn things we have no interest in. Finley will probably end up as our servant master when we reach Novum'

'That's enough, Jess,' warned their mother.

'It is unfair, though' Justin argued. 'He gets to learn about Combat and Weaponry with the most up to date technology, *and* his teacher is a member of the McGowan family. They were heroes in the Wars on Earth. No one knows more about combat than them. We don't have anything like that at the Bureau, and we're supposed to be learning how to protect people.'

'Finley didn't design the system,' their mother sighed. 'You should be pleased someone in the family has the opportunity to make something of themselves. Your father and I are very proud of Finley.'

'I think it's amazing,' Felicity, Finley's younger sister, piped up from the floor, where she was sitting crossed legged, engrossed in her battered I-Reader. 'I'd give anything to go to the Space Academy. You're so lucky, Finley. The Captain's daughter goes there too, did you know that?'

'She's in my class,' Finley replied, and Felicity's mouth fell open.

'Have you spoken to her? What's she like? She always looks so glamorous and she's *so* pretty. I want to be just like her when I'm older,' Felicity gushed.

'She's lovely,' Finley replied. 'And even more pretty in person.'

'Oh, here we go,' Justin laughed. 'Don't tell me you're in love with the Captain's daughter, Fin'

'Now there's a 'Romeo and Juliet' story for the modern era,' Jess smirked.

'I don't know her that well,' Finley defended himself. 'I was just saying ...She's nice.'

Justin and Jess exchanged a look but said no more, the burning eyes of their mother forcing them into silence.

'You'd better go and catch the lift, Finley,' his mother said to him. 'You don't want to keep your friend waiting.'

She gave him a hug and said goodbye, Felicity wrapping herself around him the moment his mum had pulled away.

'Have fun!' she squealed.

'Yeah have fun, Fin,' Justin said. 'Hopefully none of them will try and launch you into space this time.'

'Just ignore him, love,' his mum said, walking him out the door and giving him one final kiss before returning to their small apartment.

Finally alone, Finley made his way along the corridor, nodding 'hello' to his neighbours as he crossed their paths. After walking a few yards, he reached the steel lift and went inside, the doors snapping shut to seal him inside the metal box. He pressed the button for the lobby and the machine creaked into life, ascending slowly towards their destination.

After a minute or so, the lift docked, grinding to a halt and sliding open to reveal the back end of the lobby. Finley made his way past the line of recycling bins that greeted him upon his entrance and headed through the small maze of cheap convenience stores, reaching the main floor in all its shiny, marble glory.

He knew the lifts from the higher floors arrived near the entrance to the lobby, and so he picked his way through the crowds of upper-floor shoppers until he found the right area, careful to keep his head down in case someone should notice that he didn't belong.

He had only been waiting a few seconds, when the glass elevator slid into position, releasing its cluster of passengers. Among them was an excited looking Will, who bounded over to Finley with great enthusiasm, a large grin plastered across his face.

'Finley! You made it!' he greeted him.

'I did,' Finley replied eagerly. 'What's the plan, then? Are we going straight up to your apartment?'

'Well...' Will began with a glint in his eye. 'It turns out the Captain isn't going back to work until tomorrow, so we've had to put our investigation on hold.'

'Which means?' Finley probed him.

'Which means we've got a whole day to ourselves,' Will explained, puffing his chest out with delight. 'And I thought maybe we could have some fun.'

He pulled a pair of golden tickets from his pocket, each

emblazoned with a red rocket in the top right-hand corner.

'Are those...?' Finley trailed off in disbelief.

'Rocket racing tickets!' Will confirmed. 'I know you've never been to a race before, and I thought you might like to go.'

'Wow, thanks Will,' Finley beamed with gratitude, taking one of the tickets and placing it in his pocket with care, as though it were a precious jewel.

'No problem,' Will shrugged. 'My mum gets me tickets every year for Hallowed Eve. I used to take Spencer, but I'm sure you'll be much better company. Now, come on! We don't want to miss the train.'

Will led Finley away from the shops towards a gleaming set of gates, manned by a guard in smart, black uniform. He was standing with an intimidating stillness, his expression unsettlingly vacant, and Finley tried his best to avoid eye contact as he passed. His brother, Justin, had often told him tales of how the human services had been taken over by robots on Earth, until they had rebelled and started one of the many wars. As the guard checked their tickets, screwing up his nose as though he could smell something unpleasant, Finley wondered whether a killer robot might have actually been friendlier.

Once they had been approved entry, Finley and Will walked through the gates and onto a small platform where a long, open-topped train was waiting to ferry them to the rocket racing stadium. Will guided them over to the first carriage, sitting down in the front seats with the promise they would have the best view. Finley sat beside him, waiting with apprehension to find out what would happen next only half-listening as Will explained in excessive detail the individual statistics of each rocket racer competing that day.

It wasn't long before the train reached full capacity, the gaggle of excited racing fans on board talking so loudly Finley could not hear the guard's announcement as it played over the sound system.

A moment later, the carriage gave a gentle lurch, sliding forward on magnetic tracks towards a round metal door, which opened smoothly as they approached it.

Passing through the doorway, they entered an elongated tunnel with transparent walls, allowing them to see clearly into space. Finley inhaled with amazement as they glided through the blanket of stars surrounding them. Despite having grown up on *The Mayflower*, the sight of infinite space still never ceased to amaze Finley, the feeling of being a tiny part of a much bigger picture both terrifying and comforting in equal measure.

Craning his neck, Finley discovered he was able to see the rocket racing stadium a few miles ahead of them, sealed inside its protective dome that the tunnel appeared to feed into directly. The sight of it sent butterflies into his stomach, and he could hardly wait to experience his first rocket racing tournament. He pressed his cheek against the window, drinking in every detail of the dome-shaped building and was immensely thankful for whatever alien technology had made its existence possible. Will laughed as Finley's breath fogged up the glass, shaking his head with amusement. Finley didn't care how strange he looked; he was determined to remember everything about the day, knowing it would become a treasured memory for years to come.

When they had reached their journey's halfway point, Finley twisted in his seat, turning around to get a better view of *The*

Mayflower. He had never seen it from the outside before and was struck by the sheer size of the colossal spaceship. The immense grey mass spread across his entire vision as he tried to take it all in, which proved impossible. He focussed instead on the word 'Mayflower', which was adorned gaudily on the ship's side, each individual letter at least two-hundred feet tall.

Finley was completely captivated by the view, and it took him a moment to realise Will had been talking to him for several minutes without his knowledge. Hastily, he turned to sit forwards in his seat, tuning into his friend's conversation and pretending he had been listening the whole time.

'I can't wait to go back, though,' Will mused, as Finley shuffled into his chair.

'Go back where?' Finley asked, unable to hide his confusion.

'To the Space Academy,' Will replied, eyeing his friend with suspicion.

'Oh, yeah. Me too!' Finley agreed. 'I still can't believe I got in. I feel so lucky.'

'It's probably the most fun I've ever had in my life,' Will concurred. 'You know; terrifying alien monsters aside.'

'Yes, that was a slight drawback,' Finley agreed. 'Still, it could have been worse. We nearly had to have one-on-one counselling sessions with Miss Fortem.'

They both shuddered.

'That was a lucky escape,' Will reflected.

'I seem to be good at those,' Finley smiled.

They continued to chatter happily for the remainder of their journey, discussing their predictions for the race with vigour. Minutes later, they arrived at the stadium, exiting the train and riding an escalator up from the busy platform to the expansive seating area above. They found their seats and took them, Will pointing with excitement to the gigantic screen which ran along the opposite stadium walls, a countdown to the race displayed in large yellow numbers.

In the centre of the circular rows of seating was an empty space where Finley assumed the main event would take place. Finley peered over the edge, looking at the stadium floor where fluorescent lights marked the track the racers would follow. With only five minutes to go, Will accessed the interactive refreshments menu imbedded in the armrest of their chairs and ordered them both fizzy drinks and a hot dog, promptly brought over to them by a glum steward, who Finley was sure he recognised from Floor Seven.

He was halfway through eating the best hot dog he'd ever tasted, when a loud announcement echoed over their heads, causing the spectators to leap to their feet and begin cheering raucously.

'Ladies and gentlemen, please stand and show your support as we introduce today's rocket racers!' the detached male voice shouted with animation.

Several hidden doors in the stadium centre slid open, and the rocket racers zoomed out, parading around the arena in their various spacecrafts and waving to their fans from behind their heavy protective gear.

'Let's hear a round of applause for our contenders,' the announcer boomed. 'Amelia Monteiro, Zed Sinn, Symon Schoestein, Layla Atwater and Pablo Pianthus!'

Will clapped his hands together as hard as he could muster and whistled as the racers swept past them, pointing to one of the men in a glossy red rocket with adoration.

'That's Pablo Pianthus!' he yelled, his excitement carrying his voice over the crowd. 'He's the best by miles.'

Finley nodded, feigning his fervent agreement in the hopes Will wouldn't realise he had no idea who any of the contenders were.

Once the procession was over, the rockets and their racers lined up together in mid-air, aligning themselves behind a row of lights shining up from the floor beneath them.

'The rocket racers are now taking their places,' the announcer said, a blanket of anticipation descending across the stadium. He waited until each racer was still, their heads bent forward, their hands gripping their steering wheels.

'On your marks,' the announcer said in a low voice. 'Get set...GO!'

The rockets zoomed into life, their engines thundering as they whizzed in circuits around the arena, their various colours blurring into one another, Finley's hair blowing backwards as the racers rushed past him.

'How many laps are there?' he shouted to Will, his throat hoarse from the volume needed just to be heard.

'Forty!' Will yelled back.

With each passing lap, Finley grew more exhilarated, and by the time the race had reached its halfway point, he had found himself whooping and hollering along with the other spectators.

As the event came to an end, he kept his eyes glued to the big screen, desperate to catch a glimpse of the winning racer. He watched, enthralled, as Pablo Pianthus crossed the finish line, the stadium erupting into a gargantuan cheer as he was awarded first place.

'That was amazing!' Finley shouted; his cheeks flushed

with delight.

'I knew Pablo would win!' Will rejoiced, continuing to clap his hands with fury. Appearing out of nowhere, a cylindrical podium rose from the ground and into the air, allowing the top three contenders to disembark from their rockets and claim their prizes.

When Pablo Pianthus' name was announced, he removed his helmet, revealing a thick mane of chestnut brown hair that swung around his shoulders. He was much older than Finley had expected, and much more good looking. His tanned skin and carved features made him the ideal poster boy for the rocket racing sport, and Finley immediately understood his celebrity appeal.

'Thank you!' Pablo called to his fans in a thick accent. 'Thank you so much! I love you all!'

He took a deep bow and blew kisses to the crowd, who screamed and reciprocated in delight. Will was a picture of animation beside Finley, waving his hands in the air and cheering until Pablo clambered back inside his rocket, flying through stadium and into outer space beyond.

The race now over, the two boys left the stadium among the throng of excited spectators, chattering with elation to each other about the event. Their conversation continued as they boarded the train, hardly noticing as it sprung into life and began their return journey to *The Mayflower*.

'Did you see when Pianthus overtook Amelia Monteiro?' Will asked Finley, without giving him a chance to reply. 'Or when he made that impossibly tight corner! I thought for definite he was going to lose control.'

'What about when he looped underneath Zed in the final

lap?' Finley replied. 'That was incredible!'

'There's no one else like Pianthus,' Will continued, their conversation still flowing as they disembarked from the train and returned to *The Mayflower's* lobby. 'He's a genius. You can count how many times he's ever lost a race on one hand.'

They walked back to the lifts and went inside, Will pressing buttons on a screen built into the glass before standing back and clasping tightly to one of the rails.

'You might want to brace yourself,' he warned Finley.

'For what?'

Before Will could answer, the lift gave a stomach-wrenching lurch, and they began hurtling towards the ceiling at an impossible speed. Finley was barely able to keep his balance as they shot all the way to Floor One, arriving at their destination in less than a minute.

'What just happened?' he asked, his head spinning with bewilderment.

'We're here,' Will announced.

His dizziness subsiding, Finley followed Will across an impressive atrium, glancing up at an ostentatiously large chandelier hanging from the ceiling.

As they reach Will's apartment, they passed by a set of double doors marked with the number '1'. Finley's heart jumped with the realisation this apartment must belong to Lois and her father. He never dreamed he'd be so close to the Captain's apartment, nor did he expect to feel such a rush of adrenaline at the thought of being close to Lois.

Will pressed his finger to a touch sensor next to the doors marked '3', a clicking sound informing him he has approval to enter. He grabbed onto the crystal doorknobs and twisted them, opening the doors in one synchronised motion, revealing his apartment beyond.

Finley was stunned by the sight of the lavish space as they entered it, the living room at least four times the size of Finley's. The furniture was colour co-ordinated and perfectly positioned, with not a single thing out of place. There was no clutter, no piles of washing on the sofa and no shoes strewn about the floor. The kitchen surfaces were gleaming, and the dining table had been vigorously polished. Finley had never seen a place so clean in all his life, and his mother cleaned for a living. He placed his hands in his pockets, afraid that his touch alone would dirty the spotless surroundings.

On the opposite side of the room, a tall, dark-haired man was dusting a large window, the curtains drawn back to allow the apartment to be flooded with soft UV light. His white cotton shirt and plain black trousers informed Finley that he was a servant of some sort, and his heart sank as he imagined his mother in similar attire, scrubbing the floor at the Bartholemew's apartment nearby.

Before he could dwell on the depressing thought, one of the doors leading from the living room opened, and Will's mother rushed in, attaching a bracelet to her wrist with her teeth as she balanced her personal device against her ear.

'Hold on, Jarvis, I'll have to call you back,' she said, hanging up and placing the device onto her wrist strap.

'Hello' she smiled. 'You must be Finley. I'm Elsie, I'm Will's mother.'

She stepped forward, offering her hand as she smiled in Finley's direction.

Finley took her hand and shook it, the smell of sweet

perfume wafting from her wrist as she moved. As he took in the sight of this glamorous young woman, Finley was certain she was the most peculiar mother he had ever seen. She looked like the women who modelled clothes on the screens in the lobby, and made his own mother appear painfully ancient and dowdy in comparison.

'Hi, Mum,' Will said, saving Finley from his temporary inability to speak. 'I didn't expect you to be at home.'

'I'm just rushing out, darling, I've got to get back to work,' she replied, grabbing her handbag from the kitchen counter.

'How was the race?' she asked, pausing for a moment before she opened the door.

'It was good,' Will nodded. 'Pablo won again.'

'Glad you had a good time,' she smiled, as she rooted through her bag, 'Derek will look after you tonight. Have fun. Oh, and make yourself at home, Finley. Any friend of Will's is a friend of ours.'

'Indeed,' Derek said sarcastically.

'Thank you, Ms. James,' Finley nodded, suppressing his laughter as Will glowered at Derek from behind his back.

With a quick ruffle of Will's hair, Elsie disappeared through the front door. Finley watched after her as she went, attempting to understand the strange new world he had found himself in.

'Are you hungry?' Will asked, strolling over to the large fridge in the kitchen.

'I suppose so,' Finley replied. He wasn't used to eating between mealtimes, but felt it would be impolite to say 'no'.

'Hello, I-Fridge,' Will said. Finley blinked with confusion, unsure if his friend had lost his mind.

'Hello, Mr James, what can I do for you today?' the

fridge replied.

'Tell me what snacks you have'

'The snacks will now appear on screen' the fridge said.

A screen lit up on the fridge door, displaying a variety of different chocolates, fruits and yoghurts.

'What do you fancy?' Will asked him, swiping through the images to reveal the selection.

'I'll have whatever you're having,' Finley shrugged, most of the foods on screen unrecognisable to him.

'Okay,' Will nodded, continuing to browse through the items.

'That's quite an impressive fridge,' Finley noted. 'I've never seen one like that before.'

'Yeah, one of my mum's clients is Jarvis Holt, the guy who owns I-Tech. She does therapy sessions for him and he gives us all the latest stuff for free,' Will said absent-mindedly.

'Your mother forgot to tell you your favourite fizzy drink is in the cupboard,' Derek interjected. 'She bought it especially for you, so try and at least *seem* grateful. I know that might be difficult.'

'Whatever you say, Derek' Will replied, sticking his tongue out at him when he turned his back.

'I saw that,' Derek scolded him, watching Will's reflection in the window he was dusting.

'Don't mind Derek,' Will said to Finley. 'He's only the family servant. He likes to make a fuss sometimes, but we usually just ignore him.'

'Hi, Derek,' Finley said, unsure how to introduce himself. 'It's good to meet you.'

'A pleasure, I'm sure,' Derek replied, his voice dripping

with contempt.

'You don't have to talk to him,' Will laughed. 'It's not like he actually lives here or anything. He's from one of the...' His voice trailed off as he realised what he was about to say, but it was too late.

'He's from the Lower Floors,' Finley said, his voice heavy with disappointment.

'Sorry, mate,' Will blushed, rubbing the back of his neck. 'I didn't mean it like that.'

'It's okay,' Finley shrugged. 'I'm used to it.'

'Well, you shouldn't be,' Will replied. 'There's no judgement here. I should have thought before I spoke.'

'Wouldn't that be a first!' Derek exclaimed from the corner, unable to resist the opportunity to make a jibe.

'Oh, shut up Derek!" Will exclaimed, and Finley laughed, the tension in the room easing instantaneously.

The rest of the evening passed pleasantly. Will was amazed to discover Finley had never seen most of the gadgets in the apartment before, and wanted to show off some of his favourites. As a result, they ended up watching a horror film, using the 4-D system hooked up to Will's television.

It was an experience unlike anything Finley had known before, with holographic ghosts popping up around the living room and the sound of wind howling from all directions. There was even a feature that sprayed the two of them in the face with water, creating the sensation of splattering blood during the most gruesome death scenes.

When the film was over, the two boys headed into Will's room to play Earth Wars, battling each other with delight until it was time to sleep. Will drifted off within minutes, but Finley stayed awake, gazing up at the high ceiling and wondering what stroke of fortune had caused him to end up here.

He thought of his family far below him, Jessica and Felicity cramped in their bunk beds, Justin clambering over Finley's single in order to reach his own. Sprawled out on Will's large sofa bed, he imagined what any of them would give to be in his position. He felt a pang of shame, wishing he could share this experience with his siblings. He made a vow to himself, making the silent promise to raise the status of his family, as soon as he had graduated from the Space Academy and had found himself in the position to do so.

His mind growing tired, he rolled over, deciding in his last moments of consciousness that the true wealth of life was not status or material possessions, but the knowledge of what it truly meant to have a friend, for which he would be eternally grateful.

16

THE INVESTIGATION

When morning arrived the next day, Will and Finley awoke early, dressing and eating breakfast as quickly as they could. With a fumbled explanation about needing to do homework, the two boys dashed past Will's mother, running out the front door and into the atrium, arriving at Lois' apartment in ten seconds flat.

Will pounded on the door and waited, the two of them twitching with anticipation as they strained their ears to listen for any sound of movement within.

The door swung open in a startling manner, and Will and Finley jumped unpleasantly as an old haggard, woman with a broad frame and cold cruel eyes appeared before them.

'You're not Lois,' Finley gawked, the words leaving his mouth before he had a chance to stop them.

'Well observed,' the woman sneered.

'Hello, Ms. Sommers,' Will greeted her. 'Finley, this is Lois' grandmother,' he explained.

'Oh… it's lovely to meet you,' Finley mumbled.

'Lois,' the woman crowed over her shoulder. 'Some rather unfortunate boys are asking for you.'

'Coming, Grandma,' they heard Lois call from somewhere behind her grandmother's wide figure.

232

'Does your father know about this?' her grandmother snapped back, frowning at Will and Finley with as much disapproval as she could muster.

'Yes, he does. They're here to do a homework project for school,' Lois replied from inside.

'Hmph,' her grandmother sniffed, but said no more. With a final look of disgust, she pushed past Will and Finley and hobbled away, her walking stick aiding her towards the set of double doors marked with the number '2'. There was a loud 'bang' as she slammed the door behind her, the sound echoing across the quiet atrium.

'She seems nice,' Finley joked. Will snorted loudly.

With her grandmother safely out of the way, Lois and Emily appeared in the doorway, their significantly smaller figures allowing Finley to see into the apartment beyond.

Finley had expected extravagance, but the scale of grandeur was beyond anything he could have dreamed. Finley's entire home could have fitted inside the living room, which was filled with the most luxurious furnishings he had ever seen. There were soft, cream sofas, large enough to seat at least ten people apiece, each one positioned in perfect alignment to a gleaming cut-glass coffee table. On each of the four corners, sculptures of golden eagles sat, their necks outstretched in a silent cry as they stood guard of the furniture.

Finley cast his eyes to the back wall, where a white quartz fireplace had been installed, a vast, paper-thin television screen fixed in place above it. Upon the mantelpiece were genuine gold candlesticks, their impressive display embellished with an array of beautifully painted vases. Even to Finley's untrained eye, it was obvious that just one of them would cost more credits than

233

his father earnt in a year.

More wondrous than anything else in the room was the grand piano, standing majestically atop a set of carpeted steps. It rested itself proudly on four silver legs, a lion carved into each one of its feet.

'Wow,' Finley breathed.

'I know,' said Emily. 'Wait until you see the bathrooms!'

'Come on then you two, don't just stand there!' Lois laughed, beckoning them into the apartment.

'Sorry, I think Finley's a bit mesmerised,' Will grinned, as they stepped inside.

'It is an amazing apartment, Lois,' Finley nodded.

'Never mind that,' Lois said, clapping her hands together. 'Let's not waste any time. I told my dad that we have to revise for our Alien Studies exam, so he left his office open and said we could use his database. It was quite unlike him, actually. I think he still feels guilty that he had to go back to work straight after Hallowed Eve.'

'That's great,' Finley smiled, 'Maybe if we find out what that *thing* was, we can actually do some revision afterwards.'

'Really, Finley?' Will questioned him, his voice filled with disbelief.

'What?' Finley replied. 'We still need to pass our exams, you know.'

'Our exam results won't matter much if that creature kills us all before the school year is over,' Emily reminded him.

'That could happen whether we find it on the database or not,' Finley countered

'Yes, but at least if we find out some information, we'll know what we're up against,' Will replied.

'I still think we should tell someone,' Finley said, bracing himself for his friend's response.

'Don't be stupid,' Emily chastised him. 'If Allance finds out we were out of bed, we'll all be expelled.'

'And if that thing is one of Krecher's aliens, he'll get the sack,' Will interjected.

'We could tell someone else. Maybe make an anonymous report? There must be something we can do,' Finley said with desperation.

'Let's just stick to the plan, Finley,' Lois said gently. 'I think it's the only option we have.'

'Are you certain it'll be on there?' Finley asked her.

'If it's known to humans, it'll be on that database,' Lois confirmed.

'All we can do is hope it turns out to be harmless,' Finley said. 'Although if its appearance is anything to go by, I'm not going to hold my breath.'

'This way,' Lois informed them, and the three of them followed her out of the room.

She led them from the living room into a short hallway, decorated with several unnerving paintings that featured images of the dying Earth. At the end of the passage, they reached a large crimson door that had been left ajar and walked into the Captain's office. Lois sat down at a grand pewter desk and pressed a concealed button beneath it.

A moment later, a wide computer screen appeared from a hidden compartment in the wall, an accompanying keyboard springing up from nowhere. Lois began typing rapidly, indiscernible images and text flashing up on the screen.

'Here we go,' Lois said. 'I've found the alien files.'

'So, where do we start?' Finley asked.

'There's a video file here, it seems to be the only one,' she observed, pressing the 'enter' key so the clip started playing. Grainy images of Earth appeared on screen, featuring narration from a loud male voice.

'In the year 1985, humans first made contact with aliens,' the voice began. Will rolled his eyes and scoffed.

'Can we skip the history lesson?' he complained. 'We already know all of this.'

'Sorry,' Lois said, shutting down the video. She scrolled through the database, revealing hundreds of individual files on screen.

'How are we going to know if that thing's on there?' Will said with despair. 'There's thousands of files.'

'There should be a way to search by characteristics,' Emily interjected.

'In English?' Will sighed.

'It's a database,' Emily explained. 'There will be a way to search through it, hopefully by typing in what the alien looks like.'

'Go ahead,' said Lois, vacating her seat so that Emily could sit down.

While Emily was absorbed in her typing, Will began to wander absent-mindedly through the room, nosing at the shelves of dusty old books sitting behind the Captain's desk.

'Why does your dad have books, Lois?' Will asked her. 'Shouldn't they be in the museum or something?'

'I don't know,' Lois shrugged. 'He likes to collect things from Earth.'

'Maybe you shouldn't touch them,' Finley frowned, but Will

236

ignored him, picking up books at random and flicking through them to examine their contents.

'Any luck, Emily?' Lois asked her, the impatience in the room growing with each passing minute.

'I don't think so,' she sighed. 'There doesn't appear to be any aliens on here that match the description of what we saw.'

'Are you sure?' Lois pressed her. 'Maybe you missed something.'

'I can't be certain. I'd have to open every single file and read through them to know for sure, but that could take days,' she replied. 'It says here there are 300,000 entries in total.'

Finley's shoulders slumped with defeat. He looked at the others in desperation, hoping that one of them would suggest an alternative idea, but their faces appeared just as blank as his own.

'Guys…' Will said slowly from behind them. 'I think I've found something.'

'What is it?' Emily asked him, jumping up from her chair. Will rushed forward, a cluster of tattered notebook pages clutched in his hands.

'Look at this,' he demanded, and the three of them gathered around him.

'Where did you get those?' Lois asked him.

'They fell out of one of the books,' Will replied.

Finley looked down at the pages and was bewildered to see a drawing of the creature from the hallway, every feature perfectly recaptured in pencil. Its various atrocities had been labelled in an untidy scrawl, with everything from 'claw-like hands' to 'empty eyes' included in the illustration.

Next to the drawing was an almost illegible sentence, which after scrunching his eyes up tightly, Finley read as 'drawn to human emotion'.

'Look there,' Finley said, gesturing to some scribble at the top of the page. 'This person's given the alien a name; 'The Vacuous''

'Whose notes are these?' Lois wondered out loud, her face contorted with confusion.

'Aren't they your dad's?' Emily replied.

'That's not his handwriting,' Lois frowned. 'I don't recognise it.'

'Hang on,' Finley added, pointing to the top of one of the pages. 'What are those numbers?'

'2098,' Emily read. 'That must be the date these notes were taken.'

'Wait a minute,' Will mused, his eyes darting back and forth as he formulated something inside his brain. 'I've seen that date written before- in Krecher's office.'

Finley, Emily and Lois looked at him with bewilderment.

'Krecher was a teacher at the college my mum and dad went to. The Captain went there too. Krecher had a photo hanging in his office with them all in it. It had the date '2098' written underneath,' he explained.

'So… these notes belong to Mr Krecher?' Emily asked.

'I think so,' Will replied. 'He had a journal in his desk with a padlock on it. Some of the pages were missing. I'm betting this is them.'

'What were you doing in Krecher's desk?' Finley asked him. Will ignored the question.

'More to the point, why does my dad have Krecher's notes?' Lois asked. 'Do you think he knows about the Vacuous, too?'

'I think they all knew,' Will nodded. 'Your dad, Krecher and my parents. Maybe they found out about them when they were all at College Snowdonia.'

'So, what you're saying is, these 'Vacuous' creatures were on Earth?' Emily clarified. 'And your parents, the Captain and Krecher all saw them.'

'I think it's possible,' Will nodded.

'But how can we ask them about it without admitting to everything? We can't risk getting blamed for the vandalism in the hallway' Lois fretted. 'We have no way to prove the Vacuous was even there.'

'What about the cameras in the grounds?' Finley suggested. 'I know there isn't' any surveillance in the dormitories, but the Vacuous must have had to walk around campus to get inside the building.'

'There'd be no way to access the footage without clearance from Allance,' Emily frowned. 'If he found out what we needed it for, we'd be goners.'

'Forget Allance' Will replied. 'My mum wouldn't ever let me set foot at the Space Academy again if she knew there were aliens roaming about the dormitories.'

'Mine neither,' Finley realised with deflation.

'We can't tell our teachers and we can't tell our parents,' Emily concluded. 'So, what are we going to do?'

The four of them stood in silence, each attempting to conjure an impossible solution in their minds.

'There is a way we can find out what my parents saw on Earth…' Will said slowly.

'How is that possible?' Lois asked.

'The answers are in the past,' he replied cryptically. 'And I know how to get there…'

RETURN TO THE PAST

The new term at the Space Academy began with a flurry of exams, putting the plans Will had made on hold until the chaos of the first few weeks died down. In truth, the four of them had been so absorbed in their scheming that they had hardly managed to prepare for any of the rigorous tests they were now facing in every subject.

So far, they had endured a practical Combat and Weaponry exam, which involved fighting off a horde of holographic aliens in a simulated war zone, using only the weapons they had studied that term. A written assignment for the subject had demanded they type a gruelling two-thousand-word essay on the War of the Classes, which Will was certain he would have failed had he not paid attention to his mother's stories about Earth.

For their Alien Studies exam, Krecher had brought out an array of species for the class to identify, which, thanks to Finley's insistence they use Alfie's database for revision, hadn't been too difficult. Emily had prepped them all the night before their Technology exam, in which Mr Mayhem asked them to evaluate a piece of existing tech. Finley had chosen the I-Fridge, seemingly having a lot to say about the device. Will, on the other hand, had written about the serving bots in the school cafeteria, hoping to redeem himself for the embarrassing shouting incident that occurred when he had first encountered them.

For Resources, they had spent an entire day with Ms. Dido in the forest, demonstrating their abilities in foraging food, finding water, building shelters and making fire. It had been an exhausting task, and Will had complained loudly about his sore feet as they scavenged their surroundings. In truth, it was a relief for him not to be stuck typing at a desk, where he so often found his mind wondering back into the darkened hallway of the first-year dorms.

The most important exam of all came in the form of Will's Rocket Control test, the successful completion of which would mean receiving his personal licence. Mr Zeppler had taken the class out into space to fly personal rockets around a suspended obstacle course, and Will was relieved to find it exceptionally easy to navigate. He had winced from the side-lines as Finley had lost his nerve, retaking the test twice before he was ushered off the course by Mr. Zeppler.

The last day of the exam period finally arrived, and, soon, a heavy essay on the Ancient Egyptians for Civilisations was the only thing standing in the way of freedom. Will, Emily, Lois and Finley completed the task in under forty-eight hours, imprisoning themselves in the library and typing furiously on their various devices until their work was done.

With the rest of the school still pre-occupied with exams, Will called an informal meeting in his room, conducting a speech from the pillow end of his bed as he convinced the others it was the perfect time for them to find the Looking Glass. He had recounted his first experience with the mirror in vivid detail, igniting their curiosity and convincing them the answers they sought would be found inside.

'This is the only chance we've got,' he reminded them. 'The curfew's been temporarily extended to let people revise after hours. So long as no one sees us near the Ivory Tower, we should get away with it.'

'And what happens if we get caught?' Emily asked darkly.

'Well, then the Vacuous will be the least of our problems,' Will shrugged.

With Admiral Allance's threats still looming over their heads, Will assured Finley, Emily and Lois that he had studied their designated route several times, and was certain in the knowledge they would make it to the Ivory Tower unchallenged. They agreed to reconvene in Will's bedroom later that night, waiting for the cover of darkness before they initiated their plan.

When the hour arrived, Will unlocked his bedroom door, allowing Lois, Emily and Finley to enter discreetly, each of them wearing dark clothing as he had requested. They carried bags full of I-Books on their backs, serving as evidence of their late-night revision session should anyone try and stop them.

Once they had gathered themselves, they made their way out of the deserted dormitories, checking over their shoulders at regular intervals to ensure they were alone. They made it to the door without encountering a single soul and exited into the quiet grounds.

'Did Allance ever say whether they fixed the cameras' Finley whispered with worry as they set off.

'Well, if they did, we'll soon know about it,' Will replied ominously.

They navigated their way across the school campus, using the shadowy pathways Will had meticulously picked out for them, and reached the Ivory Tower undetected. They looked around, straining their eyes and ears for any alert to danger, as they prepared for their ascent to the classroom.

'Can you hear any aliens in the grounds?' Emily asked the others as they loaded into Jeff's shuttle. 'What if Krecher's still up there?'

'We've come this far,' said Will, as he started up the engine. 'No use in turning back now.'

Emily's fears, however, turned out to be unfounded. Upon arriving at the top of the tower, they found Krecher's classroom deserted. Satisfied there were no discernible signs of life in the building, the four of them headed into the office, closing the door behind them with care.

'Over there,' Will instructed, pointing to the hilted mirror in the corner.

'This is it?' Emily asked, staring with scepticism at the ordinary looking piece of furniture, which was innocently reflecting their curious expressions.

'Yes,' Will confirmed. 'That's it.'

'How do you know it's going to take us to the right place?' Finley questioned him.

'I don't,' Will admitted. 'But it showed me what I needed to know last time.'

They stood and waited, Emily, Lois and Finley shuffling on their feet and exchanging sideways glances as the mirror continued to reflect only the room around them. Will stared at the mirror without blinking, the palms of his hands beginning to sweat as he gazed at his own pale face.

'How will we know when it's working?' Lois whispered.

'Maybe it only works for one person,' Finley frowned.

'Maybe Krecher put a block on it after you broke in last time,' Emily sighed.

'Do you think we should go back?'.

'Just wait,' Will told them. 'It'll happen.'

As though the mirror had heard him, a shiny handle suddenly materialised on its surface, rewarding Will for his faithfulness and stifling any doubts.

'Woah,' Finley said. 'That was impressive. How does it work?'

'It's alien,' Will replied shortly. 'That's all Krecher would tell me. Shall we do this, then?'

The three of them nodded. Will gripped the handle on the mirror and took a deep breath, twisting it firmly to the side.

'Follow me!' he shouted, pulling the mirror open with force and running full pelt into the blackness beyond.

This time, he was ready for the gut-pulling disorientation that followed, staggering only slightly as his feet touched the ground and his lungs filled with the cool clean air that only Earth could provide. He was busy studying his surroundings, when a series of heavy footsteps behind him indicated the arrival of Finley, Lois and Emily.

'Is this Earth?' Finley asked, gawking at their surroundings.

'Yeah, this is it,' Will nodded, noting the snow-peaked mountains in the distance. 'This is where my parents went to college. If the Vacuous were here, we'll find them.'

'So, where do we start?' Emily enquired.

Will surveyed the area, scanning for clues that might suggest which path they should take. His eye was caught by an old stone building, looming upon a hilltop a few miles from where they stood. There was something drawing about its presence, and Will's gut instinct informed him it would be a good place to start.

'Over there,' he pointed, marching towards the building with the others in close pursuit.

They navigated their way through the winding streets of sleepy houses, jumping at any sign of movement and checking over their shoulders as they moved.

Keeping in step with one another, Will, Emily, Finley and Lois rounded the next corner, finding themselves on a residential street, almost identical to the others in the area. As soon as they stepped onto the smooth tarmac of the road, it immediately became clear that something was very wrong. Will's nose was overpowered with the unpleasant stench of rotting food, causing him to stop dead and recoil. The others flinched alongside him, heaving and coughing in disgust.

'What is that smell?!' Emily exclaimed, pinching her nose between her finger and thumb.

'I don't know, but brace yourselves… we're about to find out,' Will grimaced.

He pulled the collar of his black cotton jumper up to the ridge of his nose and continued forward, breathing through his mouth as his eyes watered and his stomach twisted in repulsion.

Moving further down the street, Will quickly discovered the source of the terrible odour. Every single one of the large rubbish bins positioned outside the houses had been knocked over, causing litter and debris to spill out around them. Flies swarmed in their hundreds, descending upon old discarded food in packs of dark vibrating clouds. Metal drink cans scraped across the floor and plastic wrappers rustled with every gust of wind, interrupting the silence that hung over the street.

Upon further inspection, Will noticed that one of the cars

parked next to the pavement had been bashed out of place, its wide silver rear sticking out diagonally into the road. Etched into the paint work on the side of its body were three deep claw marks, their impact so powerful a small dent had been left in one of the doors.

'I've seen marks like that before,' Lois swallowed, fear rising in her voice.

'The Vacuous…' Will said, the hairs on the back of his neck standing on end.

'It won't be able to see us, will it?' Emily fretted.

'No, we can't be seen or heard in the Looking Glass. It's like being a ghost,' Will reassured her.

'Can we move anything?' Emily queried, walking over to one of the discarded bins and attempting to pick it up. She shrieked as her hand passed through the object, grabbing her fingers to check they hadn't disappeared.

'Everything we're seeing has already happened. We can't alter the past.' Will explained. 'That means we can't touch anything. But it also means nothing can touch us.'

'We'd better keep going,' Finley said grimly, sidestepping one of the cars as he moved.

Hugging themselves against the bitter cold, they trudged through the streets, following every fork and bend in the road which led them closer to the ancient building.

Eventually, they came to an old high street, the shop windows gathering dust after being abandoned by their owners, with only a few appearing to still be in business.

They crossed the town centre, passing under an imposing grey clock tower, which chimed urgently to inform them it was midnight, and meandered through the backstreets, finally reaching the foot of the hill they had been searching for. Carved into the grassy slope was a set of sturdy stone steps, which they ascended hastily, clambering to the peak of the hill within minutes.

Once they had reached the top, they were met with a set of wrought iron gates, with two eagles carved into the flanks. Across the top, the words 'College Snowdonia' were inscribed above a motto that read; 'homo, qui discit est homo qui vivit.'

Will realised, with a giddy surge of adrenaline, that they had found his parent's college, his belief in its significance growing stronger by the second.

By some miracle, one of the gates had been left slightly ajar, allowing the four of them to enter. A short gravel path took them to the entranceway of the stone dwelling, which comprised of a set of mahogany doors under a stone archway.

The doors had also been left open by whoever had preceeded them, revealing the dim glow of artificial light from inside the college. The four of them took one last glimpse at the building, which rose from the ground imposingly above them, its twisted turrets and domed windows giving it the stately appearance of a stern church.

They walked into the main entrance, made apparent by the large reception desk in the centre of the room, which was covered in I-Tech gadgets that Will didn't recognise. The walls had been plastered in artwork created by the students, mixed with an excess of posters and flyers advertising various sports teams.

'Look at this,' Will said, reading the advertisements out loud. "Football club, players needed.' I have no idea what football is, but it sounds extremely boring.'

'What's '*Lacrosse*?' Finley asked, squinting his eyes in confusion at a yellow poster before him.

'Never heard of it,' Will shrugged.

"The Secret Society',' Emily read from beside them. "We will be meeting at the usual place at the usual time on the usual day. If you know, you know. If you don't know – stay away!"

'College was weird,' Will mused.

'Hey guys!' Lois called from across the room. 'I think I've found where we need to go.'

She was standing in a coffee shop surrounded by a small seating area, discarded paper cups littered across the tables and floor. On the right-hand side was a green door, which had been left ajar, a sign reading 'Lecture Rooms' attached to the front.

With a glance at the others to confirm they were all in agreement, Will walked through the doorway, finding himself in a long musty hallway. The walls in this part of the building were bare and painted in a faded magnolia, which had begun to chip with age. The lights above Will's head flickered, and a shiver ran down his spine. Determined to hide his apprehension from the others, he continued to move forward as quickly as he could, ignoring the knot that was growing in the pit of his stomach with every step he took.

The group reached a corner and turned, finding themselves in a second identical hallway. Before they could make sense of their surroundings, the lights faded with a loud buzz, plunging them into a pungent darkness.

'Someone get the torch out on their personal device!' Finley called out from somewhere in the blackness.

'Mine's not working,' Emily replied from Will's right.

'I don't think personal devices work in the Looking Glass,'

Will said.

'Great, so we're just stuck in the dark, then?' Lois complained.

'Ssh!' Finley hissed. 'What's that noise?'

The four of them stood in deathly silence and listened. The sound of voices echoed down the hallway towards them, distant at first, but growing louder and more frantic with each passing minute.

'It's getting away!' a male voice cried.

Heavy footsteps thundered down the corridor, reverberating noisily around the walls. Will froze, his heart thumping in his ears. He narrowed his eyes as they began to adjust to the gloom, and was certain that he could make out a shadowy figure standing a few feet in front of him.

'Where did it go?' a second voice called from around the corner.

'That's my dad,' Lois whispered.

Suddenly, bright torchlight burst into the hallway, forcing Will to shield himself from its glare. He blinked rapidly, waiting for the coloured spots to fade from his vision so he could see again. After a few seconds, his sight returned to normal, and his blood ran cold.

Directly in front of him was a Vacuous, identical to the one they had encountered in their dormitory. Its misshapen head was cocked slightly to the side as it emitted hissing noises, twitching its sharp claws and staring through its hollow eyes. Will froze with fear, overcome by the powerful feeling that the Vacuous could see him.

'There it is!' Elsie shouted, as two more beams of torchlight flooded into the hall. Will peered around the Vacuous to see younger versions of Alfie and his mother, accompanied by his father, Austin.

'What's it doing?' Austin asked, unable to see Will and the others standing petrified in the creature's wake.

'It's looking at something,' Alfie frowned.

'But there's nothing there?' Elsie said with confusion, waving her torch in different directions to illuminate the corridor.

The Vacuous was startled by the sudden movement of light and turned away, letting out a bloodcurdling screech. It spun around and began to run on all fours, moving exceptionally fast on its powerful limbs.

Will, Finley, Lois and Emily jumped out the way as it passed them, the force of its weight thudding deafeningly through the corridor each time it hit the ground.

'Let's go!' Austin shouted, sprinting after the creature at full speed, with Alfie and Elsie close on his tail.

Will followed them, running as fast as he could to keep up as they darted out of the building and back into the night. The cold air hit Will's face like needles, a painful contrast to the warmth of the building inside, but he continued to pursue Alfie and his parents, his determination driving him forward.

He pounded down the stone steps with Emily, Lois and Finley a few paces behind him, and raced through the back streets of the town, passing invisibly through a small crowd of people who were emptying from a high-street bar, wrapping themselves in coats and scarves to keep out the cold.

Mercifully, Alfie, Elsie and Austin ground to a halt in front of the clock tower, doubling over to catch their breath. Will copied, gasping as he desperately tried to fill his lungs with air, his stomach knotting uncomfortably as his chest burned with exhaustion. Finley, Lois and Emily thundered to a stop alongside him, wheezing and panting with the exertion of running long distance, which none of them had ever had cause to do before.

Feeling dizzy, Will sat on the ground to listen, as Alfie and his parents began to speak.

'Did you see where it went?' Austin puffed, leaning against the clock tower, his face dewy with sweat.

'No,' Elsie replied with deflation.

'Damn it!' Austin cursed, banging his fist against the tower's stone base. 'I can't believe we let it get away.'

'They'll be other chances,' Elsie soothed him.

'I've been thinking,' Alfie interrupted them, his tone sombre. 'I don't think hunting the Vacuous is such a good idea anymore.'

'What?' said Austin and Elsie in unison, exchanging a look of bewilderment.

'I think we're wasting our time,' Alfie re-iterated.

'How can you say that?' Austin demanded. 'Nothing is known about these creatures. Not even Professor Krecher can figure out what they are. We need to find out why they're here. It could be the difference between human extinction and survival!'

'Yes, that's what we keep telling ourselves,' said Alfie bluntly. 'But aliens have been visiting Earth for over a hundred years. Just because we've never seen this species before, doesn't mean that they're harmful. I mean, look at the facts. Every time we see a Vacuous, it runs away from us. We've never seen or heard of anyone being hurt by one.'

'Not yet... but look at them! Their clawed hands, their sharp teeth, the way they can move... They're built for killing.' Austin argued.

'We can't base all of our assumptions on their physical appearance,' Alfie replied. 'It's not enough evidence to justify what we're doing.'

'We've been following the Vacuous for nearly a year. You've been convinced we were right up until this point,' Austin countered.

'Look, I'm just trying to be realistic,' Alfie sighed. 'We stumbled upon these aliens and started tracking them down, convinced we were saving the world in the process, but the truth is, we have no idea what we're doing.'

'Then we need to ask for help. We need to contact the government again,' Austin insisted. 'Something needs to be done! We need answers!'

'I told you, there's nothing the government can do. We haven't been able to provide any evidence that the Vacuous pose any kind of threat. Think how many fanatics must have come out of the woodwork since the Split was made public,' Alfie answered. 'They're bombarded daily with false reports from people who are trying to stop it from happening. They're not going to take us seriously.'

'Elsie, tell me you don't agree with this!' Austin pleaded with her.

'I don't know,' Elsie said uncertainly. 'Maybe we should talk to Krecher again.'

'Krecher doesn't know anything, he's just as confused by this whole thing as we are. I supported going to him at first, but it hasn't helped. Showing him the Vacuous did something to him. He hasn't been the same since,' Alfie replied.

Elsie frowned, contemplating his words carefully.

'Look, I know I'm right about this,' Alfie pushed. 'If we

carry on doing what we're doing, we're going to mess up our graduation and we won't get places on *The Mayflower*. It's not going to matter what the Vacuous are if they're here on Earth and we're up in space. They can't follow us to Novum.'

'How do you know for certain? The Split could be part of their plan,' Austin pointed out. 'The great conspiracy says *The Mayflower* isn't safe. Maybe it's referring to the Vacuous. Maybe they want Novum for themselves.'

'That seems a little far- fetched…,' Alfie frowned.

'Does it?' Austin demanded, his eyes wild, his breath coming thick and fast. 'Do you think we're the only species that have wrecked our home planet? I'm betting we're not. If the Vacuous somehow found out about Novum, they could see it as a second chance for their own kind. It doesn't seem that impossible to me. Why else would they be skulking around a college? They must know educational institutes are working with *The Mayflower* to create skilled workers. They're trying to find out how to get on board! I'm telling you… I can feel it in my gut.'

Elsie and Alfie exchanged a look of concern.

'Perhaps this has all gone too far,' Elsie said after a moment. 'It's turning into an obsession. I think it's time to let it go, Austin. All we're doing is chasing shadows.'

Austin slumped to the ground in defeat, resting his head between his knees for a moment as his breathing slowed back to normal.

'Of course you would side with him,' Austin said darkly.

'I'm not siding with anyone,' Elsie insisted, 'and it's only because I care about you that I'm saying this. The Vacuous have ruled our lives for long enough. Imagine how good it would feel to be normal again; to go back to how things were before we knew they existed. Regardless of what happens, there isn't much time left on Earth. I'd rather spend it being happy than chasing aliens that may or may not be dangerous.'

'Fine,' Austin conceded. 'If you tell me to stop, then I will. There's no use in me trying to do this on my own. But if I'm right...'

'Then we'll write you a long letter of apology,' Alfie grinned.

'I think it's for the best,' Elsie said, sitting beside Austin and placing an arm around his shoulder. 'Let's just be normal nineteen-year-olds again. We can save the world another day.'

'So, we're all in agreement then?' Alfie insisted. 'No more Vacuous and no more 'great conspiracy'. It all ends tonight.'

'Alright,' Austin nodded reluctantly. 'I suppose it ends here, then.'

Elsie squeezed his hand, looking up at him with shiny adoration.

Will got to his feet. A mirrored door had materialised next to the clock tower, informing him they had seen all that the Looking Glass wished to show them.

'Time to go,' he told Finley, Emily and Lois. They silently trailed behind him as he opened the door and stepped through, returning to the present day in Krecher's office.

As soon as they arrived, Will made his way out of the door, through the desolate classroom and into the shuttle, flying it to the ground without speaking a single word. Sensing his dark mood, Finley, Lois and Emily said nothing, waiting until they had retreated across the school grounds and reached the safety of Will's bedroom before they dared to speak.

'Are you alright?' Emily asked him, swinging herself up to sit on his desk, as he hunched over the end of his bed, twiddling his thumbs together with agitation.

'It's weird seeing my mum and dad together,' Will frowned. 'Especially knowing he abandoned her so soon afterwards.'

'It was weird seeing my dad, too,' Lois agreed, curling her legs up on one of the armchairs. 'Back then he almost seemed like an actual human being.'

'At least we got some answers, though,' Emily pointed out. 'We know the Vacuous were around on Earth.'

'Yeah, but that's all we know,' Finley disagreed. 'We still don't know whether they're dangerous or not, or what one was doing hanging around our dorms in the middle of the night.'

'And I don't think we should try and find out either,' Will stated bluntly. 'The Captain said they'd never seen a Vacuous hurt anyone, and that all they ever seemed to do was run away. We might not know why there's one at the school, but I think if we try and find out, we're going to put ourselves at risk.'

'At risk?' Emily asked, folding her arms.

'For being expelled, for getting hurt,' Will clarified. 'For seeing things that we might not want to…'

'Will, the Vacuous we saw didn't run away' Emily argued. 'It came after us. Don't you think it's a bit of a strange coincidence that the Vacuous were hunted by your parents and now they've turned up at our school?'

'Coincidence or not, it's not worth the trouble to find out,' Will insisted. 'If the Vacuous are dangerous and they're wandering around the school, Allance and the teachers will deal with it. In the meantime, I think we should follow the Captain's advice and leave alone what we don't understand.'

'But your dad-' Emily began.

'My dad's dead,' Will interrupted. 'His obsession with the

Vacuous drove him to make some horrible decisions and eventually killed him. If that isn't a clear enough sign that we should leave this alone, I don't know what is.'

There was an awkward silence. Finley and Lois shifted uncomfortably in their chairs as the words from Will's outburst lingered for a moment in the air.

'If you're sure that's what's best...' Lois said uncertainly.

'I am,' Will replied with force. 'If my dad had done the same then he might still be alive.'

'Okay,' Finley said hesitantly. 'We can drop it.'

Will stared at Emily, who was chewing her lip, her arms still folded against her chest.

'Fine,' she huffed. 'We'll forget about it.'

With their new decision in place, Emily, Finley and Lois traipsed off to bed, leaving Will to stew in the fresh feelings of anger the Looking Glass had brought to the surface of his mind.

In truth, he knew Emily was right. His parents hunting the Vacuous in college and then one turning up outside his room fifteen years later had to mean something, but his desire to honour the promise his father had broken was stronger than any need to unravel the truth. In his mind it was very simple; Vacuous or no Vacuous, he would never make the same mistakes as his father. Of that, he was determined.

THE HAPPY INTERLUDE

Lois sat in the Dining Hall, drumming her fingers against the table and staring unwaveringly at the blank screen on her Student Planner, ignoring the delicious smell of French pastries that was wafting over from the breakfast buffet. Any minute now, her planner would beep, delivering the dreaded message that contained her grades for every subject so far.

After a few minutes of sitting alone in abject terror, Lois was joined by Finley, Will and Emily, whose appearances reflected the tired dishevelment that Lois felt. They bleated 'good morning' half-heartedly, each producing their own planners and resting them delicately on the table, eyeing them fearfully as though they were bombs about to explode.

'I'm guessing you guys didn't get much sleep either,' Lois observed.

'Not a wink,' Will replied.

'How could we?' Emily stressed. 'If we don't get good grades in these exams, we won't be able to come back to school next year.'

'We have our final projects, too, remember?" Finley reminded her. 'They count towards our overall marks.'

'Yes, but we hardly revised for our exams at all!' Emily continued to fret. 'We were so distracted.'

There was an awkward pause as they were all reminded of their promise to Will not to mention the Vacuous, or anything related to their previous ordeal.

It had been difficult at first, with Lois, Emily and Finley forced to discuss the situation in secret whenever Will wasn't around. Over time, however, their inclination to talk about the subject had faded naturally. Nowadays, Lois found the Vacuous only entered her mind when she was alone at night, vulnerable to the chain of unsettling thoughts her brain liked to present her with in the silence of darkness.

'Remind me one more time how the grading system works,' Emily said to Finley, running her hands through her already unkempt hair.

'You get a score from one to five,' Finley explained calmly. 'One is the best and five is the worst. Three and above is classed as a 'pass,' whereas four and five are 'fails'.'

'And how many subjects do we need to pass to get back in next year?' Emily asked him, despite knowing the answer.

'All of them,' Finley replied morbidly. Will groaned and sunk his head into the table. Emily sighed in an exaggerated fashion, and Lois began massaging her temples, pulling the skin around her eyes a little too aggressively for the act to be relaxing.

'Don't worry,' Finley laughed, in response to their reaction. 'You won't have done *that* badly!'

'Easy for you to say, Fin,' Will grumbled. 'You're top of nearly every class.'

'Well, I still messed up in my Rocket Control exam,' Finley reminded him.

'At least Mr Zeppler let you retake it,' Lois pointed out.

'He only did that because we're supposed to go out in space

this term. If I don't get my licence, I'll have to stay behind every lesson while you all go off flying,' Finley said.

'What time is it?' Will complained, not wanting to take his eyes away from his planner.

'7:59,' Finley told him.

'One minute to go!' Emily squealed.

Lois' heart began to beat heavily in her chest. Despite all her dad's excessive funding into her education, she had never been the brightest in her tutor group and had always struggled to apply herself properly in her lessons. The curriculum at the Space Academy, however, fascinated her beyond belief, and she could only hope she would be allowed to continue studying it.

The sickening sound of beeping erupted around the hall, and the entire student population seemed to draw in breath as one. Lois, Will, Finley and Emily looked at each other, their eyes wide as saucers as they realised the message of their fates had been delivered.

'All together?' Will suggested and they nodded, picking up their Student Planners in unison.

'One, two, three....'

Lois winced, opening the message and turning her face away from it slightly, as though reading it would blind her. She skimmed down the page quickly and was immensely relieved to see there were no fours or fives in any of her subjects.

Her fear subsiding, she read through the page carefully, making sure not to miss any details. The page stated:

'Lois Sommers,

Mid-Year Examination Results:

Alien Studies ~ 1

Arithmetic ~ 2

Civilisations ~ 2

Combat and Weaponry ~ 2

Rocket Control ~ 2

Resources ~ 3'

'How did you do, Lois?' Finley asked her.

'I got a 'one' in Alien Studies!' she gushed. 'I got 'two's in everything else, except Resources which I got a 'three' in.'

'Well done!' he congratulated her. 'I knew you'd pass.'

'What did you get?' she asked him.

'I got a 'one' for everything, but a 'three' in Rocket Control,' he replied happily. 'I was convinced I'd failed that exam.'

'I got four 'ones',' Emily interjected. 'In Alien Studies, Technology, Combat and Weaponry and Arithmetic! The rest were 'twos'.'

'Nice,' Finley smiled. The three of them looked at Will, who was staring down at his Student Planner in disbelief, his face frozen in an expression of shock.

'Everything okay?' Emily asked him.

'I got a 'three' in Civilisations,' he replied flatly.

Lois looked at Finley and Emily, unsure how to react.

'I can't believe Miss Fortem passed me!' Will laughed with euphoria.

'Did you get any 'ones'?' Finley asked him.

'Yeah, in Alien Studies, Rocket Control and Combat and Weaponry,' he answered merrily.

'Seems like Mr. Krecher was very generous this year,' Finley noted.

'I know. It makes me feel a bit guilty, considering we broke into his office…' Lois admitted.

'I can't believe we all passed,' Will beamed, changing the subject. 'All we have to do now is not mess up on our final projects and we'll be coming back in September.'

Just as Will spoke, Rudy and his followers passed by the table, overhearing his announcement.

'Isn't that nice?' Rudy said to his posse, his voice heavy with sarcasm. 'Emily and her boyfriend together for another year.'

'He isn't my boyfriend,' Emily blushed.

'It's a shame we won't be partners for our final projects, isn't it, Emily?' Rudy continued to taunt, ignoring her completely. 'You and I made a great team looking after that Beakin thing.'

'You hardly did anything, Rudy. Monster would have starved if it wasn't for me,' Emily snapped back.

'Well, if you find yourself missing me, you know where I am,' he winked, before sauntering away.

'He really isn't very bright, is he?' Finley mused after him.

'At least I didn't have to fight him this time,' Will smirked.

'Now that's all over, let's eat!' Emily exclaimed, and the four of them strolled over to the serving station together, each asking the robots to pile their plates high with celebration food.

Back at the table, they sipped merrily on sweet, cold orange juice and chewed on buttery warm croissants, their conversation flowing as they basked in the glory of their success.

Half-way through their breakfast, Emily's older brother, Charlie, strode over to their table, sitting down assertively between Finley and Lois and squashing them to the end of the row.

'Guess what?' he grinned, not bothering with greetings

or introductions.

'You passed your exams?' Emily ventured.

'Well, yeah, obviously,' he waved his hand dismissively. 'I got 'ones' in everything. But, no, that isn't what I meant. What I was going to say is, we're passing by a sun.'

'What do you mean, Charlie?' Emily sighed.

'The school!' he exclaimed with frustration. 'We're passing by a nearby sun in whatever solar system we're travelling through.'

'So?'

'So, it means we get real sunlight!'

'What do you mean?' Will asked him, his brows furrowed in confusion.

'Give me strength,' Charlie sighed, rolling his eyes. 'We are flying past a sun in a see-through dome. Therefore, we will experience real, genuine sunlight for a few days.' He enunciated each word carefully, as though speaking to very young children.

'That's never happened before on *The Mayflower*,' Finley frowned.

'Well, of course not, there aren't any real windows on *The Mayflower*. It only happens here at the school,' Charlie replied. 'There's nothing else like it. You can even swim in the lake and sunbathe. Trust me, once you feel genuine sunlight, you'll never forget it. That fake UV stuff has got nothing on the real thing.'

'How do you even know about this, Charlie?' Emily asked him with suspicion. 'None of the teachers have announced anything.'

'I have contacts in all the right places,' he winked.

Just as he spoke, a pinging noise rang out across their heads, travelling over the Dining Hall and provoking an instant reaction of silence from the students inside. The noise seemed to be coming from an intercom that Lois had never realised was there.

'Here we go,' Charlie whispered.

'Good morning, Space Academy,' Admiral Allance's voice boomed through the speakers.

'First, allow me to congratulate you all on your excellent exam results. I am sending this message to the school through every television screen and sound system to make absolutely certain every student knows how truly proud I am of their achievements.'

Lois couldn't see Allance's face, but his flat tone of voice greatly contradicted the expression of pride he was trying to convey. Had she headed out into the school and found a T.V screen, she wouldn't have been surprised to find him reading his speech from a piece of paper.

'Secondly, I would like to inform you we will shortly be bypassing a sun on our way through the Irodonius solar system. If you would like to make your way outside in an orderly fashion, you will be able to witness the magical moment we are bathed in natural light.'

The Headmaster's announcement ended, and the hall erupted with the noise of benches scraping against the floor as everyone rushed to their feet to observe the spectacle. Lois, Finley, Emily and Will joined the stampede, converging with dozens of students in the Reception Hall as they pushed their way towards the school grounds.

Searching for a decent spot among the gathering crowd outside, Lois and the others planted themselves on the lawn opposite the school's main entrance, turning their faces towards the black sky, where an orange glow had already started to appear.

In the distance, thousands of miles above their heads, the planets of the Irodonius system were visible. They ranged in colour- from deep magnificent blue to rich emerald green, each one floating enigmatically in perfect orbit around their sun. Rings of dust could be seen swirling around one of the celestial bodies, forming a hazy layer of cloud around the planet's burnt yellow surface.

Captivated by the fascinating sight of the solar system, Lois almost missed the moment the grounds were flooded with brilliant bright light. She felt the warmth spread across her body, and closed her eyes, basking in the pleasant heat.

She was amazed how the light of a single burning star could carry such instantaneous happiness in its rays. She remembered something her mother once told her about all humans being made from stardust, and wondered if that was the explanation for the wonderful sensation which spread steadily through her bones.

Opening her eyes again, she looked about the grounds with a new perspective; as though she was seeing them again for the very first time. In the new sunlight, she could make out shades of colour she had never seen before, the school illuminated with new life and vibrancy.

The golden logo of Novum above the navy-blue doors glinted as the sun reflected from its large spherical surface, blinding anyone who gazed at it for too long. The glass windows shimmered, the Resources Biodome sparkled, and the smooth metal roof of the school Observatory swam hazily in the distance, visible waves of heat rising from its metal shell. The grass Lois stood upon was suddenly a bright shade of green, looking far more realistic than it ever did under the black sky. Even the asphalt paths that provided passage around the school looked beautiful in the sun's rays, glittering in hues of charcoal and silver.

As well as bringing the light, the sun also bought several days of bliss, with many of the teachers deciding to move their lessons outside to celebrate the natural phenomenon. Mr Krecher took the opportunity to showcase one of his favourite alien specimens; a beautiful, four-winged creature with crystal skin that refracted the sunlight, casting rainbows onto the floor as it flew above them.

'This is an *avem de lumine*,' Krecher informed them, watching with boyish delight as the bird-like alien flew above their heads. 'I never thought I'd get the chance to show it to you. Take in its beauty. The sight of it is a rare thing to behold.'

In between lessons, Lois, Finley, Emily and Will spent their time by the lake, sunbathing and dipping their toes into the cool clear water, easing the effects of the intense heat. When they weren't relaxing outside, they confined themselves to the library, where they found their good spirits had even managed to make Mr Mayhem's uncharacteristically boring final project on 'How the early intervention of aliens in the 1980's greatly advanced the space travelling capabilities of humankind' a relatively bearable task.

In the wake of her new positive attitude, Lois had been persuaded by Emily to accompany her to the book club she attended every Friday, insisting, despite Will and Finley's teasing, that her membership had nothing to do with the librarian, Martyn, or his charm and good looks.

Lois went along obligingly, and discovered a great joy in reading the famous works of antique literature, never having realised what true pleasure could be found by holding a real book in her hands. As a result, she had taken to spending the evenings curled up on her bed, reading novels in the sunlight and turning their crinkled pages in her hands, inhaling their musty aroma. She would read until her eyes blurred and itched, refusing to put her book down until the shutters in her bedroom closed at ten p.m., blocking out the sun and forcing her to sleep.

It was as though they had left reality and entered Utopia, where there were no troubles and no negative feelings at all. So wonderful were the days of sunshine that Lois was filled with a genuine depression when Admiral Allance announced they were soon to pass through the solar system, leaving the warmth of the sun's presence behind.

To temper the sting of her disappointment, she invited Will, Finley and Emily to her room after dinner, under the premise that they would start work on the lengthy project Mr Krecher had set them. Their task was to pick five different species of alien and explain how humankind had discovered them. In truth, Lois didn't want to be alone for the moment the darkness resumed, and was willing to pretend to be enthralled as Finley explained in great length about the trade deals humans had made with aliens, so long as it meant her friends would be with her when the sun disappeared.

All too soon, the light finally faded, darkness enveloping the school once more. Will yawned and stretched, complaining of a dead leg and mumbling something about homework being bad for his health. Emily got up from her crossed-legged position on the floor and cricked her neck, heading to the drinks machine to pour herself an icy beverage. Finley rose from the bed next to Lois and strolled absent-mindedly to the window, staring out at the inky blackness that had made its return outside.

Lois was in the middle of tidying the blankets that were strewn across her floor, when Finley let out a cry of horror, causing her to drop everything she was holding and rush to the window, Will and Emily close behind her.

They gathered together, united in confusion as they scanned outside for the source of Finley's distress. Lois could not take her eyes from his face, which was paler than she had ever seen it, his mouth frozen open in terror as he pointed wordlessly to a shadowy corner of the grounds.

All at once they saw it, gasping in horror as they reeled from the terrible sight. Standing by the lake was a Vacuous, its bone-white skin shining like a beacon in the gloom. Its long spindly arm was outstretched, the claws of its hand grasping thin air as though it were frozen in some sort of strange and dramatic tableau.

'It's back,' Will whispered, his pupils wide with fear.

'What's it doing?' Lois shuddered, hardly daring to breathe. 'It looks like its holding something.'

'Not something...' Finley said darkly. 'Someone'

Lois scrutinised the scene again, straining her eyes to distinguish the shapes among the shadows. At that moment, she saw what Finley could see, the blood draining from her face as the trauma of the sight took hold.

Letting out a scream, she covered her mouth and staggered backwards, her stomach heaving at the realisation of what she had witnessed. The Vacuous's gnarled claws were not clutching thin air, but were clasped around the throat of a man, who was dressed head to toe in dark clothing.

As she watched, the Vacous released its grasp, letting the lifeless body of its victim slump horribly to the ground. Lois fell backwards, fear overpowering her as she lost control of her legs. Will and Emily ducked beneath the window, crouching on all fours to avoid being seen. Finley, however, remained standing, his face ghostly white as he stared paralysed by the awful scene before him. Will tugged firmly on his clothes, knocking him off balance and dragging him to the ground and out of sight. He sunk to the floor, shaking uncontrollably as he looked at his friends with wide eyes.

'It saw me,' he swallowed. 'It looked right at me.'

'Are you sure?' Lois asked him desperately.

'I'm sure,' he replied with harrowing certainty.

Will leapt to his feet, locking the door and barricading it behind him with Lois' bed. Emily pressed a button beside the window, snapping the shutters down and concealing them from anyone watching outside. Lois went and sat beside Finley, putting her arm around him to comfort him as he continued to tremor, his skin freezing cold to the touch.

'Okay,' Will said, struggling to level his tone. 'What do we do now?'

'We have to tell,' Emily replied with resignation. 'We don't have a choice.'

There was a long pause as the statement resounded across the room. Will began to pace, walking back and forth with such a fury that Lois was surprised he didn't wear a hole in her carpet.

'Did anyone see who it was?' he asked. 'The man who the Vacuous...'

He trailed off, unable to bring himself to say the word

'killed'. The three of them shook their heads in response.

'We haven't got any evidence,' he frowned, 'and we can't name the victim. Who are we going to tell? Who's going to believe our story?'

'Someone just got murdered on the school grounds, Will,' Emily reminded him, flinching as the words left her mouth. 'There'll be a missing person's investigation. There'll be a body. We have to go. We have to tell someone what we've seen. We don't have time to waste!'

'You want to go now?' Will said with disbelief.

'The longer we sit on it, the worse it's going to get,' she warned him. 'This goes way beyond expulsion. People found guilty of a crime get thrown off *The Mayflower*. Failing to come forward as witnesses to somebody dying would definitely constitute that.'

'Lois' dad is the Captain,' Will protested. 'Do you really think he'd let his own daughter get thrown into space?'

'What about the rest of us?' Finley fretted.

'We've got to go straight to Allance,' Emily pressed. 'We need to tell the person right at the top. He'll know what to do. We can't carry this secret, Will. It's too much. We have to tell him everything, and then face the consequences.'

'Where will he be?' Will surrendered, frantically gathering his things as he prepared to depart.

'I know where the teacher's live,' Emily replied, putting her shoes on and tying a knot in her laces. 'Charlie's pointed it out to me during the first week. It's not far from here.'

Lois jumped to her feet and rushed to her wardrobe, pulling a hoody over her uniform and following Will and Emily to the door.

They were about to leave, when they realised Finley hadn't moved from his position on the floor. Lois turned back to see him rising to his feet unsteadily, his complexion now a shade of green as he balled his fists up tightly.

'You can't go out there,' he warned them. 'It's too dangerous.'

'We have to,' Emily insisted.

'That thing saw me!' Finley exclaimed. 'It knows I witnessed the murder. It could be waiting out there in case I try and tell someone.'

'We can't just sit here and do nothing,' Will argued. 'And besides, it saw you in this room. If it was going to come after you, this would be the first place it would go. The quicker we find Allance the better. We'll be safe with him.'

Finley shook his head profusely.

'Lois,' he pleaded with her, knowing she was his last hope. 'You can't go.'

Lois hesitated. As much as she wanted to stay and comfort him, the thought of the Vacuous making its way towards them while they were trapped in her bedroom was too much to bear.

'We all have to go, Finley,' she encouraged him. 'We're in this together now.'

Finley took in a deep breath, nodding slowly as he acknowledged the truth of her words. He stepped forward and placed his hand into hers, the moistness of his palm informing her how truly scared he was.

With a meaningful look at Will, Finley gave his silent consent for them to leave. They opened the door of the bedroom and began to run, hurtling towards the dark of night and the fate that awaited them there.

THE ADMIRAL'S CONFESSION

Finley sprinted as fast as his legs would carry him, the sound of blood pounding in his ears and as he raced with Lois, Emily and Will to find Admiral Allance. He dared not look around, petrified of seeing the Vacuous lurking in the dark, waiting pitilessly to kill him. Instead, he kept his eyes forward, focusing on Emily's back as she ran ahead, leading them to the building where the teachers slept.

'It's just up ahead,' she called out. She pointed to a bland high-rise block a few yards in front of them, which had almost no distinguishable features, save for the small replica of the school logo attached to the very top.

As they approached the building, Finley's heart began to soar with hope. He could see the front door beginning to take shape. If they could just find a way in, he was convinced the Headmaster would be able to stop the Vacuous before it hurt anyone else.

His joy turned to terror as something large and pale white caught the corner of his eye, causing the air in his lungs to turn to ice. With sickening fear, he looked towards the silvery figure, everything around him slowing to a glacial pace.

The Vacuous cocked its head to the side as it regarded the group of children running a few metres in its wake. As soon as it realised it had been seen, its empty black eyes connecting with Finley's fearful brown ones. It began to run towards them, its muscular limbs carrying it at an impossibly fast pace.

Finding his voice, Finley yelled out in panic to alert the others, who had continued dashing forward with no idea of the imminent danger that was approaching them.

In unison, they turned their heads towards the Vacuous and screamed, chaos descending as they all ran in different directions, scattering like pieces of shattered glass. Finley knew what he had to do.

Instead of fleeing with the others, he set his sights firmly on the building ahead of him and dashed towards it as fast as he could. Given how quick and agile the Vacuous was, he was almost certain it would intercept his path before he reached Admiral Allance, and he braced himself, flinching with every step as he anticipated the pain of its sharp claws on his skin.

Somehow, he reached the building unscathed, and was surprised to find the front door had been left slightly ajar, meaning no fingerprint identification was needed for him to enter. He paused briefly before going in, scanning his surroundings wildly for any sign of the Vacuous or of his friends. Seeing nothing, he called out in hopes that someone would hear him.

'Lois! Emily! Will!' he yelled, cupping his hands around his mouth to project his voice.

'Finley!' Lois' voice echoed from out of sight.

'Get to safety!' he called back. 'I'm going to get Allance!'

Without waiting for a reply, he hurried inside, aware that he had just alerted the Vacuous to both his location and his intentions.

He found himself in a small lounge, furnished only by two

white armchairs, a coffee table and a large plant. At the back of the room was a lift, and Finley made his way over to it, reading from an inscription of names and numbers on the wall beside it.

He scanned down the page, noting the names of 'Miss Veronica Fortem, Mr Albert Mayheim, Ms. Helen Dido and Mr Kurt Krecher,' until eventually he found the Headmaster's name, his information written simply as 'Admiral Allance- 6A'.

Armed with this knowledge, Finley jumped inside the lift, pressing the button for the sixth floor and shooting up to the top of the building. He tried to ignore the eerie elevator music playing in the background, keeping his mind focussed on the task at hand. When he arrived on the correct floor, he exited with determination, finding the door to Admiral Allance's apartment with ease. He hammered on the outside, his fist turning red with the force.

After a few seconds, he heard a clicking noise coming from the door's mechanism and it swung open. Finley was greeted by the sight of a confused Admiral Allance standing in the entrance to his apartment, dressed in his midnight-blue suit and silk tie despite the late hour.

'Sir,' Finley began, the words tumbling from his mouth before the Headmaster had a chance to speak. 'I'm sorry to disturb you. I know it's late, and that students aren't supposed to be here, but I really need to speak to you. It's an emergency.'

'Yes, yes of course,' Admiral Allance replied, eyeing Finley with concern. 'Come in then, boy. Finley, is it?'

'Yes, sir,' Finley nodded, following him inside.

He stepped into Admiral Allance's lounge, which was surprisingly simple and bare. Most of the room had been left empty, with only one reclining black leather chair and matching stall perched on top of the cream coloured carpet. Shelves had been installed on the walls, but had been left empty, the absence of photographs and books painfully noticeable. On the windowsill sat a dead plant in a chipped magenta vase, its leaves wilted and brown from neglect. The only part of the entire set-up that mildly resembled what Finley had expected for the Headmaster was the large window on the back wall, which allowed for a spectacular view of almost the entire school and the stars beyond.

'Sit down,' Allance instructed him, gesturing towards the leather chair. Finley obeyed, and Allance moved across the room, locking the door and turning the handle to ensure they would not be interrupted. He turned back to Finley, raising a thick silvery eyebrow and placing his arms behind his back, echoing the military stance of the Captain.

'So, Finley, would you like to explain to me what you're doing knocking on my door in the middle of the night?' he asked. 'As you know, there are strict rules regarding the student curfew, which was almost two hours ago.'

'Yes, sir, I understand,' Finley replied calmly. 'I'm here because I witnessed a murder.'

Admiral Allance blinked, his authoritarian demeanour slipping for a moment as he regarded Finley with shock.

'I'm sorry?' he said gruffly. 'Did you just say you witnessed a murder?'

'Yes, sir,' Finley nodded. 'I saw a man be killed, and so did my friends, Emily, Will and Lois. It happened here on the school grounds. The killer was...' he paused, knowing he was about to share the most unbelievable element of his story. 'The killer was an alien, sir.' He swallowed. 'The most horrifically terrifying alien I've ever seen.'

The Headmaster rubbed the bridge of his nose and began to pace the room, processing the information Finley had given him. An expression of acute stress pulled at the edges of his mouth and he frowned deeply, his brows knitting together more determinately than Finley had ever seen them.

'You saw an alien kill someone?' Admiral Allance clarified.

'Yes, sir' Finley confirmed.

'And when did this happen?' he probed him.

'About thirty minutes ago, sir.'

'And you say your friends also saw this attack?'

'Yes, sir.'

'And where are your friends now?' the Headmaster said, pausing to watch Finley closely as he answered.

'They ran off. When we were on our way to find you, we saw the alien again. It's still out there, sir! It chased the others away. If we don't catch it soon, it could kill someone else!' Finley exclaimed, hoping the wealth of questions the Headmaster was directing at him meant that he believed his story.

'I see,' Admiral Allance replied bluntly. 'And the victim of this crime... it was a student?'

'I don't know, sir,' Finley bowed his head. 'We couldn't see properly. It didn't look like a student, though. It looked like an adult man.' A lump grew in Finley's throat as he recalled the awful moment, and he closed his eyes, forcing himself to keep it together long enough to gain the Headmaster's help.

'Well, naturally this is very concerning,' Allance sighed. 'If one of Mr Krecher's aliens has escaped confinement and committed such an atrocity, then there will be severe consequences for both himself and the specimen involved. I'll contact him now to discuss the matter. Perhaps he can help us track down the creature before it hurts anyone else.'

'I don't think it's one of Mr Krecher's aliens, sir,' Finley interjected, stopping the Headmaster as he began tapping on his personal device.

'What makes you say that?' he asked, his tone darkening.

Finley hesitated. He desperately wanted to explain everything but feared confessing he had learnt about the Vacuous through a magic mirror in Mr. Krecher's office would earn him a one-way trip to the Psychiatric Ward on *The Mayflower*. Worse than that, he could get Mr. Krecher and his friends in trouble, and he would never be able to forgive himself if he lost them their places at the Space Academy.

'It doesn't look like a creature anyone would want to study. I think it's too strong to be kept in confinement. It's intelligent. Mr Krecher would never be able to control a thing like that. I'm worried about my friends, though, sir,' he re-iterated, growing concerned by the Headmaster's lack of action. 'They're still out there with that creature. It could have caught them...'

'Yes, of course,' Allance concurred, beginning to sound flustered. 'I will alert the other teachers immediately and we'll form a search party. I'll make sure you're escorted safely back to your dormitory. We'll make sure we find your friends, and we'll retrieve any evidence we can pertaining to this horrible crime. I'll go to the lake myself to see if anything was left behind. Does that satisfy you?'

'Yes, sir. Thank you, I-'. Finley stopped mid-sentence, an unsettling realisation tugging in the pit of his stomach.

'What is it?' the Headmaster asked impatiently.

'Sorry, sir, it's just ... I don't think I mentioned the lake...' Finley replied slowly, his legs beginning to lose feeling.

'What?' Allance snapped, waving his hand dismissively. 'Of course you did. How else would I know that's where the crime took place? And anyway, all the bedrooms on the top floor of your dormitories have a view of the lake. It's part of their design.'

'Except... my bedroom isn't on the top floor, sir. Lois' is. It was her room I was in tonight when I saw the murder happen. But how could you know that? Unless... you were there,' Finley looked up at him darkly.

The Headmaster's eyes flashed with fear, fury and exasperation in a matter of seconds. His body slumped with defeat and he shook his head, rubbing his temples and licking his lips with irritation.

'Oh, foolish boy, if only you had left it alone,' he muttered, strolling over to his desk and removing a thick rope from one of the drawers.

'I don't understand,' Finley said, jumping to his feet in panic, his eyes fixed wildly on the rope. 'How could you have been there? There was nobody else around.'

Allance laughed mirthlessly, positioning himself between Finley and the door and blocking any chance of his escape.

'You still haven't worked it out, heave you?' he mocked. 'Oh, child, and to think, I went to all the trouble of getting you a place at this school. They told me you were intelligent. That's why I held a special assembly to deter you after you saw me in the hallway that night. Now I see that needn't have bothered. You and your little friends aren't as clever as I gave you credit for.'

'Saw you in the hallway? You mean… you're the …' Finley trailed off, the end of the sentence too terrible to utter out loud.

'I'm the creature you saw, yes,' the Headmaster replied bluntly. 'At least, that is my true form in all its glory. Beautiful isn't it? This human disguise is so restricting. I don't know how you go around all your lives like this. No one wonder you're all so miserable. There wouldn't have been half as many wars on your home planet if you had known the power of a form like mine.'

'But…how?' Finley said pathetically, his words failing him, the breath seeming to evaporate from his body.

'How? You really want me to explain the complicated process my species undertook to emulate the DNA of human beings? Because I can assure you, it's extremely boring, and in any case, I need to be getting on with your disposal,' Allance answered, approaching him with the rope in his hands.

'I think perhaps the question you meant to ask me was 'why' not 'how'. Why am I here? What do I want? Why was I in your dormitories in the middle of the night, and who did I kill beside the lake? These are all fascinating questions with equally enthralling answers,' he continued as he began to wind the rope around a petrified Finley's limbs.

'The fact you're tied up in all this – that is, both the situation and this rope- is an unfortunate mistake. It's my fault, really. After that idiot Mayheim knocked the cameras out with his failed experiment, I couldn't resist taking the opportunity to roam the grounds as my true self, free from the limitations of this human form. The first couple of hours were glorious. I remained completely undiscovered, and I'm certain that no one would ever have known the truth, had I not been drawn to your dormitories that night by a huge surge of pathetic human emotion. I had forgotten about all the raging hormones and complicated feelings adolescent humans have. Such chemicals are like a drug to my kind. I was taken like a moth to a flame.'

The Headmaster paused, securing the ropes around Finley's arms and legs as he pushed him down onto the leather sofa.

'It's a shame I have to do this, Finley,' he sighed. 'I try not to kill unless necessary. Murdering a student will be a particularly messy affair. I'll have to do well to cover this one up. Taking you to a nearby planet and leaving you there is out of the question, considering our current position in the galaxy. Let me think what story I can invent. Perhaps one of your peers took a dislike to you being at the Space Academy, resenting your low status, and decided to finish the job Josie Jones started at the beginning of the year. Or maybe the condescending looks and harsh judgements finally got too much for you, and you flung yourself into of space, unable to bear the pain of not fitting in any longer.'

'Did you know I have my own private launch bay?' Allance smiled. 'It leads straight from my apartment into space. How about you and I should go on a little rocket trip. I must warn you, though; only one of us shall be returning.'

'It won't work,' Finley challenged him, the prospect of impending death inspiring him with new courage. 'Lois, Emily and Will know I'm here. They've seen everything I've seen. If I go missing, they'll know it was you. They'll figure it out. Would you really risk murdering the Captain's daughter to cover your tracks? Imagine what he'd do to you when he found out.'

Allance faltered, his face falling slightly as he digested this information.

'Very well,' he said after a moment. 'In that case, there will be a different narrative.'

He began twitching his hand, and Finley watching in horror as it transformed into the gnarled claw of the Vacuous. Allance strolled over to the window and smashed it with one fell swoop, shattering the glass into hundreds of razor-sharp pieces without flinching. He took his claw and tore at his own clothes, slashing his suit and undershirt and scratching the skin underneath to draw blood. When he was finished, he morphed his hand back to human form, and returned to loom above Finley.

'How terrible!' he cried, his face wrought with emotion. 'The vicious alien creature burst to my apart and attacked me. I tried to fight it, but it was too powerful. It snatched you, fleeing into space before I could do anything to stop it. It must have known you had witnessed its crimes and kidnapped you as a result. How sad for you family. It will break their hearts to know you are lost forever, never truly understanding what happened.' He snapped out of his despair and grinned, his eyes cruel and cold. 'How does that work for you?' he chortled, double knotting the rope around Finley's ankles.

Finley fell silent, his body slumping with defeat. The cover-up was perfect, all angles considered. Even Lois, Emily and Will would be none the wiser. It was over. The truth would die with him, and Allance would go on as Headmaster, his secret identity concealed until they reached Novum, where Finley suspected the Vacuous would rise to take over. A single tear rolled down his cheek as he thought of his mother, the unimaginable pain of knowing he would never see her again ripping at his heart like knives.

Admiral Allance grabbed the rope that was tied around

Finley and pulled. He fell off the chair, hitting the ground with a sickening thump. Allance began to drag him across the floor, hitting his head on the doorframe as they moved from the lounge to a long hallway, running its way through the apartment.

The light was dingy, but Finley could make out the strong muscles of the Headmaster's back as he hauled his body forward. Even in his human form, there was no way Finley would be able to fight him. He was completely at his mercy. His head began to throb, a lump forming from the impact of the doorframe. Finley let out a whimper, unable to hide his distress from his captor. Allance did not react, moving forward with unwavering purpose.

They reached a metal door at the end of the hall, a 'caution' sign drilled into its front. Finley knew without having to look that this was the entrance to the Headmaster's private launch bay. Allance used his fingerprint to access the room and bumped Finley across the threshold. He winced as the cold steel of the floor rubbed against the burn the carpet in the hallway had inflicted onto his back.

From his position on the ground, Finley could see several small spacecrafts parked in the steel hangar – each one big enough to carry two or three people. At the end of the room was a tunnel, not dissimilar to the one Mr. Zeppler used in Rocket Control. He thought about how Will had come to his rescue that day, saving his life with heroics. Finley wished he could be as brave as his friend, certain that Will would know what to do in this situation.

It pained him now to think of him. Finley had been strangely grateful to Josie for attempting to send him into space. Despite her malicious intentions, she had indirectly brought him to Will, Emily and, eventually, Lois; the only friends he'd ever had. He imagined them grieving for him, never knowing the truth of how he had died. After a while, they would continue their life at the Space Academy, completely unaware of the danger lurking beneath Admiral Allance's façade.

As the Headmaster loaded Finley into a small red rocket, he closed his eyes. He longed to reach for his personal device and send a message to his mother, telling her that he loved her and that he was sorry he didn't listen when she told him to come home.

He wished he could speak to Justin and tell him that he was worth more than he believed himself to be. He wished he could tell Jessica that she was the funniest person he'd ever known, and to look after Felicity; the best little sister he could ever have asked for. He thought of all the things he would trade just to see them one last time, his mother's smile and his father's bellowing laugh appearing vividly his mind. He braced himself for death, hoping it would be quick and painless.

'Stop!'

The voice echoed across the launch bay, resounding from every wall.

At first, Finley thought he had imagined it. His brain was playing out some rescue fantasy stop him from experiencing the true horror he was facing. From his current position, he was unable to see anything but the interior of the rocket. He held his breath, nonetheless, praying for the voice to speak again and prove that its owner was real.

'What are you doing to him?!

'Let him go!'

Finley's whole body exploded with euphoria. He recognised the voices immediately. It was Will, Emily and Lois. By some miracle, they had come to save him. He cried out in relief, thanking whichever twist of fate had led them to him.

Suddenly, he realised they did not yet know the truth, and he was instantly grateful that the Headmaster had forgotten to gag him.

'Allance is the Vacuous!' he called out to warn them. 'It's him! He's the murderer!'

His voice was interrupted by the sound of a crash and the loud purr of an engine, causing him to jump as he assumed the Headmaster had started up the rocket he was lying in. When he realised he wasn't moving, he guessed that Allance had escaped in a different spacecraft. Relief poured through his body as he allowed himself to hope that he might live, so long as the Headmaster didn't return to finish the job he had started.

Finley watched as a pair of feet, which belonged to Will, swung into the rocket beside him. Will began tapping his fingers furiously on the control panel, starting up the rocket quicker than Finley could comprehend.

Seconds later, Emily and Lois jumped in, Lois rushing to untie Finley the moment she entered their spacecraft. The engine hummed into life and they began ascending slowly, Will guiding them towards the tunnel that would carry them out into space.

'Wait!' Finley called to Will. 'We haven't got any gear!'

'Emergency seal, remember?' Will winked, pressing the button Mr. Zeppler had shown them after the Josie Jones incident. A glass dome sprung over their heads, sealing them in a protective bubble as they hovered in mid-air.

'How many minutes of oxygen did Mr Zeppler say this would give us?' Finley asked.

'About fifteen! No time to lose,' Will replied.

They flew through the tunnel in seconds, Will steering with expert precision as they made the transition into space. Their rocket soared through the stars in pursuit of Allance, who Finley saw was only a few hundred yards ahead of them.

'How are we going to stop him?' Finley shouted to Will. 'We haven't got much time!'

'Leave it to me!' Will nodded.

'Finley,' Lois addressed him, her voice thick with worry. 'Are you alright? What happened in there?'

'Allance told me he's the Vacuous,' Finley replied darkly. 'I saw him transform his hand into a claw right in front of my eyes. Once he knew his secret was out, he tried to kill me. He was going to take me into space and make it look like it was an accident.'

'That's awful' Lois gasped.

'I didn't think anyone was coming,' Finley admitted. 'I thought I was dead.'

'Do you really think we would have saved ourselves and left you?' Lois shook her head. 'Of course we came back. We had to know if you were alright. We had no idea Allance was the Vacuous.' She shuddered. 'How is it even possible? What is he trying to achieve?'

'I don't know,' Finley said. 'But whatever it is, he would have succeeded if it wasn't for you guys.'

Finley smiled at her thankfully and she smiled back, the two of them forgetting where they were as they lost themselves in the warmth of each other's eyes.'

'I don't mean to spoil your moment, guys,' Will called from behind the steering wheel. 'But I think you might want to see this.'

Finley scrambled to his feet, hurrying to the front of the rocket with Lois and Emily by his side. Looking through the window, they watched as Allance stopped his spacecraft in mid-flight, turning it around to face their own.

'What's he doing?' Will muttered to himself, bringing their own rocket to a halt.

They waited in silence, holding their breath collectively as the Headmaster smiled at them. A pair of bulky cannons appeared on either side of his rocket, his deadly intentions suddenly apparent.

'He's going to shoot!' Finley yelled.

Two pale blue balls of fire sprung from the canons, hurtling towards them with ferocious speed. Will grabbed the steering wheel, veering sharply to the left, just in time to avoid the impact. The rocket tipped and the four of them smashed hard into the steel wall, Finley winded by the force of his fall.

As they rotated through the air, one of Allance's fireballs clipped their wings, sending them into an even faster spin. They tumbled sickeningly, hitting against each other's bodies as the rocket lost control, rolling chaotically through the depths of space.

'Somebody grab the wheel!' Will shouted, as Finley felt the vomit begin to rise in his throat. He was so dizzy, he could hardly see, and he struggled to discern what was space, what was rocket and what were the blurry shapes of his friends.

Just when he thought he would certainly lose consciousness; they were unexpectedly pulled level and out of their spin. He collapsed against the wall, breathing deeply to steady his stomach, as he waited for his giddiness to subside. His vision came back to him, and he saw Lois clasping the steering wheel in her hands, her body shaking and her eyes wild with the surprise of her success.

'Lois, you saved us,' Emily gasped.

'Allance is getting away,' Lois panicked, pointing to his rocket now several miles in the distance.

Will rushed over and took the wheel, putting the spacecraft into the highest gear and setting off at full speed.

'Will, maybe we should go back,' Emily said with worry. 'We don't know how much oxygen we've got left.'

'We have to catch him,' Will shook his head. 'We need proof. If he gets away, no one will ever know what he was. They won't believe us. We need to stop him. If the Vacuous can disguise themselves as humans, we'll all be dead before we reach Novum.'

'Is there some way we can communicate between the rockets?' Lois asked, struck by sudden inspiration.

'There's a radio system somewhere in the control panel, but I'm not sure how it works.' Will replied.

'Get hold of Allance and get him to confess,' Lois commanded, tapping on her personal device with fury.

'What? Why?' Will asked with confusion.

'Just do it,' she asserted. 'Emily, can you work the radio?'

'I can try,' Emily said, as she scrambled forward.

'Bottom right of the control pad,' Will instructed her, not taking his eyes from the Headmaster's rocket.

'There's a button that tunes the frequencies,' Emily said, biting her lip with concentration. 'I just need to find the right one.'

She set to work, twisting and turning the button as she navigated through the static white noise on the radio.

'I've got him!' she cried victoriously.

'Allance!' Will called through the radio. 'Can you hear me?'

There was a brief crackling noise, followed by the sound of the Headmaster's voice projecting into the rocket.

'It's no use, boy, I'm not going to stop' he hissed.

'Why are you running? There's nowhere for you to go,' Will responded. 'It doesn't matter where you are- the Captain will find you.'

There was a moment of silence as the Admiral contemplated Will's words. Capitalising on the opportunity, he continued to speak, Lois holding her personal device up to the speakers.

'Just turn yourself in,' Will pressed him. 'The Captain is a decent man. I'm sure he'll show you mercy if you do the right thing. Surely anything's better than dying out here in space?'

Allance laughed, the cold, hollow sound sending chills down Finley's spine.

'If I turn myself in, I'll be executed,' he snapped back. 'Perhaps I should just kill you all and then continue with my plan?'

'You don't have a plan,' Will mocked him. 'You have no idea what you're doing, Allance. Anyone can see that. Look at you. If you're so clever, what are you doing in the middle of space, fleeing from a bunch of children?'

'Watch your tongue, boy,' Allance snapped. 'You have no idea what you're talking about. This goes ways beyond what your tiny mind can comprehend. Your species is pathetic. So ruled by your emotions that you cannot think clearly. You waste your time tearing each other apart, instead of furthering your collective interest. It's no wonder your home planet fell to pieces around you. You were all too busy arguing with each other to notice it had died. You don't deserve Novum, but we do. Once we have taken over *The Mayflower*, we will rid the Universe of the infection of human beings. All life shall be pure once more.'

'Take over *The Mayflower*?!' Will scoffed, his eye on Lois' personal device as he hounded Allance into revealing more. 'Do you know how many guards there are? How much security you'd have to defeat to even get close to the control room?'

Allance laughed again.

'Foolish, foolish boy,' he said. 'There are a million ways I could access that control room, but I found the version that's the most fun. Mr Holt and his partners at I-Tech have been developing a very interesting piece of technology. The computerized weaponry allows control of the minds of any living organism of your choice. Imagine it. An army full of Space Academy students storming *The Mayflower*! Do you think the guards would shoot and kill their own children? We would be unstoppable!'

'You can't do that!' Finley cried. 'It's sick.'

'Don't you worry, my boy,' Allance laughed. 'Your peasant family will be safe down on Floor Seven. They'll do nicely as our slaves, once we are in charge.'

'But why now?' Will asked him. 'You've had thirteen years to take over *The Mayflower*. Why wait this long?'

'I got impatient,' Allance confessed. 'I grew sick of surrounding myself with children, so infantile in their needs. The place was like a hot-bed of emotion all the time. It was growing harder to conceal myself, when I was high from the fumes of your teenager despair. How anyone could expect me to go on like that, denying myself while I pretended to actually *care* for the snotty little brats at that diabolical school? It was an insult, and I decided enough was enough.'

'You won't get away with it,' Will warned him.

'Are you sure about that, child?' Allance taunted. 'Who do you propose is going to stop me? So long as nobody knows my plan, I will succeed. After I've killed you, no one else is going to find out what's happening. Not until it's too late.'

'It's already too late,' Lois said, her voice low with hatred.

'Who's that? What are you talking about?' Allance demanded.

'I've been recording this entire conversation on my personal device,' Lois replied. 'It's being sent in a live stream to my father as we speak. I should imagine his forces will be here in about...' she looked at the time on her device. 'Five minutes?'

Suddenly, Allance's rocket stopped ahead of them, suspended statue-still in the star-strewn sky. The protective seal across the roof came down, and Allance stood up, his foot poised on the edge of the spacecraft as he prepared to fling himself overboard.

'Wait!' Will shouted.

With one final look of contempt in their direction, Allance jumped from his rocket, drifting at a horribly slow speed into the never-ending abyss of space. Finley, Will, Emily and Lois watched as he floated away, his human form fading as he transformed back into a Vacuous.

His slender, white body heaved as it pleaded for air it would never find. His terrible empty face twisted into an expression that conveyed his agony, despite his lack of features. After a moment, his elongated arms fell to his side and he became still, his fight finally over as he shrunk into the distance.

Finley stood in silence with his friends, each of them rendered motionless by what they'd just seen. Despite Allance's evil nature, Finley could not help but pity him dying in such a long and painful way.

'Why would he do that?' he asked Will breathlessly.

'I suppose he knew it was over for him anyway,' Will shrugged, turning the rocket around and speeding back towards the safety of the Space Academy, the first of the Captain's fleet appearing as tiny silver dots over the school.

20

HOMECOMING

The days after Admiral Allance's death were a chaotic blur. The Space Academy grounds had become swamped with security from *The Mayflower* within hours, and a full investigation into Allance's crimes was ordered by the Captain. Will, Emily, Finley and Lois were subjected to extensive interviews, with various high-ranking guards probing them on what they had witnessed until they were completely exhausted.

By the time their part in the proceedings was declared over, they were deeply relieved to be sent back to their lessons and return to normality, concentrating on their final projects and end of year results.

In the final week of term, rumours that a body had been pulled from the lake began to circulate among the students, the identity of the victim heavily speculated upon. Fortunately, Will's classmates had enough sense not to question him or his friends on the matter, despite their involvement in the whole saga being incredibly well-discussed. Even Rudy maintained a respectful silence, giving Will the occasional dirty look, but otherwise keeping his distance.

The teachers also seemed to have been given instructions not to discuss the incident, conducting their lessons without a single mention of Allance or the murder that had taken place.

On several occasions, however, Will caught some of them staring at him with concern, as though expecting him to break down at any moment.

Indeed, the only person who was brave enough to mention the situation at all was Mr Krecher, who pulled Will into his office after Alien Studies one day and forced him into an armchair, thrusting a hastily made cup of tea into his hands.

'Are you alright, my boy?' he asked, as soon as the first sip had slid down Will's throat.

'I'm okay sir,' he replied, adding a weary smile for a conviction.

'No use starting that 'sir' business with me now,' Krecher told him. ''Mr Krecher' will do fine.'

'Sorry,' Will said with embarrassment. 'Force of habit from all the interviews with the guards.'

'Ah yes, of course,' Krecher frowned, pacing around his office. 'I don't suppose you mentioned anything about the Looking Glass in those interviews?'

'No, Mr Krecher,' Will replied honestly. 'I'm not sure how I'd explain it- even if I wanted to.'

'I see,' Krecher's face filled with relief. 'That is good news. I've been beside myself with worry. If the guards find out I've got an unregistered alien artefact, I'd be in serious trouble. Not to mention the fact it would be confiscated from me. Such a device could do a great deal of damage if it fell into the wrong hands.'

'Don't worry. I won't tell anyone,' Will promised. 'Nor will the others.'

'The others?' Krecher repeated. 'What others?'

Will's cheeks flushed crimson.

'My friends Lois, Emily and Finley,' he confessed. 'I brought them back here one night, and we all went into the Looking Glass. It was after we had seen the Vacuous for the first time. We thought we could find some answers in the past. I'm sorry.'

'Lois is the captain's daughter,' Krecher fretted. 'What if she tells her father?'

'She won't,' Will shook his head vigorously. 'I trust her.'

'If you're certain...' Mr Krecher replied.

'I am,' Will assured him. Seizing upon the opportunity to speak to him alone, he added; 'there is something I wanted to ask you, Mr Krecher.'

'Yes, what is it?'

'When we were in the looking glass, we saw Alfie and my parents talking. They said they'd gone to you for help about the Vacuous, and that you'd seen them too. Is that true?'

Krecher sighed.

'Yes, I must confess they did rope me into it all. They joined my Alien Studies class, you see, shortly after they encountered the Vacuous for the first time. Once they had decided they could trust me, they showed me images they'd caught of it, asking if I recognised the species. I told them that I didn't. Whatever they were, the aliens they described to me were unknown to humankind.

'Afterwards, I became obsessed by the entire thing, hunting the vacuous by myself in secret. They were terrible creatures, horrifying beyond anything I'd ever seen. It drove me mad, in the end, trying to work out what they were and what they wanted. I gave up my research when we left Earth. I never dreamed there'd be a Vacuous here at the school,' he frowned.

'You didn't know about Allance then?' Will confirmed.

'No, no, of course not,' he denied. 'If I had, I would have contacted the Captain straight away. I don't expect he would be pleased to hear from me. I suppose I remind him and your mother of things they'd rather forget, but if I had known what was going on, I wouldn't have hesitated to involve them.'

'There's something else that's bothering me,' Will frowned. 'Everything that happened, the things Allance said… it means that my dad was right about everything.'

'Forgive me, I don't follow?' Krecher replied.

'My dad's belief in the 'great conspiracy', Will explained. 'He knew *The Mayflower* was unsafe and he suspected the Vacuous had something to do with it. He was right all along, and no one believed him.'

'Your father was a very passionate man,' Krecher reflected. 'Once he got something into his head, there wasn't much that would make him let go. Still, at least you have the comfort of knowing you stopped the Vacuous. The Captain won't rest until he's certain he's captured them all. You've finished your father's legacy. He spent most of his adult life searching for the truth, and now you've found it.'

'The great conspiracy might have been real, but I still can't forgive my dad for what he did,' Will said slowly. 'He abandoned me and my mum, not knowing whether we'd live or die. Nothing can ever change that.'

Will stared at the Looking Glass standing innocently in the corner, and began to relive the scene of his father's death it had shown him.

. 'You've seen much more than a boy your age should,' Krecher sighed. 'My advice to you is that you move on from all of this. You've done your part. Leave the rest to the Captain and his forces.'

'Trust me, Mr Krecher, after the year I've had, I'll be happy to spend the holidays as a normal teenager. No more Vacuous, and no more trips into mirrors,' Will replied sincerely.

Krecher smiled to himself and then dismissed him, bidding him well until they met again.

The announcement of final results provided a much welcome distraction for Will, and he was both shocked and delighted to find that he had passed the year, receiving an overall '2' grade along with a formal invitation to return the following September. Despite facing two separate attempts on his life, Finley had managed to obtain a '1' in his results, an achievement which was celebrated by an evening of playing Earth Wars in Will's room, at Finley's request.

All too soon, the morning of their final day at the Space Academy arrived, and they found themselves trailing their suitcases across the grounds gloomily, their hearts heavy with the prospect of leaving their new home for ten whole weeks.

Waiting in line with the other deflated first-years, Will studied his surroundings with precision, his eyes drinking in every detail of the main school building and the grounds, as though he would never see them again. Even the fake grass that covered the floor suddenly felt like a novelty he would deeply miss. He only hoped that come next year, he would be able to truly appreciate studying in such a unique and wonderful place, with no distractions from murderous aliens or, indeed, magic portals to the past.

The shuttle journey back to *The Mayflower* seemed to pass twice as quickly than usual, and in the blink of an eye, they had reached the platform, unloading en-masse into the waiting crowds of parents, who were incredibly anxious to see their children's safe return. Will was surprised to see his mother standing with both Finley's family and Emily's parents, huddled together in a stance of mutual concern. Emily's father stood haughtily in the background, deeply embarrassed to be part of such an emotional display. When they saw their children, the mothers rushed forward, pulling them into bone-crushing hugs as they babbled incoherently about how worried they'd been.

After a few minutes of being suffocated, Will was released by his mother, who kept her grip firmly on his arms as she bent down to address him.

'Will, my darling,' she said frantically. 'I'm so sorry for what you've been through. Alfie told me what the Headteacher looked like when they found his body in space. We'd seen that type of alien before, back on Earth, but we had no idea how dangerous they were! If only you had told me what was going on... I could have helped you. I feel terrible you had to do this alone!'

'I wasn't alone,' Will smiled, looking towards his friends.

'We didn't know the aliens could take human form!' his mother cried. 'It's awful. Derek's been arrested. Apparently, he was one of them.'

'I knew there was something wrong with him!' Will exclaimed victoriously, his look of triumph fading when he saw his mother's expression.

'Alfie's going to make a speech about everything he knows,' Elsie continued. 'Is Lois with you? He asked me to pick her up and bring her with us.'

Will pointed to where Lois was standing, twiddling her thumbs awkwardly as she watched the intimate embraces of the parents and children around her. Will called her over, and she looked relieved to have been noticed, accompanying Will and Elsie as they manoeuvred towards the exit, Finley and Emily's families following close behind.

They walked briskly down the corridor and into the lift, riding it all the way down to the lobby, where a colossal crowd had gathered around the huge screen in the centre. A guard escorted them to the front of the ensemble, standing protectively nearby as Alfie's face appeared in gigantic proportions on the screen.

'Good morning, citizens of *The Mayflower*,' his voice boomed over their heads. 'I am making this important address in light of the recent events that occurred at the Space Academy, of which I am sure you are all aware. I know that many of you have questions, and I hope to provide you with as many answers as I can by sharing what we have discovered through our investigation.

'As you may have heard, Admiral Allance, the school's renowned Headmaster, was discovered to be a rare species of alien in disguise. His body was retrieved from space and examined in its true form, the results of which have been studied. When I saw his appearance, I realised he belonged to a species that I had, in fact, encountered personally on Earth. Back then, we referred to the specimens as 'the Vacuous', a name which describes the empty features that are characteristic of their breed. This name has now been officially registered, and the Vacuous have been added to our database of known alien creatures.

'We have discovered the Vacuous are capable of taking human form, something which has been unprecedented among alien beings until this point. A specially trained team have been assigned to try and work out how their transformation may be possible. A full-scale enquiry has also been launched across *The Mayflower*, and several Vacuous have been caught already. Through special means of interrogation, we have managed to confirm their motive.

'They had plotted to take control of *The Mayflower* so they could take Novum for themselves. Their false identities were so elaborate that many of them could be traced back for years on Earth, attending colleges and working in high-profile jobs, in order to gain places on our ship. 'Most shocking of all our discoveries is that two adolescents, going by the human aliases of 'Kyan Smith' and 'Josie Jones,' turned out to be members of the vacuous species'. These young aliens were students at the Space Academy, positioned there, we believe, to help Admiral Allance with his plot, until Josie attacked a fellow student and forced him to expel her to cover their tracks.'

Will exchanged a wild look of surprise with Lois, Emily and Finley.

'We believe this indicates the younger Vacuous are less able to control their murderous urges, making them easier to identify,' Alfie continued. 'The captains of the other spacecrafts have also been informed of everything we know so far, and we will be taking a number of steps to ensure the safety of their citizens. Our priority is to maintain the integrity of humanity's mission to Novum, and to ensure our safe passage to the planet remains guaranteed.

'Unfortunately, before Allance could be stopped he claimed the life of one victim, whose body was retrieved from the lake at the Space Academy about a week ago. I can now reveal the identity of this victim as Mr Jarvis Holt, a dear friend of mine, and the CEO of the Interactive-Tech company.

'Mr Holt was an incredibly intelligent man, and a deeply valued passenger on *The Mayflower*. His death comes as a severe blow to both his friends and family, and to the innovation of our future technology. A memorial will be held for him in the Commiserations Hall next Monday to celebrate his life's achievements, and to give his body a safe and dignified send-off.

'For those who are wondering why Allance chose to murder Mr Holt, I can reveal an extensive search of his office uncovered his plans to gain access to some experimental technology I-Tech had been developing. He intended to use the technology on the children at the school, essentially turning them into robots he could use to take over *The Mayflower*. He knew the higher officials on board would not shoot at their own children, and had he not been discovered, his plan may well have been unstoppable.'

A gasp of horror rang around the lobby, as parents clasped their children tightly.

'It is thought that he lured Mr Holt to the school with the objective of offering him a significant amount of credits from the school budget in exchange for use of the technology. When Mr Holt refused, he was murdered. It is therefore paramount that Jarvis is remembered as the hero he truly was, protecting that which we hold most precious, even at the cost of his own life.

'Now, despite the dark circumstances that have surrounded the school this year, the board of Governors and I have decided that the Space Academy should remain open, and that term will resume as normal in September. We feel it would be unjust to allow the actions of one twisted individual to ruin the chance the more- able children to experience the excellent education the school provides. I have appointed Miss. Fortem as Headteacher, a position which she will formally accept following a thorough background check, and have set up regular inspections at the school to guarantee its pupils' safety in the future.

'Now to end on a positive note,' he smiled through the screen. 'I would like to give a special thanks to my daughter, Lois Sommers and her friends, William James, Emily Pannell and Finley Campbell. It was these four students who uncovered Allance's true identity, and it was only through their bravery and initiative that he was stopped before he could put his terrible plan into action.

'It is remarkable that these young teenagers could face down such an incredible adversary and win. Even more impressive is the fact they all managed to pass their academic year, with Mr Campbell achieving one of the highest grades in the entire year group. As special congratulations, and as a show of our gratitude, I have decided to elevate the Campbell family to Floor Two, offering Finley's father the prestigious position of Governor of Maintenance.'

Will looked over with jubilance at Finley, who was staring open-mouthed at the screen, unable to believe what he was hearing. His mother and father were crying with happiness, while his younger sister shrieked and hugged her stunned older siblings.

'I conclude my address today by making a promise to you all that I will go above and beyond to ensure the safety of every innocent passenger aboard this ship. Any and all Vacuous found hiding among our population will be punished with the severest consequences, and we will not rest until we are certain they have all been discovered. In the meantime, I urge my citizens to be vigilant, and to immediately report anything suspicious to a member of security, no matter how small it may seem. We are only powerful when we work together. Thank you for your time.'

The screen turned to black and the lobby erupted into a roar of loud discussion. Passers-by stopped on their way towards the lifts to point and stare at Will and his friends, causing a number of guards to rush over and form a wall around them, urging the spectators to move on. The four of them converged into a huddle, congratulating a shell-shocked Finley on his promising new status.

'I don't feel like I deserve it,' he said, shaking his head in disbelief. 'Lois, please thank your father for me. I don't know how I can ever repay him.'

'You don't need to repay him. You earnt it!' Lois replied. 'You're the one who went to find Allance and worked the whole thing out.'

'Well, only because he told me he was an alien. If you hadn't all shown up, I'd be dead. Besides, Will's really the one who stopped him,' Finley blushed.

'Me? No way!' Will argued. 'All I did was chase him through space and shout at him. I wouldn't have been able to do anything without all your help, especially Emily fixing that radio.'

'It wasn't *that* hard,' Emily said bashfully, though she looked extremely pleased to have been complimented.

'You all did brilliantly,' Lois told them sincerely. 'Who knows what would have happened if Allance wasn't stopped.'

'You were brilliant too, Lois,' Finley reminded her. 'Streaming

Allance's confession to your dad was a fantastic idea.'

'We make a good team,' Will concluded, and the four of them smiled warmly at each other, lost in a moment of silent comradery.

'I can't believe Holt is dead...' Emily said, her eyes filling with tears of grief for her hero.

'I know,' Lois said sadly. 'He was a good person.'

The four of them bowed their heads as they reflected on Allance's hideous crime.

'Do you think I'll still get my work experience at I-Tech?' Emily wondered out loud.

'Emily!' Will scolded her.

'What?' she replied indignantly. 'I was just asking...'

'We'll still see each other over the holidays, won't we?' Lois implored. 'No matter what happens?'

'Of course,' Finley beamed.

'Promise?' Lois pressed them.

'Promise,' they all agreed.

'Now, Finley,' Will said, placing an arm around his shoulders. 'Let's go and have a look at your new apartment. I have to tell you though, if it's nicer than mine I'll have no choice but to never speak to you again.'

'I understand,' Finley laughed, and the four of them walked away, united in a bond they felt certain would last forever.

THE END